BLOODLINE

BLOODLINE

Priscilla Masters

SEVERN
HOUSE

First world edition published in Great Britain and the USA in 2025
by Severn House, an imprint of Canongate Books Ltd,
14 High Street, Edinburgh EH1 1TE.

severnhouse.com

British Library Cataloguing-in-Publication Data
A CIP catalogue record for this title is available from the British Library.

ISBN-13: 978-1-4483-1476-8 (cased)
ISBN-13: 978-1-4483-1587-1 (e-book)

All Severn House titles are printed on acid-free paper.

Typeset by Palimpsest Book Production Ltd.,
Falkirk, Stirlingshire, Scotland.
Printed and bound in Great Britain by
TJ Books, Padstow, Cornwall.

Praise for the Joanna Piercy mysteries

About the author

Priscilla Masters is the author of the popular DI Joanna Piercy series, as well as the successful Martha Gunn novels, a series of medical mysteries featuring Dr Claire Roget and the Florence Shaw mysteries. She lives near the Shropshire/Staffordshire border. A retired respiratory nurse, Priscilla has two grown-up sons and two grandsons.

www.priscillamasters.co.uk

ONE

'**G**o back to sleep, Jo. Please. You've a few hours yet.'

But she felt too restless, anticipating the day ahead, feeling the excitement rise like bubbles in soda, and finally she slid out of bed to have a shower, slip on her dressing gown and check on Jakob, who was sleeping the noisy, gurgling sleep of an infant who neither knew nor cared what the day ahead held. She returned with two mugs of coffee before their son woke with his usual roar and dance around the cot. Jakob Rudyard Levin was a child who demanded to be noticed.

Matthew reached out and took the mug from her. 'Excited?'

'I can't wait,' she admitted. 'It's been so long, Matt.'

He eyed her sleepily. 'Nearly a year.' He curled an arm around her shoulders while anticipating her next response, waiting for the confession he'd heard all too often.

'I still feel partly responsible.'

He tried to reassure her, as he'd done before on numerous occasions. 'Joanna, it wasn't your fault. The accident was the fault of the person driving the car, who deliberately went for him. And now you're about to get him back.' He gave her a cheeky grin, bent to kiss the top of her head, her hair still damp from the shower, before reaching out to touch her hand. 'And still with two legs.'

'Thank goodness,' she breathed. 'At one point it all seemed so hopeless.' She kissed her husband's bristly cheek, ruffled his honey-blond hair, which was getting a little long for a pathologist, then sat up, dropped her legs to the floor and headed for their wardrobe while she wondered. What was the right outfit to wear to welcome a loved colleague back after a year's sick leave?

She ran her hand over the various outfits, mainly sober-coloured trousers, jeans, shirts and sweaters, a couple of party dresses. She smirked to herself. That would cause some interesting comments, but she ran her hand past them. Nothing quite so obvious, she thought, but still decidedly festive. Because she had something so wonderful to celebrate that she felt like dancing all the way to the station. Which would cause even more comments.

In the end, she settled for a pair of well-fitting black trousers and boots with a low heel but gave in to a pink sweater with a hint of sparkle in the wool. It was raining hard, which gave her the perfect excuse to use the car rather than head in on her bike.

TWO

7.30 a.m.

Less than three miles away from Briarswood, an early morning mist shrouded the lake. A blushing pink sun was trying to find a way through the gauze to illuminate the water, but it was losing the battle. The rain was getting heavier, turning the muddy track that led from the lake up to Cloud Mansion into rivulets of fast-flowing water, loosening stones, deepening potholes, making the track even less passable.

On the side of the hill, the shadows of trees stayed stubbornly black as rain dripped from the branches, adding to the flow of the rogue stream. The harsh calls of a few gulls which swooped down to the water's surface accompanied the drumbeat of the rain, turning them into a symphony of nature, blending with the backdrop of the weather. The Lake House, which projected thirty yards into the lake on a pier, came briefly alive as the morning sun found a gap in the clouds and then disappeared.

Doreen Caputo stared out at the weather then turned to her dog. "Fraid we do have to go out for the morning walk,' she said, 'whatever the weather.'

Stevie Wonder wagged his tail. He didn't care about the rain.

Joseph Holden was also staring out of his window, his gaze angling down towards the lake. Like his neighbour, the view never bored him. Water never portrayed the exact same image – ripples, waves or glassy stillness, the lake's surface was ever changing. He could watch it forever.

He smiled. Down at the water's edge, the pennants topping a couple of tilted sailing dinghies fluttered in the breeze then drooped as they became heavy and waterlogged. After a few more minutes, Joseph turned away as something registered. Something felt different today, but he couldn't work out what it was. It was giving him an uncomfortable feeling, yet he didn't know why. He frowned, scanning the familiar panorama. Nothing had changed surely? But Joseph was a believer in the power of instinct. It had saved his life on occasions, particularly when there had appeared no rational reason for an alert.

He peered harder through the window, searching for a clue. The weather was typical – the lake surface choppy, the trees bending and waving, the track down to the water's edge a muddy stream determined in its effort to find an outlet. He stood perfectly still for a moment, controlling his breathing, scanning each frame as he tried to work out what had alerted him.

He found nothing, but the feeling of unease intensified. And then he realized. It was *not* something in his line of vision. It was a sound that rumbled underneath the pounding of the rain. A car struggling with its descent down the steep track that led from the road to the back of the house, through a pair of rusted gates which stood permanently open.

Joseph was used to interpreting noises – their implications and their warnings – and assessing their significance. There had been a time when interpreting sounds had meant the difference between living or not. And this one alerted him because it was unexpected.

He analysed the possibilities. He was expecting no deliveries, and the postman always left his letters in a box on the road side of the gates. He could find no logical reason why somebody would be driving a car down the track, which was tricky and hazardous, particularly in today's sodden weather. The turning yard at the bottom was tight, even for his small van. Cloud Mansion was isolated, visitors few. Built of heavy granite blocks, it stood guard as a sentinel over the lake and had been built to withstand the harshest of weather. Vehicular approach was tricky, which was one of the reasons he had bought the house in the first place. He didn't want visitors. Isolation and poor access had been, for him, a desirable feature.

The front of the mansion was a steep climb up from the lake, through woodland along an unmade track that turned into a rogue stream in the lightest rainfall, and to the rear, a precipitous rough descent from the Horton Road. At the top, there were gates he could have kept padlocked, but they were rarely closed – a last resort to protect his isolation. The house was unheralded; there was no signage. It hosted no casual visitors and only a select few invited guests. None of whom were expected today. Which meant the vehicle struggling down the rocky track from the higher road towards the back was uninvited and unexpected. Very possibly unwelcome.

And now his mind was on full alert, his stress level notched up to high. He felt himself tense as he tried to find an acceptable explanation.

His neighbour called every morning, but she walked up from the lake. Clarice, his cleaner, came once a week, catching the bus from Leek into Rudyard village and tramping up through the woods, often arriving with muddied shoes which she changed for indoor footwear. As far as he knew, she didn't have a car. If she had, she would have driven surely?

Besides, Tuesday was not her day.

Other dog walkers and hikers passed his front door, but ramblers and dog walkers didn't drive; they climbed the track from the lakeside parking. It took deliberation and firm intent to visit here.

He stood still and listened as the car's engine stopped.

A car door slammed. Footsteps followed. Determined, ominous. Someone was here.

Joseph crossed the study, moved to the hall, stood behind the front door, braced himself and waited for the inevitable hammering of a fist. But it didn't come.

There was sudden silence as the wind and rain waited too. Joseph's instincts warned him: this guest was definitely unwelcome. Keep the door between you.

He sensed the stranger's breathing matching his own, both of them catching the last moments of tranquillity.

What Joseph couldn't know was that the stranger had doubts too as he'd been caught off guard. He hadn't expected geography to play its part in the hostilities. He hadn't anticipated the atmosphere of the house or the wildness of the environment, which seemed conspired to beat him away.

He looked around him, unnerved, then stretched out a hand and touched the cold granite blocks. It was a fortress, he was realizing, a fortress with no need of a moat to repel all aggressors. The house did the defensive work efficiently.

A gargoyle spat at him, and for a moment he hesitated. Once the door was opened, it would begin. He'd planned his assault with great care, but he hadn't counted on the fact that fear and apprehension, a moment of doubt, would infect him too. He gripped the gun with both hands, stood in combat mode and knew that behind the stout door, the man was aware of his presence. As the prey senses the presence of a snake just before it strikes, the man inside knew he was here. And so he brushed away that faint intrusion of doubt and raised his hand.

While, on the other side of the door, all of Joseph's instincts screamed at him not to open it.

THREE

8.45 a.m.

Leek police station

They were watching the clock as the minutes ticked by, eyes drifting towards the door. No one spoke.

But they were all thinking the same thing. He wouldn't be late. Not on his first day back surely?

Joanna stood motionless. Matthew had taken Jakob to nursery, leaving her free to focus on reaching the station in plenty of time.

So they all waited, eyes on the clock, gravitating towards the door, full of anticipation.

8.50 a.m.

The door opened to a cheer. And Korpanski was standing there, grinning around the room, his eyes resting longest on Joanna. Who'd vowed she wouldn't be emotional. She wouldn't hug him. She wouldn't cry. She wouldn't make a spectacle of herself.

But she couldn't stop herself moving forward, throwing herself into his arms and feeling that reassuring bulk. Slightly reduced but still unmistakably Detective Sergeant Mike Korpanski. She'd almost forgotten the feel of him, the crisp scent he emitted. His very presence. She suppressed tears and mumbled into his chest. 'Good to see you, Mike.' Her voice was husky with emotion.

She took a deep breath in. The axis had shifted. Now all seemed right in the world.

He patted her shoulder and, clearly suppressing the joy he felt at being back, muttered, 'DS Korpanski, reporting for duty, ma'am.'

She forgave him the *ma'am*, took a step back and met those dark eyes, and now that grin was even wider than usual.

'Jo,' he said tenderly. Then: 'Bloody hell. You nearly knocked me over.'

'Sorry.' But she knew he was teasing her while trying to regain his equilibrium. DS Mike Korpanski was back to normal. Almost.

The last time she'd visited him at home, she'd suggested he and Fran take a holiday. 'Somewhere hot,' she'd said. 'Not with the kids. Just the two of you. Quality rest time.' It looked like the Korpanskis had obeyed. Mike had a dark tan which showed even darker against a pale blue sweatshirt, its sleeves pushed up. But even the tan couldn't quite hide his underlying anxiety, the shadows under his eyes – or the fact that he'd lost weight. And, glancing down, she could see, through his jeans, that one leg was still slightly thinner than the other. The accident had left its indelible mark.

He broke the silence that had dropped between them like a gate, replaced by awkwardness. 'Hope you haven't dressed up like that for me.'

She was quick to respond lightly. 'Of course not. It's wear-some-sparkle-to-work day.'

He raised his eyebrows, his mouth twisted in amusement. Which gave her an opportunity to launch a counter-attack on his jeans. 'See *you* haven't followed suit.'

He gave a great big belly laugh. 'I don't suit anything sparkly.'

And now the others all joined in. It was good to have him back – even if it was on 'light' duties. Not one of them could imagine Detective Sergeant Mike Korpanski on 'light' duties. The laughter that rippled round the room was a tonic. Things were back to normal, the rapport between DI and DS restored.

FOUR

7.31 a.m. An hour and nineteen minutes earlier

And yet Joseph had – he'd opened the door to the hard knock. Curious, apprehensive, his first mistake of the day. And now he was angry with himself. His antennae had been up, his senses on high alert. But he'd opened the door. He'd question why later.

It took a while to register fully, as though his brain could only absorb one detail at a time. In front of him, rain sheeting down behind him, a man stood, framed by the front door. Medium height, somewhere in his thirties, black hoodie and trousers, his face set, determined, hostile, dark eyes staring boldly into his. Legs apart, in combat stance, both hands gripping a gun. Joseph took a moment to absorb the details of the gun. A Glock. His eyes drifted back to the man's face. Mediterranean features. A sharp pointed nose. Very dark brown eyes. He ran through the possibilities. Moroccan? Maybe Spanish, Egyptian. Possibly Middle Eastern? Turkish?

'Who are you?'

The stranger didn't answer but stared at him while Joseph waited, apprehension stealing through him, which wasn't solely down to the gun. It was the man himself. And his soldier's stance.

The man waved the gun at him, indicating the hallway behind. 'Back,' he said in a faint foreign accent.

Joseph tethered the information in the hope that the picture formed would tell him what he needed to know.

The old questions. Who, why, what, when? How?

He took two steps back into the hall, his eyes on the muzzle of the gun, his mind slowly churning, the stranger keeping step with him, his foot slamming the door shut behind him.

The hallway was tall, airy and spacious, the light provided from above by a glazed oculus. They seemed like two tiny figures watched by a suit of armour standing at the side of the bottom step.

The intruder ignored everything, his eyes trained solely on Joseph, who was shuffling backwards, his slippers making a soft slapping sound over the tiled floor.

At the base of the stairs, he stopped. The hall was cold in all weathers and filled with echoes which wafted upwards. Joseph forced his mind to think. Behind him, the stairs, a door which led into the kitchen, another to a small cloakroom. In the kitchen were knives. Potential weapons. Could he? He eyed the gun again, met the stranger's eyes and rejected the idea. The smallest pressure on the trigger would release the safety. He watched it as he asked a question which would haunt him for the next few days. 'What do you want?'

The stranger's eyes moved from side to side as though looking for something. He made no attempt to answer. Finally his eyes looked left, into the study, which had tall windows facing downwards towards the lake. Following his gaze gave Joseph some hope. His nearest neighbour would soon pass, as she did every morning. They invariably had a brief chat, either through the window or when he opened the front door. Doreen Caputo would see what was happening. She could alert the police. Who would . . . And there his mind stopped.

The stranger indicated the doorway. 'In,' he said.

And despite the fact that he didn't think the stranger was going to answer, Joseph asked again, 'Who are you? What do you want? Why are you here?'

The man stared at him, his face impassive, and provided not one answer.

Feeling the gun pressed against his spine, Joseph walked inside. The study was a room he was as familiar with as his own hand. It was a room crowded with his treasures, mementoes of his journeys and adventures. He spent most of his days in there, sitting at his desk, his back to the window, his face to his computer screen or else reading in the armchair. As he stood in the centre of the room, a long-forgotten phrase he'd often used to shore up his men wafted into his mind.

Never let them feel your fear.

The stranger was scanning the room now, looking at the cabinets of curios, the pictures, the objects mounted on the walls.

Was he a thief? Joseph wondered. A burglar?

He kept trying. 'Who are you?'

The stranger's eyes now returned to him. 'Who am I?' It was a blatant mockery. 'You will know in time.'

Joseph was starting to gather facts that might come in useful. The stranger's accent was foreign but not markedly so. No one except a born-and-bred Briton spoke English without remnants of the accent of their motherland. It was always there – a trace, a hint, a lisp, an inflexion. In a slightly unusual emphasis, in a word difficult to pronounce, the order of words in a sentence. Something always lingered of one's mother tongue which, in this case, wasn't English. One got caught out the more one tried to hide it. Usually Joseph could pin down an accent, return it to its native geography. Perhaps the stranger had been born elsewhere but educated in the UK.

Joseph was building a picture.

The more you knew about your adversary, the greater chance you had of defeating them.

He tried to gain comfort from the familiarity of the room. So familiar he believed he could have found anything even in the dark. But today, it was absorbing the stranger's presence, so books, shelves, desk, ornaments looked subtly changed. Old friends turned into old enemies. Nothing looked right.

The stranger's eyes moved to the window as though it surprised him. Keeping his weapon trained on Joseph, he crossed the room and peered out of it before pulling the curtains tight shut with only the tiniest crack of daylight visible. Now the room was dingy.

The stranger returned to the desk, swivelled the chair around so it faced into the room and gestured for Joseph to sit. Joseph dropped into it. So now he had his back to the familiar item at which he had sat for hour after hour, reading, working, sinking back into bygone memories. The back of the chair was heavily carved, the sharp ridges uncomfortable against his spine. Another old friend turned hostile.

Holding the gun in one hand, the man fished around in his pocket, drawing out a few plastic zip ties. 'Put your arms here.' He indicated the arms of the chair for Joseph to lay his forearms along. Then, eyes watchful, using his teeth and his one free hand, he secured Joseph's wrists, checking they were tight enough for him to have little movement and no chance of slipping down the side and sliding his arms free. Only then did he draw up one of the window chairs to sit opposite him, the gun resting now on his lap, his eyes flicking towards Joseph periodically. All the time he had a fixed concentration, each action measured, disciplined, deliberate, rehearsed.

He was staring at him now, disdain and dislike clearly visible in the dark brown eyes, but also some curiosity, his head tilted to the side. The silence crossing the room was unnerving, magnifying to a roar as something passed between captor and captive. But Joseph couldn't have told anyone what it was.

He broke into the silence. 'If it's money you're after, I don't keep much around the house. Just a few—' He stopped right there. It wasn't money the stranger was after but something else. Proven by the fact that the stranger smirked and blew out his mockery in a huff.

Joseph sank back into the chair.

Now he had him safely tethered, the man was relaxed, spending time looking around the room and surveying the contents in leisurely fashion, his eyes resting on items long enough to appraise them before moving on. Joseph's eyes followed his. He hadn't found what he was searching for? Or was he deciding which pieces were most valuable? Which the most portable? Which the easiest to sell on?

Finally, his captor's eyes returned to him. 'You have quite a collection, Mr Holden. Some interesting pieces.' There was a hint of derision in his tone.

Joseph's mind was still sifting through possibilities. If the man wasn't here for a simple theft, what other options were there? Was he waiting for an accomplice? He'd already realized this was no ordinary burglary. It wasn't just the professional way his captor held the gun. And being armed was, in itself, an alert. There was something leisurely about him; calm, unhurried, displaying an economy of movement. Something controlled.

Then, abruptly, the man stood up and moved to an outline on the wall, above a Chinese cabinet, a pale patch where something had once hung, leaving a barely discernible outline. And as Joseph continued to watch him, he felt an almost suffocating sense of panic, as though a shadow was moving across the light.

The man turned around sharply, eyebrows lifted, head tilted to one side. Joseph stared back.

'You have many trophies,' the stranger said.

And despite the circumstances, Joseph nodded. The stranger was right. In this small room were treasures from all over the world. Scattered casually on surfaces, crammed into cabinets, festooning the walls. Clocks from France, bijouterie from Russia and Austria, ivories from Burma, celadon ware from China and Korea, Indian idols, Japanese and African weapons, carvings and masks. And what the eyes couldn't see, hidden in drawers, were other treasures: opals from Australia, rubies from Burma, diamonds from the deep mines in South Africa. Upstairs, every room was crammed with more. Carolean tapestries, seventeenth-century stump work, miniatures painted on ivory. Some he'd paid for. Others he had not. He'd walked through markets, villages, churches and palaces with a collector's passion, an eye for quality or the unusual, the bizarre and the frankly sinister, like the shrunken head which screamed upstairs on a small table by his bed. The thrill of acquisition had burned inside him like a furnace, while he'd justified this heaping up of treasures as being provision for a comfortable old age. Now Joseph mocked his plan. So this was the future he'd been saving for?

He came to and watched as the man seemed to visit his thoughts, dipping inside them, walking alongside this violent memory lane, seeming to sense the power of the objects themselves and the means Joseph had used to acquire them.

As Joseph watched him, following his eyes, taking in what caused him to rest on one or another of the pieces, he wondered.

What was his plan?

Murder?

Perhaps sensing his questions, the man turned round and looked at him.

Joseph scrutinized him, trying to divine his purpose. Was there hatred there? If there was, why had he not simply burst in and shot him? He could have been in and out of Cloud Mansion in minutes.

Again he wondered . . . Was he waiting for someone? An accomplice to help him?

The man stood now in front of him, his silence unnerving. It spoke of control.

Joseph saw granite hardness, a bloody determination that twitched in his memory, like a wounded man. Joseph recognized the stillness, the control of every single muscle in that taut body as well as the suppression of emotion in his face. He knew that immobility. It was the instinct of a soldier, a man who had swerved to avoid death and collected his reward: life.

For now.

FIVE

'I suppose we'd better get some work done.'

She gave him a cheeky smile and waved an admonishing index finger at him. 'Don't forget you're on light duties.'

Korpanski scowled and then his grin widened. 'Same old, same old,' he said before he read the top name on the list on the whiteboard, Cherie Glover, and her age, fourteen. He looked up.

'School bullying,' Joanna said. 'Suicide.'

'Oh shit.'

They were alone in what passed as her office – in reality a corner of the room allocated, begrudgingly, by the fire department to the police. Little more than a desk, a couple of chairs, computer terminals and the ever-ready whiteboard on which were penned current caseloads. These were as varied as the weather and numerous as the number of potholes in and around local roads: check up on the aftermath of domestic disturbances (a current priority), fraud involving substitute car parts, fake cigarettes and vapes pouring in from Albania (some of them containing lethal toxins) and details of computer romance scams which had resulted in some lovelorn, optimistic women losing money to their 'Romeos'. One of the IP addresses had been tracked down to Leek, though it could be a mule, one in a chain of customers, who would pass the details from one to the other. But it was a link worth checking on which might prove valuable.

Cherie Glover was the saddest case on the whiteboard, a fourteen-year-old girl who'd been callously trolled by some year ten pupils at one of the local comprehensives and had hanged herself. Joanna had been asked to speak to Cherie's schoolmates to try and persuade them to see that what had started out as teenage jealousy (Cherie had been a very pretty girl) and teenage teasing had ended up in tragedy. She'd read some of the texts on the girl's phone and had been shocked at the vitriol. But while they were nasty, in a way, they were also pathetic. Silly little insults about her breath smelling, having legs like sticks, bad teeth and so on. And yet the result had been tragic, her parents so devastated they hardly knew what to do with themselves and these days were almost unable to function. Both were receiving counselling. Cherie had been their only child, achieved after years of IVF.

Joanna had been dreading the trip and had put it off. Because, a mother herself now, she couldn't imagine how terrible she would feel if something like that had happened to her beloved Jakob. And Matthew would be destroyed, as Cherie's parents had been. He lived for the child. But Cherie's parents had begged the police to speak to the girls who were responsible for their daughter's death so they could learn where their childish actions had led. 'Don't let any more parents suffer this.'

Witnessing their anguish and seeing the scars that would never heal had determined Joanna to do at least this for them and their daughter. And so she'd agreed to visit the school. But in a fit of cowardice, she'd delayed the visit until she had Mike at her side (who would prove a distraction to the teenage girls). And give her moral support.

But however well she and Mike performed, they both knew Cherie Glover wouldn't be the only teenager to kill herself because she was being trolled. And so she sighed.

''Fraid so, Mike. Leek doesn't change.' She managed a smile. 'This moorlands town might be untouched by events in the wider world, but it has its own microcosm of criminal activity. Here the criminals never retire but return to their bad old habits and their bad old haunts. So predictable. The usual traffic offences, troublesome families. ASBOs. We're linking up with the major investigative unit over cybercrime. Just about reaching our targets on domestic violence, stalking' – she tossed the list aside – 'that sort of stuff. Nothing major, but Cherie . . .'

Again, his eyes returned to the whiteboard and he lifted his eyebrows, questioning. So she told him a few more details about Cherie Glover and watched his face pale while his responses mirrored her own, turning the events inwards. 'If that happened to Ricky or Jossy . . .' His voice trailed away. He couldn't vocalize his thoughts, but his face sagged. 'You want me to come along?'

She nodded, secretly pleased he'd been the one to suggest it.

'So. Priority for today?'

'Light duties, Mike,' she reminded him. 'Remember?'

'How could I forget?' There was a hint of bitterness in his voice. 'Who's going to *let* me forget?'

'It's for your own good,' she said softly. 'You know how physical front-line duties can be . . .' She didn't add that some local villains would sense and exploit any weak points. She couldn't take the risk.

He was scowling now, so she mollified him with, 'You can come to the school with me. You know how teenage girls take to you.'

'Before this.' He glanced down at his leg, and she read, for the first time, vulnerability in his face. Something she never would have connected with all six feet and three inches of Detective Sergeant Mike Korpanski.

The attention had drifted away from them, officers getting on with their own work. A chance for a more intimate exchange. 'So how are you, Mike?' She asked the question quietly.

He responded equally softly, privately, something between the two of them, not meant for a wider audience. 'Getting there,' he confessed, 'but I'm not there yet. Not sure if I ever . . .' His eyelids flickered dangerously. 'Confidence eroded. Well, you know what I mean. I'm just thankful—'

Emotions threatening to overwhelm them both, they each looked away, and she tried to make a joke of it. 'Not sure I'd have fancied having a one-legged hop-along for a colleague.'

And he teased her back. 'Sure that's in our new, politically correct, ultra-kind, woke new guidelines?'

'Oh, don't you get all PC on me,' she warned, 'or even light duties will be denied you. You'll be confined to a chair sat in front of a computer terminal.'

He put his hand on her arm; kept it there for a moment, frowning. 'Put it like this: I've seen things from another perspective since the accident. Hobbling around on crutches isn't much fun. Everything,' he sighed, 'is so much more difficult. Getting in and out of a car, holding shopping, climbing stairs. I'll take none of it for granted ever again.'

'So in that way . . .?' She was watching his face for his response.

'No,' he protested. 'I'm not glad it happened, but it's put something into my life that wasn't there before. A sort of . . .' He cast around for the right word. 'Awareness.'

She nodded. 'We should get going. The school day has already started and they're expecting us later. But first let's see how King is getting on with his search for the online Romeo who's conned so many women out of their life savings.'

SIX

9.38 a.m.

Being unable to move was playing odd tricks with his mind. The stranger's scrutiny of his collection was conjuring up a memory from when he was a boy. His parents had been religious, almost puritanical with an insistence that he pay attention to Bible teachings. And now he remembered a passage from Luke which, even as a boy, had chilled him. Something about a rich man who needed to build bigger barns to hoard his wealth.

I will pull down my barns and build greater.

As a boy he had applauded the sentiment.

But now it was the follow-on he was paying attention to.

The mockery of God. His eyes roved the room, seeing its contents in a different light.

Then whose shall those things be, which thou hast provided?

Thou fool.

His lips moved as he remembered the words.

Thou fool, this night thy soul shall be required of thee: then whose shall those things be, which thou hast provided? He closed his eyes, and when he opened them again, it was to see the man standing in front of him, as though he had read his mind and now was providing the answer. Mine.

His eyes shone with a glint of mockery.

Thou fool, this night . . .

The silence was tense between them, thick and poisonous.

'Joseph!'

The voice sang into the silence, breaking the tension. Startled, the stranger gripped his gun, searching Joseph's eyes for an answer. 'Who is that?'

Joseph, however, felt relief and a certain triumph. With this one visitor he had gained the upper ground – momentarily.

'Doreen, my neighbour.'

Doreen Caputo was his nearest neighbour. She lived in The Lake House, the house that projected on a jetty out into the lake. She walked her dog, Stevie Wonder, every single day come rain or shine, heatwave or snow, past Cloud Mansion, her route never varying. And every single day, as she passed, she called out to him. If the weather was good, they exchanged a few words through the open study window. At other times, they chatted at the front door. The conversations followed well-worn topics: Stevie Wonder, the weather, her husband's health. Luca Caputo had Parkinson's disease and Doreen looked after him devotedly. But she found caring for him hard emotionally and heavy physically, and confided in her neighbour who sympathized – daily.

The stranger crossed to the window and peered through the crack in the curtains. Joseph's hope flickered. Doreen would know something was wrong. She would raise the alarm. The police would come swarming in and this nightmare would be over.

But the stranger had other plans.

Doreen was rapping on the window, puzzlement turning his name into a question. 'Joseph?'

The stranger looked at him, and Joseph's hope flickered into life. This was unanticipated, and his captor was unprepared. Whatever the stranger's plan was, it had a flaw.

'Joseph?' The sing-song tone had been replaced by a note of concern.

'Joseph?'

He knew she was standing just the other side of the window. He knew she waited as Joseph sensed the stranger's hesitation, his search for a response which would deflect this intrusion.

Joseph said nothing but waited for his cue, fearful there was a chance that Doreen would be dragged into this terrible situation – a tied-up hostage faced with a gun.

Could he warn her? Somehow?

She spoke again, anxiety raising the pitch of her voice. 'It's Doreen. I'm just taking Stevie Wonder for his usual walk.' The dog gave a confirmatory bark. Or maybe he'd picked up a stranger's scent and was trying to warn his mistress.

The stranger's eyes were roving around the room, searching for a prop before finally returning to Joseph. 'You normally respond?'

'Yes.'

The gun was jabbed into his sternum. Joseph tried to stifle his mind. If the man pulled the trigger now, ribs, lung, heart would explode. The trajectory of a bullet rattled through organs, bounced off bones, found purchase, maybe in the spine, in less time than it took to blink. You felt it before you heard it. Joseph knew the damage a bullet could do.

'Then respond.'

'I usually go to the window.' He eyed the curtains before meeting his captor's eyes and sensed indecision.

He grabbed at a chance. 'If she can't see me,' he said, looking boldly into the man's face, 'she goes round to the front door.' He shook his head, watching him closely. 'She won't give up. We speak every day.'

'Not today.' The stranger bent down so they were eye to eye, tension mounting, as Joseph waited for his move.

It came quickly. In one fast, smooth action, he pulled a knife from his waistband and sliced through the plastic ties. 'Go to the door,' he said. 'I will be behind you. Don't think of trying anything. It won't be just you I aim at. It will be you, her – and the dog.'

Joseph pressed his hands against the chair arms to help himself stand and struggled to his feet, rubbing his wrists, while the man pressed the gun into his spine. 'Walk,' he said.

Joseph stood behind the front door and calmed his voice. 'Hello, Mrs Caputo. Can't open the door right now. I'm a bit tied up.' He spoke quickly, was even able to smile at the irony, while he hoped she would pick up on the anomaly before he gave a theatrical cough. 'Got a bit of a cold.' He sniffed and gave another pantomime cough while from behind the door he sensed her suspicion. She'd picked up on his use of Mrs Caputo, he was sure. For years now, she had been Doreen while he had been Joseph.

'Joseph,' she said slowly, and he sensed her puzzlement as well as the enquiry. 'Do you need anything?'

'No,' he said quickly. Too quickly because her next sentence was heavy with doubt.

'You're sure?'

'I'm sure.'

He held his breath. Had she also picked up on the fact that his curtains, always open, were closed?

From the other side of the door, there was an uneasy silence, while behind him he sensed the man's finger was tightening on the trigger, and he prayed to a God he didn't even believe in anymore: *Go, Doreen. Get away from here. Go and raise the alarm that a madman with a gun is threatening me. Get far away, out of range. You are in danger too. Don't let him realize you're suspicious.*

The tension between the three of them was as thick as a radio-active cloud. Even Stevie Wonder was silent now except for a low bubble of a growl.

The gun jabbed even harder into his back. He braced himself for a shot which didn't come. He sensed Doreen's hesitation as she wondered which path to take. Challenge or retreat?

After a brief pause, Joseph heard her dubious response. 'OK. But if you need—'

He cut her off short, speaking quickly, sending her on her way. 'No. Nothing.' He didn't want anything to happen to her. She was garrulous and sometimes talked for too long. But she was his neighbour and he was, actually, fond of her. He understood she was lonely, isolated by her husband's incapacity, while he was isolated by choice.

'Thank you, *Mrs* Caputo.' Again, he stressed the formal use of her name, another signal.

He heard her footsteps crunching over the gravel then fainter as she passed his house, receding into the distance until he couldn't hear her at all. And he was left with a sense of disappointment, an opportunity lost. And an alien emotion: loneliness while he was beset with doubts. Maybe his hint had been too subtle for her, and his story, though weak, had actually convinced her.

He turned round, and the stranger poked him in the ribs again. 'Back,' he ordered. 'Chair.'

And he obeyed. He walked towards the study and settled back into the chair he was beginning to hate.

The pistol whip came without warning. The first thing he felt was a cracking pain in his temple. There had been no sign it was coming. No change in the stranger's face. It had been done almost casually and was all the more terrifying for that. Had his wrists not been tethered he would have fallen to the floor. As it was, the chair had saved him this time.

The stranger had chosen his target well. The temple was a good place to inflict pain and ensure maximum damage, with little more than a thin shard of bone protecting the eye sockets. And he knew why the stranger had done it. He'd sensed his appeal in the exchange with his neighbour.

Joseph gripped the arms of the chair to steady himself, his mind and body dealing with the nausea and the sharp pain in his temple where he felt the bone had been cracked. But even in all this, he still felt the ring of triumph. The stranger might have the upper hand, but he didn't hold all the aces.

Maybe Doreen would raise the alarm. And if not, there might be another opportunity.

He closed his eyes and moved his head from side to side, searching for answers.

When he opened them again, he saw the stranger had parted the curtains just enough to peep out and was keeping watch along the track in case of a further intrusion. But the day was rainy and dull. Few would pass this way today.

After he'd kept watch for a few minutes, the stranger returned to him. He bent down, his face so near to Joseph's that he could pick up a faint scent of exotic spices. 'Where is your mobile phone, please, Mr Holden? I would like to use it.'

His very politeness was chilling.

Joseph tried to force his brain to visualize the last place he had seen his phone. He was careless where he put it down and often had to use the landline to locate it.

'I don't know.' He despised his voice – weak, vulnerable, pathetic: a frightened old man. He watched the stranger's knuckles whiten as his hand tightened around the pistol grip, and he braced himself for another blow. He looked at the floor. 'I'm sorry. I don't use it much. I don't always know exactly where . . .' His voice tailed off, and he realized he had to do better. 'Maybe it's by my bed.' He tried to inject some credence into his tone. 'Yes. By my bed.'

But then they heard a dog's soft bark.

SEVEN

Through the window, Joanna could see DC Alan King's long fingers tapping away on a keyboard.

'Call me an optimist,' she murmured to Mike, 'but is there a modicum of excitement in the boy's fingertips?'

Korpanski's response was cautious. 'Maybe.'

She pushed open the door. 'Got anything, King?'

King was your typical computer geek. Tall, skinny, prematurely rounded shoulders. Intense and not only a whizz kid on the computer, he was also a linguist, fluent in French and Spanish, and although they hadn't tested it, he could probably get by in German too. His bony fingers could dance across the keyboard and uncover all sorts of secrets. In Joanna's opinion, he was typical of the type the police were lucky to recruit. Dyspraxic, bumping into desks as he passed, he was bordering on dyslexic. And he was also a genius. The force relied on him more and more as techno crime barged into all their lives, skipping across countries' borders and time zones.

King's response to her casual question was typical. Without taking his eyes off the screen, he answered with the tap of a few keys so fast neither Joanna nor Mike could have said which ones he'd pressed.

'I have the bank account details where Romeo's money was lodged – which is a start. Plus the IP address. Not quite as sophisticated as most. Kept it local. Here.' He tapped a few more keys and brought up a pudgy-faced teenager.

Joanna and Mike stared at it. Joanna spoke first. 'Is that who I think it is?'

A few more keys exposed a police record, and Joanna felt her mouth drop open. 'Tell me that isn't Finley James.'

King turned his head round, a big smile spreading across his thin face. 'Yep,' he said, a degree of satisfaction in his tone. 'The very one who was in a young offenders' institution, but in an attempt to change his ways, he was sponsored by a well-meaning philanthropic charity to gain expertise in computer sciences. And this . . .' He turned back to the screen and presented a series of messages exchanged between Finley James age 'twenty-three' and his victim, who called herself 'Hayley', aged 'nineteen', who had turned out to be a lady called Julie Trent, forty-one years old. The picture she'd used was of a pretty nineteen-year-old female, but the style – big hair, orange pinafore dress, false eyelashes and heavy eye make-up –suggested it was probably thirty years out of date. King leaned forward. 'This is the actual person. We lifted this from a Facebook share.' And now they confronted the lined face of a woman somewhere in her forties who looked as though a diet of alcohol and cigarettes had done their worst. King swivelled round in his chair, laughing. 'Neither of them was quite what they claimed to be.'

Mike moved forward. 'Yeah, but I'm guessing only one of them lost money.'

'Yep,' King agreed without a hint of sympathy. 'Fifty grand.'

'Fifty thousand?' Joanna couldn't help herself. 'Where did she get that sort of money from?'

'Remortgaged her house,' King said, eyes still on the screen, 'maxed out on her credit cards and, I'm guessing, borrowed money from friends, though that,' he said regretfully, 'doesn't show up.'

'How did the little toad convince her to part with so much money?'

'Posed as . . .' His fingers performed another trick and a picture appeared of a good-looking man with ruffled blond hair, and an even-toothed American grin. He looked somewhere in his thirties. 'That's the character he posed as – very convincingly, I have to say.'

He swivelled round in his chair to grin up at Joanna. 'Sure it wasn't just computer sciences Finley was learning? He's proper imaginative. Had a great backstory lined up. Good enough for a Hollywood blockbuster. Said he was being held by the Russians having fought on the front line near Dnipro with the Ukrainian army and been taken captive.'

'That figures,' Mike growled, his eyes drifting towards the messages.

King continued, 'Said if a ransom was paid he'd be released and by her side in a matter of days. Poor old "Hayley" lived on hope.' Now he did sound regretful and genuinely sorry for her. For all his attachment to computers, Alan King was soft-hearted.

'Any chance of her getting her money back?'

King shook his head with conviction. 'Not a hope in hell unless he's kept some of it in a UK bank account, but as far as I can see he hasn't, so that's that. God only knows where it's gone.' He pressed a couple more keys. 'Disappeared.'

'We'd better go and have a chat with Mr James,' Joanna said, 'and maybe "Hayley".' She gave a last, regretful glance at the picture – nineteen years old. Once upon a time, she thought.

10.15 a.m.

Doreen had returned, but this time she hadn't called out. Only Stevie Wonder had. They'd both heard the dog's soft bark, as though asking a question. They'd waited, but dog and mistress had left.

The stranger had found the mobile somewhere and was currently charging it up. He was going to use it to make contact with someone.

The obvious answer was a partner in crime, someone who would bring a van and help clear out the house. It was one possibility.

But there was another. If his intention was to use Joseph as a hostage, then the natural next step would be to make demands. And the usual demand was for money. But who would pay to have him freed? He had no rich relatives; neither did he have a whole lot of cash in a bank account. He managed, most of the time, on his pensions. If the house needed a repair, then he sold an item or two – as he had late last year when his roof had leaked.

The man had dragged a chair towards the window and seemed able to sit, motionless, for long periods of time. Not asleep but not quite awake either. He kept his grip on the gun while seeming in a trance, his eyelids drooping. But if Joseph made even the smallest movement, his eyes would fly open, instantly watchful, ready for action.

His mind stumbled over the many questions. Why the delay in whatever he was planning? Each hour surely put him in more danger of being discovered? Maybe he was safe for now. Maybe Doreen Caputo hadn't registered the significance of her suspicions. When she did surely she'd raise the alarm. And then what?

His captor was in no hurry, but Joseph was sure he had a definite plan and was waiting patiently to execute it. He had to be waiting for someone or something.

He turned his attention to the gun. A Glock semi-automatic. A good gun for a professional. Austrian made, nice pebble grip, safety on the trigger.

Perhaps sensing his scrutiny or maybe following his thoughts, the man's eyes opened, and for a moment they stared at each other. Then the man grew restless and started pacing the room. He seemed to be focussing on the varied objects again, possibly just to pass the time. But he wasn't here for a museum trip. He stopped to study the pale patch high on the wall, as he'd done before, before dropping his gaze down to the cabinet. Which gave Joseph another possibility. Could he be waiting for an expert to help select the more valuable pieces? Or was he looking for something specific?

Joseph's thoughts were turning round and round as he tried to find a more comfortable space for his back. Why the wait? When knowing that every minute he spent holding him hostage, even in an isolated house with few passers-by, the risk of someone realizing something was wrong increased. Which made Joseph reflective and a little sad. Who came by apart from Doreen Caputo?

He looked longingly towards the door. It wasn't even very far away. Four long steps would do it. He pulled against the arm restraints, but he could hardly wiggle his fingers and there was no movement at all in his wrist. Even if the stranger's gaze wasn't directly on him, Joseph knew he was watching all the time. And he could hardly have dragged the chair across the room. He strained again against the ties, but it was hopeless.

Now the man had finished roaming the room and had returned to sentry duty in the chair in front of the window, his eyes peering through the narrow crack in the curtains. Perhaps he was watching for the return of his neighbour. Or maybe he was simply keeping an eye on the track down to the lake. Or maybe he was waiting for his confederate. At times he caressed the gun with the familiarity of an old friend; at others it lay loosely on his lap. The room was silent. Joseph could hear the heavy tick of the long case clock in the hall as time moved forward slower than usual. And now they avoided looking directly at one another, as though each wanted to deny the other's existence. But it didn't work. Both were searingly aware of the other.

The man's lips moved. Was he talking to himself? Praying? *Thou fool.*

Joseph watched his eyelids droop.

He managed to shift the chair a little, turning his head very slightly, but enough to see the surface of the desk behind him. Which gave him hope.

If the man fell asleep or left the room, even for just a moment, was there something he could use to free himself? But all he could see, out the corner of his eye, was a scatter of papers, the computer turned off, showing a black, empty screen. He closed his own eyes, and for a moment, the room was silent except for the two men breathing.

Even the hall clock seemed to have stopped.

EIGHT

11 a.m.

Finley James lived in a rented room in one of the terraced houses which had once belonged to mill workers. Leek's history had been influenced by the silk industry as well as the French prisoners of the Napoleonic Wars paroled to Leek in the nineteenth century. The house where Finley lived looked run-down and neglected, with rotten window frames and one window covered with a sheet of cardboard. The front door looked as though it had been kicked in a couple of times, its wood splintered in places. No one was hanging around the street, which felt like a dystopian ghost town. This was the sink end of Leek, the area where people kept largely indoors. Curtains were drawn even though it was the middle of the day.

Korpanski banged on the door with his fist then turned to Joanna with a broad grin. 'That feels good. It's something I've really missed – the heavy knock of the long arm of the law.'

Joanna too was smiling. She took a moment to peer into her colleague's face before they heard the sound of a scuffle inside; the door was opened, and a young guy looking as though he'd just woken up faced them. His chin was covered in stubble, his T-shirt many sizes too large for his skinny frame, and he had an unhealthy pallid complexion. That fitted with someone who spent their days hunched over a computer keyboard. Maybe Finley James had known this day would come eventually. He even held out his wrists.

Joanna didn't need to ask his name, but they did need to caution him before they arrested him.

Finley gave a long heartfelt sigh. 'Thought it was too good to last,' he said before spoiling the penitent effect with a cheeky grin. 'Nothin' quite like it though, when a fish takes the bait.'

It was one way of putting it, but Joanna's thoughts and sympathies were with 'Hayley', fifty grand out of pocket for a shattered dream. She didn't have the glamorous boyfriend. Just a heart full of regret and years of penury. Would she try again? Joanna wondered. Or would she give up on true love?

Finley gave her another cheeky grin. 'Thought even you might be tempted, Inspector, with the juicy images I posted.' He obviously hadn't heeded the *You don't have to say anything* bit in the caution.

'I'm married,' Joanna said shortly, while Korpanski looked as though he was about to throw a punch. She followed that with, 'We'd better get you down to the station and record all this.' And they escorted him to the car.

But Finley hadn't finished taunting them. 'I wonder what training you'll sort out for me this time round.'

'Whatever it is,' Joanna responded, 'if it leads to a crime, we'll catch up with you. We have you marked, Finley. And' – she turned round in her seat – 'you're not smart enough to pull it off.'

There was this strange connection between the police and the habitual petty felon. They weren't friends, but neither were they quite enemies. More like boxers dancing around the ring, each waiting for the other to make a mistake. There was a sort of grudging respect between them.

Joanna wanted to ask him about the money. If Julie Trent was to be subjected to humiliation in a public court, hopefully she would at least be able to recover some of her funds.

But Joanna stayed silent. Best to do all this under PACE regulations. It didn't do to step out of line. Lawyers were such experts at exploiting breaks in regulations. She sighed.

Mike was in the back while she was driving. He leaned forward to speak very softly in her ear. 'You don't seem very pleased we've got him.'

'I'm thinking about the victim. Shattered dreams and all that.'

'Yeah. I thought that was probably it.'

He leaned back in his seat while she made up her mind. Charging, interviewing and filling in the forms online would take a while even with Alan King's input, but when all that was done, she vowed she would speak to Julie Trent herself. As it was, they were due at the school in a little over two hours.

NINE

11.30 a.m.

J oseph could feel every knob and angle of the carving in the back of the chair. The irony was that the carving – deep, original, seventeenth century – had been one of the main reasons why he'd paid so much for it. Another irony was that at the time, he'd appreciated the solid frame which now seemed designed to torture and imprison him. He remembered running his fingers over the arms, trying to lift it, but it was a heavy piece – he'd had trouble transporting it out to his van and lifting it in. Now its design seemed to mock him: the carving, the weight, the structure – everything he'd loved then now seemed designed to trap and torture him. It had become a prison, its arms stout enough to restrain him. He scorned the pride he'd once felt for it. He'd like to bloody well burn it.

Thou fool.

He shifted his weight again, testing it. It refused to budge. It didn't even creak, its joints holding fast. He had an image of his younger self, strong, powerful, agile, running helter-skelter down a hill, leaping over tree stumps, avoiding rocks and stones as skilfully as a gazelle, sliding through mud, dodging bullets and pursuers. An image replaced with reality. He was an old man now, powerless and weak, bound to an ancient, treasured possession, held hostage by . . .? And that was where he stopped. Who was his captor? His gaze met hard eyes. What was he doing here?

He'd found the mobile phone and was scrolling through it. While he was absorbed, Joseph tried to work out the man's ethnic origins again. Maybe that would give him a clue. Earlier, he'd thought he could be North African – possibly Moroccan or Egyptian; that he might have had Arab blood. But now he studied his face in profile, he wasn't so sure and shifted his guess further south . . . African blood. His skin was light, which had initially misled him; the accent overlaid with an English education reminded him of something. Not a specific person. A place. His mind flicked through memories until he found it then quickly shut it down, sealing his ears from unwelcome sounds. He seemed to feel sand between his fingers and shifted uncomfortably, worrying that he'd located it.

He frowned and closed his eyes against the bad, sick feeling. He hadn't felt this anxious when he'd opened the door to the man holding a gun. He'd been curious but not panicky. Now he felt the chill of the floor creep into his feet, stealing up through his body until it reached his brain. And he felt even more powerless and terrified. His observation of the man had stirred up dark memories. Joseph wrenched his wrists in frustration. Even though he was a non-believer, he closed his eyes for a moment and begged for mercy, but heard only the response, *Thou fool.*

When he'd paid cash for Cloud Mansion, locals and the estate agent had all asked the same question in different, roundabout ways. Where did the money come from? He'd had his answer prepared.

I earned it. He'd never said how.

Now he reassured himself, justified his past, applying a liberal salve to his conscience, the conscience he'd suppressed successfully over the past years. No one made this sort of money or acquired such treasures without breaking a few rules. Looting and pilfering was, surely, a perk of the job? The spoils of war surrounded him: large house, souvenirs, treasures. His just reward for the risks he'd undertaken. But – his eyes swivelled back to his captor, still engrossed in the information held on his phone – what was stolen by you could be stolen by another. Joseph made a silent vow. *I will not beg; neither will I plead.*

And now he turned his mind to the journey which had led him there. The rain which had trickled from stream to river, from river to sea, money and the possessions that now adorned the mansion. He closed his eyes for a minute and seemed to smell evocative, exotic scents: jasmine and patchouli, sandalwood and frankincense. His head dropped forward, and he dreamed.

He was in a market. It was noisy, bustling, colourful, everyone jostling, pushing and shoving, the cries of vendors, the buzzing of a million flies, metal ware clanging in the fronts of shops, everything moving and banging together as people passed and knocked against them, their clothes moving in a kaleidoscope of vivid colour. He breathed in the sweet scent of meat hanging in sunshine on butcher's hooks, the flesh not pink but black with flies, no matter how hard the children tried to beat them away with the tail of a donkey. He caught the swish of *djellabas* and the slap of sandals in dust, and there it was again, puffing across from the ladies' *guntiinos*, another elusive scent, this time saffron and turmeric, chilli peppers and cinnamon, the sound of food spitting fat from the cooking pots. He opened his eyes and waited for the sensation to fade, but when he scuffed his feet, he still half expected to raise a cloud of market dust.

He knew the place. *Somalia*.

He felt fear as fate ran to catch up with him, but sitting on its wings was a hot, furious anger. He'd been careless, and that would cost him his life, because now he was dipping into his past, he realized this could have only one end. This man had come to kill him.

His eyes flickered open to look straight into the stranger's, which were focussed on him now, dark and cold, hostile and cruel, but also with the tilt of a question. He searched in the dark irises for pity and found none. Only a granite hardness. But he still puzzled over the question. Why wait?

He'd located his quarry. Tracked him down like a professional, incapacitated him. Tethered him to the chair like a decoy duck giving him no option but to wait for the shot.

The stranger moved back to his guard post, keeping watch through the narrow crack in the curtains, stroking the Glock on his lap as though it was a much-loved friend.

As Joseph watched him, ignored now by his captor, he felt an overwhelming sense of shame that overtook his fear. He'd left a trail of breadcrumbs for the man to follow him here then opened the door to the stranger. Had he been accepting that fate had come to visit? Worse, he'd made no attempt to defend himself.

Not only a fool but a coward.

He dropped his chin on to his chest. He had no fight left in him.

All he had left was impotent curiosity and shame.

TEN

Joanna and Mike were also feeling uncomfortable. Joanna acknowledged that she'd brought Mike along partly for moral support but also as a way of getting into these girls' mindsets. In days gone by, his physique had impressed, possibly overawed, the boys, while the girls had drooled over the handsome detective with his neat black hair and engaging manner. But he wasn't quite back to strength yet. She had to accept it. The accident had changed Detective Sergeant Mike Korpanski. Some of his confidence had gone. And that overwhelming physical presence was diluted. Maybe he'd get it back, maybe not. But he was still Mike, her loyal side-kick, and she knew he would continue to put his life on the line for her as he had in the past.

As she headed through the school gates, she shot him a look, trying to inject some of the appreciation she felt towards him. It was difficult. Detective Sergeant Korpanski wasn't someone who accepted compliments easily.

Perhaps sensing some of her thoughts, he glanced across but quickly looked away. There was a moment's heavy silence between them before he spoke. 'Not looking forward to this.'

The moment passed. 'Me neither.'

His face cracked. 'I'd rather face a pack of wolves than a roomful of teenage girls.'

'Really?'

They both chuckled, and she knew they were back to their old banter, relationship preserved.

'Come on,' she said, striding out, 'let's face the wolves together,' as a middle-aged woman in a tight black skirt and red cardigan headed towards them.

They introduced themselves, and she smiled. 'Laura Fieldman,' she said. 'For my sins, I'm the headmistress of this place.' She wafted her hand around to indicate the campus before her face changed. 'We were devastated when Cherie—' She stopped for a moment, recovering herself. 'When the full extent of what had happened—' She tried again. 'I hadn't realized how vulnerable—' She paused. 'How she'd been affected. I think now—' She replaced that with, 'I had to do something. So thank you for coming and talking to the pupils.'

Joanna and Mike gave her a warm smile of sympathy. Not for anything would they have been in her shoes.

The school was a two-storey sixties building that looked as though it was made of glass and cardboard. Ms Fieldman hadn't quite finished her effusive thanks. 'Really. Thank you so much for coming,' she continued, walking briskly ahead of them, leading the way through the doors into a large hall, presumably doubling up as a gymnasium, as there were climbing bars along the walls and apparatus shoved into a corner. The place was full of kids jostling each other, shuffling their feet, and the noise was off the scale – until Laura Fieldman, tailed by the two detectives, climbed the three steps on to the stage – when, remarkably, the room fell silent. Joanna eyed the sea of youngsters, all looking at the floor now in collective guilt.

One day, she was thinking as she scanned the room, Jakob would be one of those kids. That was when the reality hit her again. How would she feel if . . .?

The thought snatched at her heart. 'We have to make this work,' she muttered to Korpanski. 'We have to stop this . . . somehow.'

He nodded his agreement, perhaps, like her, thinking of his own children.

Most of the youngsters had stopped looking at the floor now and were shooting defiant looks at them as though they were their parents, about to give them a telling-off. But Joanna and Mike knew they had to find another way into these youngsters' minds than simply wielding their authority. Maybe it had been a mistake to try to speak to three classes at a time. The hall was packed, but they couldn't spare more than an hour away from work at the most; they had multiple ongoing investigations and they'd wanted to reach as many of the pupils as was possible. So they were addressing years nine, ten and eleven, the years either side of Cherie Glover's age. At a guess year eleven, the fifteen-year-olds, would be the biggest challenge. Joanna remembered herself at that age and smiled. She'd been described on her end-of-year report as 'rebellious'.

She eyed the faces lifted towards her, searching along the rows before speaking.

'I expect you think I'm here to warn you about the dangers of the Internet.'

A few of them looked up, but a good half of them retained their disdainful expression, avoiding her eyes. Whatever this cop had to say, they either already knew it or they weren't interested.

'Have a think about this,' she said, 'just for a minute. If you had known that these messages could have caused Cherie to kill herself, would you still have sent them?'

Most shook their heads but not all. She picked on one of the most defiant starers. A redhead, arms folded, hard stare.

'What's the worst message *you've* ever received?'

The girl's mouth dropped open. She'd expected a lecture. Not an invitation to share.

'Someone . . .' The girl's voice was little louder than a whisper and yet clear enough that everyone in the room could hear. They were all looking at her. 'Someone said that I smelled.' She dropped her eyes after this sharing. Wasn't looking around now, inviting her mates to join in the derision. In fact, there was a ripple of sympathy around the room.

'It's not always something or someone obvious,' Joanna said. 'You can send out hundreds of negative messages. But if just one strikes home . . .' She addressed the girl again as though only the two of them were in the room, as though no one else could hear, although she could tell all were listening, including the headmistress, who was frowning. Maybe this hadn't been the talk she'd anticipated. 'When was this?'

'Months ago.' The girl was mumbling now.

'And it still hurts?'

The girl nodded.

'Did you know who sent it?'

She shook her head, eyes fixed on the floor.

'I take it you *never* knew who'd sent it?'

And now Joanna addressed the entire room. 'Do you think it's better if a nasty message is anonymous or from someone you know?'

A boy at the back wearing black-framed glasses spoke up. 'Both have their downsides.'

'Yeah.' She paused. 'You know what? I've read the messages that caused your school friend's suicide. We've identified some of the people who sent those messages and will be speaking to them and their parents at some point in the future. But myself and my colleague have come today to include *all* of you in this warning. The messages on Cherie's phone . . . to be honest, they weren't that bad.' By her side, she knew Korpanski was watching the room intently. Later they would share their instincts. She continued. 'They contained stuff saying she didn't wash, that she'd pinched someone's boyfriend, that she was . . . strange. Most of them clearly weren't true. But you don't know when a message will find vulnerability. And that's what makes them so dangerous. Just think on this: Cherie will never grow up, never marry, as many of you will. She won't go to university or have children, again, as many of you will. She was the only, beloved child of her parents. She was their hope for the future. And now that's gone.'

There was a shocked silence. Even the headmistress shuffled her feet – a sure sign she was uncomfortable at this graphic description of the Glovers' future lives.

'And the worst thing is it wasn't one person who caused this but a collective responsibility.'

Heads down, the whole hall fell silent. Some of the girls sniffed while the boys shuffled their feet.

Joanna moved away from the lectern, and Korpanski stepped forward. They'd choreographed the entire talk earlier at the station. She watched the girls eyeing him up while the boys also took his measure, a few of them, chins in the air, squaring their shoulders as though ready for a fight – except they weren't. Not really. She sighed. They were just kids.

'So what can you do about it?'

No one, apparently, had any suggestions. Or if they did, they weren't sharing them.

Korpanski moved on. 'I wonder if you have anyone you could turn to who might help you get through a horrible problem like bullying messages?'

Some looked bemused, others wary as though Korpanski was setting a trap. A few looked even more worried.

Korpanski waited for them to think this through before grinning. 'Personally I'd be ready to take them on. But that isn't the way, is it. So what is?'

Now he looked around the room. His grin broadened. 'Come on,' he encouraged. 'Give me some ideas.' He paused. 'Preferably less physical.'

Hands shot up.

'Block the number.'

'Ignore it.'

'Text back you're a worm.'

That caused a release of laughter.

And finally a small, timid girl speaking quietly said, 'I'd take my phone to the police and ask them to track down the sender and have a word with them.'

That resulted in silence, during which Korpanski nodded.

'They're all correct answers,' he said, flashing his signature grin at the girl, who instantly turned pink, before he turned round to face the whiteboard. 'So, as the police, what can *we* do? What should we do?'

2 p.m.

Doreen Caputo was running through her morning encounter. *Mrs Caputo?* she was thinking. She turned to her husband to whom she'd relayed her misgivings. 'Luca,' she said, 'what do you think?'

Her husband's speech was slurred. Parkinson's made speaking increasingly difficult, but she understood his meaning.

'Nothing.'

Yes, she thought. *That was the right answer. But tomorrow, if I still think something's up, I'm contacting the police.*

2.05 p.m.

Korpanski was writing on the whiteboard, answering his own question.

Track down the sender and talk to them.

Warn them that if they continue, we will press charges.

Work with the service provider to have the texts blocked.

File a restraining order.

Issue a fine and, in extreme cases, the sender can go to prison.

There was a shocked silence as the pupils read the last line.

Joanna turned back to the watching faces; the kids were now fully engaged. 'So how can we stop it?'

The red-headed girl spoke, loudly now, with a hint of aggression. 'We can't.'

Joanna lifted a finger. 'No – you're right. We can't. But we can stop sending them ourselves, can't we? Think of the consequences before you press send.' She heard the note of appeal in her voice. 'I'm guessing many of you knew Cherie.' She'd deliberately framed this as a comment rather than a question. 'So you know what the end result can be. And you're right. We can't stop it.' She paused. 'Have any of you ever heard of the hydra?'

That resulted in blank looks and head shaking.

'It was a many-headed beast in Greek mythology. When Heracles cut one head off, two grew in its place. And so the heads proliferated.' She frowned and scanned the room. 'This is a warning. Some things get worse when you try to tackle them alone without giving it some thought. How do you think Heracles finally defeated the hydra?'

There was plenty of shrugging as the teenagers looked at each other.

'Heracles got his nephew to help by cauterizing each stump as soon as he cut the head off.' Joanna paused. 'This is the first thing you can do. Ask for help. Doesn't matter who from. It can be a friend or a parent. Even the parent of a friend who can put things into perspective.' She asked another question. 'Why do you think people send these malicious messages?'

Two girls put their hands up. One had blonde plaits and cow-like eyes fixed on Detective Sergeant Korpanski. The second girl wore the same school uniform, but her hair was styled in a rather severe short, geometric cut.

'Jealousy,' Cow Eyes said, and Joanna nodded.

'Yeah. A lot of the time.'

'Spite,' was Geometric Cut's offer.

Joanna stood up, ready to leave. 'I think you already know all these things,' she said, smiling now. 'You just needed me to remind you.' And then she slipped back into her official role. 'When we are faced with a young boy or girl's suicide, their mobile phone is one of the first places we look for an explanation. If we find messages or pictures streamed that we feel have contributed' – and here she paused – 'we do take action, and we will.'

She skewered them with a stare. 'Charges can result in a criminal record, which can have an impact in later life.'

At which point the entire room was subdued.

They were leaving the school and climbing into the car. 'Not quite lost your sex appeal then.' Joanna couldn't resist pulling Korpanski's (good) leg.

He grunted, but she noted he'd flushed and looked awkward so she changed the subject. 'You know what really pisses me off?'

He waited.

'It was all lies. That girl died because of a pack of silly, adolescent lies. Jealousy, spite, girls ganging up. It wasn't even true, so a girl died because of someone's made-up tales.'

He looked across at her, surprised at her vehemence.

They were back at the station where Joanna had to stop herself from repeatedly glancing across at him to reassure herself that he really was back. He really was OK. He caught her glance and bounced it back with a broad grin. 'Thought I'd never get here,' he confessed sheepishly, looking around. 'I so wanted to make it back.' His face warmed then crumpled. 'But now I'm ready to moan about the paperwork.'

'Which unfortunately never goes away. We don't just have to work, Mike. We have to prove that we are – every minute of every day.'

Korpanski grunted then turned back to his computer screen and the online form he was filling in. 'I just wish, for once, they'd stick to just one set of guidelines and priorities instead of changing them every couple of months. This month it's cybercrime, which was, I suppose, why we had to visit the charming Mr James before making fools of ourselves at the school.'

'You think that's what I did?' She felt herself bristle.

Korpanski hastily retracted. 'No of course not. I'm just not sure it'll do any good.'

'You don't think teenagers can have the intelligence to see what damage a few words can cause?'

He knew he was being forced to retract his statement. 'It's not just girls, Jo,' he said. 'The whole thing is so pernicious. And so hard to police. It all seems so unreal. Just fiddling with the keys on a screen. It's hardly like threatening someone with a knife or a gun, is it?'

'But the results are real enough,' she said. 'Cherie Glover dead at fourteen, and impoverished, impecunious, disillusioned Julie Trent who's lost her life savings.'

'Well, she hid behind a false persona too.'

'Yeah.' She was thoughtful now. 'That's true. Neither was who they said they were, but she was the one who lost money.'

Korpanski turned back to the screen – and his grumbling. 'Car

crime over the summer.' He swivelled round on his chair and gave
her a cheeky grin. 'More than a hundred thefts from vehicles in
July and August. Very poor percentage of arrests, Inspector.'

'Get back to writing your report on speaking to teenage girls
about online abuse,' she warned, 'before the government changes
its mind again. And, Mike,' she said, throwing out a challenge,
'we'll see if the clear-up rates improve now you're back.'

It felt good having Korpanski back to throw the gauntlet at. He
took the hint, and for the next half hour, their corner was quiet until
he resumed his grumble.

'Next month: domestics,' he trotted out. 'The month after it'll be
house burglaries while the government assures the gullible general
public that every single victim of crime will be' – he affected a
pompous, public-school voice – 'thoroughly investigated and each
victim will be visited – in person. In person, mind, by an officer of
His Majesty's police force.'

Had she a rubber on her desk, she would have thrown it at him.
But she couldn't chuck the mouse or she would lose all control of
her already misbehaving computer. So she substituted, 'Yeah, it's
nice to have you back too – even if you are Mr Grumpy.'

He glanced across at her, his face split in a wide grin. 'I'm not
really grumpy,' he said. 'Just recognizing the day-to-day reality of
our work. When I joined the police force, I thought I'd be solving
crime, fingering the collars of criminals, not sitting at a computer
facing statistics, watching the government make targets for Stop
and Search, teaching us how to treat ethnic minorities.'

She turned and faced him then. 'Mike,' she said, arms folded,
'they *have* to put us through courses to prove that when things go
wrong, it wasn't through lack of education but an officer's failure
to adhere to the rules.'

His mouth twisted into a cynical grin. 'So what courses have you
been subjected to, Jo, to save our senior officers' embarrassment?'

'I,' she responded with more than a hint of pride and dignity,
'have done a course on hostage negotiation run by an expert, a guy
called Robbie Callaghan, who's managed to free shedloads of
victims.'

Robbie had looked ex-army, with an uncompromising stare,
cropped hair, legs apart, camouflage clothing and an air of super
confidence. He had a wealth of experience in dealing with hostage
crises, which meant the class had been subdued into silent respect.

He'd freed fourteen people being held at gunpoint at a night club, a unique case for the UK of a school hostage situation and, on another occasion, a crowded restaurant of diners who'd been threatened by a terrorist wearing a suicide vest which had turned out to be corrugated cardboard and no explosives.

'But the ground rules,' he'd claimed, brown eyes scanning the room, seeming to pick on each individual, 'are all the same. Calm has to be your mantra.' He'd singled out Joanna for special treatment. 'Don't get impatient.' (He'd obviously sized her up pretty quickly, maybe watched the feverish way she tried to take detailed notes.) 'Even if their demands are ridiculous, go along with them. Above all, fix on your goal: safety of the hostage and eliminating the threat to the wider public. The hostage takers know they won't get away. They can't. Any money agreed will never reach them. They'll never be able to spend it because they'll never be free. So don't lose sight of your goal.'

Korpanski leaned back in his chair and gave a couple of slow, sarcastic claps. 'Well. Now that is impressive. We have so many hostage situations out here in the Staffordshire Moorlands. You're bound to use that training one of these days.'

She bridled. 'You can take the piss, but one of these days you might be glad of my skills.' Then she was forced to be honest. 'Though I didn't exactly score the best marks even though I did do a thesis on negotiation during my psychology degree.' She was anxious to drop the subject. 'And now it's nearly five o'clock. It's your first day back and we don't want to tire you.'

His face was a visual groan.

'While I'm off to see my cyber victim Ms Trent, aka "Hayley Smith", you need to go home and get some rest.'

'Thank you very much for that.' His face assumed a mischievous look. 'Though I sense the subtext is that our newly poverty-struck lady won't welcome a bloke turning up to keep her up to speed.'

'Yeah,' she agreed. 'I think a woman might appear more sympathetic.'

'Even you?'

She put her face close to his. 'Even me.'

He picked his jacket from the back of the chair, hesitating before he spoke. 'It *is* good to be back, Jo.' He looked around him. 'There were times I thought I wouldn't make it.' He grinned again. 'At least not on two legs.'

'Me neither,' she admitted. 'But here you are.'

For a moment, they gazed at each other, each realizing how close this friendship was, how much it meant to them.

'See you tomorrow.'

And then he was gone.

ELEVEN

6 p.m.

'I need the toilet.' In reality, he didn't, having had only two cups of tea and a sandwich since morning. But if he didn't move, he would go mad. His arms, legs, body were slowly seizing up.

The stranger grunted and looked up as though he'd forgotten Joseph's presence. He'd been staring into his own iPhone while Joseph's had been left charging in a wall socket at his feet. He glanced across, put away his phone, picked up the gun and took his knife out of his waistband. With two brisk cuts, he sliced through the arm ties, and Joseph tried to move. God, he was stiff.

It took him a few moments to stand; a few more to get his balance. But now he was upright, his eyes on a level with the stranger's. He stared right into them, trying to divine the man's purpose and intention. Strangely there was no anger there, no hatred or fury. In fact, nothing except a cold, calculating impassivity as he stared right back, his fingers on the pistol's trigger. Joseph recognized that expression. He'd seen it in the mirror, felt the same cold emotion in himself. The man had a job to do, and he would do it. He had no doubt his captor wouldn't hesitate to shoot if he needed to. But for now, his overriding emotion was patience, sticking to his plan – whatever it was. He had to be waiting for something or someone. Perhaps an instruction on his phone?

So Joseph asked himself as he stumbled towards the downstairs lavatory: what or who was he waiting for?

He stared at his reflection in the mirror over the sink and noted the bruise on his temple, a slight indentation. And he read his own response. Curious now rather than frightened. He too was waiting.

The stranger stood outside, not objecting even when he'd locked the door behind him. He must have reconnoitred the cloakroom and knew that the window was too small for him to crawl through. Which told of professionalism and a certain confidence in the ultimate success of his mission. Which was? The question went round and round inside his head.

He realized he'd lapsed into military talk, military thinking, outcomes, objectives.

He looked around the tiny room, hardly big enough for the corner sink and the toilet. As he flushed, he briefly considered refusing to come out, barricading himself in here, until he looked around and rejected that idea. The room was tiny, and the Glock could fire through the door as easily as through a piece of paper. Besides, the stranger could easily force the lock with one well-aimed bullet or a hard kick. It would be pointless and would surely only serve to anger him.

Don't waste your energy, he exhorted himself.

He washed his hands, massaging warm soapy water into his wrists, relieving the soreness temporarily, then towelled them dry as he tested theories. The intruder was here for a robbery and was awaiting his accomplice. He settled with that explanation, because behind it he recognized another, greater fear . . . retribution.

It was a fear which lay dormant at the back of his mind, surfacing only occasionally, but when it did, it scratched inside his head, like a mouse trying to emerge from its hole but too frightened to escape. He was the same. He'd needed to stay hidden too in his mouse hole. It was one of the reasons he'd chosen Cloud Mansion, where few people passed, a house that rose high over the surrounding countryside, and with a tricky approach from the rear. Easy to defend, he'd thought. But someone had found his hiding place, and he was realizing his safety had been an illusion.

He opened the cloakroom door. His captor stood right outside, his head jerking in the direction of the study. Joseph passed him, averting his eyes, because he didn't want to read something there. The truth.

Retribution could take many forms. He, of all people, knew that. He'd watched retribution in painful, cruel, sadistic action. People paid.

'Back,' his captor said, breaking into his thoughts. 'Get back in the chair and I will bring food and a drink.'

The study was gloomy, darkened by the closed curtains, with only a sliver of early evening light allowed through. Joseph paused on the threshold, not anxious to return to the torture chair, until he felt the gun jab into his back and he knew worse possibly awaited. So he sat, even going so far as to lay his arms compliantly along the arm rests, keeping them still, while his captor pulled the new ties tighter, punishing him, it seemed, for the trip to the bathroom.

Joseph stared at the floor, hating himself for his compliance, angry with the chair for its tortuous projections, trying to fight his growing sense of fear. He tried to tense his flexor muscles up, but the zip ties held firm. His head ached from the sharp pistol whip across his temple, and to add insult to injury, he sensed his captor was mocking him with a surreptitious smirk, his mouth tightening on one side.

He disappeared into the kitchen and returned with a tray holding a cup of tea and a cheese sandwich, balancing them on a chair he'd pulled up for the purpose. He released his wrists and watched him as he ate and drank.

Joseph was neither hungry nor thirsty, but he ate and drank because didn't know when he would be given another chance and he needed to stay alive. The food gave him strength to ask again, 'Why are you here? What do you want?'

The captor gave a huff of laughter. 'You will find out soon enough, Mr Holden.'

'How soon?'

The captor raised his hand, patting the air. 'When I decide the time is right.'

'How long must I wait?'

The man didn't answer, only stared at him, studying his face. And the expression Joseph read this time was more disturbing than all the other components: the gun, the imprisonment, the threat, even that one crushing blow which was still ringing on his temple. Because the expression Joseph read now was pity. He searched again, hoping he'd misread it, but there was no doubt. He'd read it right. This robotic stranger, who had seemed to possess no emotions, actually felt pity for his fate. It jarred Joseph into a new depth, where he floundered in dark, terrifying water. Desperate to escape, tempted now to beg, terrified his ankles too would be tethered to the chair legs.

He slid his feet along the floor. The man met his eyes for a second, brief moment while Joseph checked his expression, hoping he'd been mistaken. He hadn't, and, as the man stood up, again Joseph caught the scent and sound of something exotic, something even more evocative that reminded him again of unwelcome memories: dusty streets, sandals slapping through markets, the cries of vendors, the scent of spices and meat hanging on hooks in a too-hot sun. He followed the dusty sandals to another place: a warm, calm sea, brilliantly coloured fish darting through turquoise waters, hot sand underfoot, blood sitting on its surface for a moment, sticky and sweet, before soaking away, leaving a rusty stain that soon would also disappear.

He closed his eyes and followed the memory down the dark passage he'd sealed off before a portcullis dropped down replacing the vision with thick black iron bars. His captor turned away as though he didn't want to face him anymore. He settled back in his chair by the window and continued scrolling down his phone screen, Joseph's mobile on the floor by his feet.

Joseph watched him for a while before scanning the contents of the room again. But that proved a mistake. Every object evoked a memory, every memory a story in itself.

Some memories now gave him physical pain and something else he hadn't experienced at the time – guilt.

Thou fool.

TWELVE

6.45 p.m.

'Hayley Smith' looked even worse in real life than in her recent picture. Dressed in a pink bathrobe, she opened the door of a house that smelled strongly of cigarettes.

She looked at Joanna's ID listlessly, and Joanna could read her mind. Her expression was twisted with cynicism that asked wearily: *What are the police going to be able to do?*

Perhaps restore her money – or at least some of it, Joanna hoped, realizing at the same time that the police would be able to do nothing to restore her self-belief, her trust, the replacement of the sparkling fantasy romance with a dull, depressing reality. Both faced each other recognizing the cruelty of the Romeo scams: the shameful exposure of desperation and loneliness, the scrubbing away of make-up, the stripping of hair dye, any semblance that disguised the person underneath, a lonely woman past her youth seeing despair on the horizon.

Julie Trent didn't offer her a drink and had given Joanna's ID card only a cursory glance before she led the way into a small, stuffy sitting room. And rather than looking at Joanna with any hint of optimism, her face leaked the fact she believed there would be no news she could interpret as good.

Joanna did her best. 'We have the guy behind those messages, Julie.'

She nodded a response, but there was no corresponding light of hope in her eyes.

'He's here in Leek,' Joanna continued, trying to inject a single ray of hope into her voice. 'But his victims are from all over.' When there was still no response, she added, 'He isn't who he said he was.'

Julie nodded, but it was a dull, hopeless gesture.

'Your money . . .'

Julie hovered on the edge of hope for just a moment, shifting to the edge of her seat before sinking back.

'We hope to recover some of it.'

'Hmm.' There was a brief silence until she said what was really on her mind. 'Will it all come out?' Her voice was soft, ashamed, the depression in her voice now overlain with anxiety.

'Not if he pleads guilty. If it doesn't go to trial, most of the facts need not come out.'

Julie gave another nod, this time an acceptance.

'I'm so sorry. It must have been—' She didn't get to finish.

'Yes, it was.' Her eyes lingered over Joanna's wedding ring and her engagement ring, a black pearl with shoulders of diamonds.

Finally, she blurted out, 'I feel such a bloody fool.' The bitterness in her voice was sharp and ugly. 'I saved all my life for that money. Scrimped and saved, went without. Thought I could pay my mortgage off – one day. Maybe even treat myself to one of those wall-to-wall sunshine holidays people seem to rave about. It's not a huge amount to ask out of life, is it?'

It was a genuine question.

Joanna shook her head, tempted to pat the woman's hand. 'If it's any consolation, you're not the only one – not by a long chalk.'

She responded by lighting a cigarette with angry, shaking hands.

8 p.m.

Home at last, and judging from the BMW in the drive, Matthew had beaten her to it. She let herself in. Upstairs, she could hear him talking to Jakob and mounted the stairs to the bathroom, savouring the sight. Matthew was kneeling beside the bath, ducking and playing peek-a-boo with his son. Both were laughing, and she felt she'd entered a new world where plastic ducks swam, where the climate was warm and humid, and the sight of his father's head popping up over the side of the bath was enough to cause her son to erupt into gales of laughter.

Then both of them spotted her. Matthew stood up, met her eyes and straightaway asked her the question he knew would have occupied her focus all day. 'So how did his first day back go?'

'He's different,' she admitted, kissing suds off his soapy mouth. 'Goodness, have you been drinking the Infacol?'

'Practically. Blame Jakob.'

Their son responded with a giggle and a splash.

'In what way different?'

She was shaking her head as she answered, finding it difficult to put into words. 'Not so confident. A bit . . . tentative.'

'That's natural.'

'Still managed to charm some schoolgirls.'

'Ah well, that's Korpanski for you.'

'Daddy, Daddy.' Their son was holding his arms up and clamouring for attention. Matthew picked him out of the water and wrapped him in a towel. The next half hour would be the extended practice of bedtime. Pyjamas, story, bottle of milk, tucking up. More story.

It was a ritual Matthew revelled in. He always did his best to join in bath time.

'I'll sort dinner out.'

She kissed the top of Jakob's head, touching the honey-coloured hair he'd inherited from his father along with those perceptive green eyes as bright as a cat's. He gave her a contented sleepy smile.

Then she went downstairs to make tea.

THIRTEEN

9.30 p.m.

'**U**p.'
Joseph had been dreaming. He'd been at the market, haggling over a small statue of a lion wearing a feathered headdress. The lion of Judah. He hadn't been certain it was genuine, so, in his dream, he'd been nervous, palms sweating, but still determined to have it. At any cost. He came to with the pain in his back and the order.

His captor was cutting the ties. 'Up,' he repeated. 'Get up.'

Still sleepy and confused, Joseph stood, holding on to the arms of the chair to steady himself.

'Upstairs.' Another jab in the spine.

He walked. Outside now it was dark, the hall hardly lit by the two dim side lights. He turned around, waiting for instructions.

'Up,' his captor said again. And when Joseph had climbed each step stiffly, clutching the banister, his captor indicated the bathroom.

Cleaning his teeth and sluicing his face made Joseph feel almost normal. And when he peered at his reflection in the mirror, he looked pale, the bruise darker now, but otherwise, he reassured himself, he looked very much himself. He smoothed back his hair, once thick and blond, a feature he'd always been proud of, unlike his nose, which he'd always hated. He tried to smile into the mirror, but now his captor was knocking on the door. He waved the gun towards one of the bedrooms. 'In,' he said. 'Bed.'

Joseph obeyed, and then he heard the key turn in the lock.

Again, the man had done his search thoroughly. The front bedroom was the only one with a lock and key.

Oddly enough, being alone, untethered and in his own bedroom calmed him; gave him a moment to reflect. He sat on the side of his bed and considered his options. Not a lot. There were windows, but they were too high for him to jump from without hurting himself. His captor must have examined each room, checked each potential escape point, every window – and what was beneath it – checked for a lock and key before deciding which room to put him in. He wondered if he might be able to catch Doreen's eye from the window, but one false move and he would be back downstairs.

Joseph lay back on his comfortable bed and closed his eyes.

10 p.m.

They'd eaten the pasta dish Joanna had knocked up and were drinking a glass of wine in the sitting room. It was a treasured time of day. All was peaceful upstairs. Jakob, after the usual exhausting day, was flat out. They were on the sofa, Matthew's arm loosely draped over her shoulders. He was holding an iPad in the hand of his other arm, reading, while she was uncharacteristically quiet, reflecting on the day just passed, the comfortable feeling of having Korpanski back at her side, the Romeo scam and the short, unhappy life of Cherie Glover who hadn't lived beyond fourteen. Finally she came to. 'What are you reading?'

'It's a weird article,' he said, closing his iPad. 'Bicycle traumas. Some nasty ruptured spleens.'

She turned to face him. 'I hope you're not trying to stop me getting on my bike?'

'It's enough to make me worry.' He ran his finger over a page which had an image of a CT scan that, presumably, illustrated his point.

'You're getting things way out of proportion.' But she was smiling as she leaned in against him. A career in forensic pathology made her husband cautious. Overcautious, some might say. 'So does it try to assimilate figures on heart attacks prevented by exercise, obesity and depression reduced, air pollution improved or any of the other benefits of cycling?' she teased.

He chuckled and pressed his lips to her hair. 'You win, Jo. So how was it really? You said he's lost some confidence?' Matthew bent down and now kissed the back of her neck. He'd always been physically affectionate. It had been one of the characteristics which had made him irresistible to her.

'Yes. He's like . . . eighty per cent of himself.'

'It'll come back.'

'Does it?' She was openly curious now, asking him as a medic.

'In time,' he said, honest as ever, 'most of it does.' He smiled at

her. 'Not quite all. Injuries leave scars both physical and mental.'
He tried a truism. 'But he'll always be the Korpanski who'll run to
your side.'

It didn't quite console her.

She moved into him, feeling his arms tighten around her. She
wanted to say something neutralizing about Korpanski's loyalty and
add that it was her husband who was always at her side, but she
couldn't find the right sentences or put the words into the right
order. Besides, Matthew had already moved on to another subject
which was occupying his mind.

'Don't forget Eloise's graduation,' he said, 'a week on Saturday.
You'll be looking after Jakob for the day.' She knew he was skating
quickly over the words. 'I promised Eloise I'd book us a hotel in
Birmingham for the night. Kenneth too. Then we won't have to
worry about driving after our meal.' He gave a mischievous grin.
'So we can get well tanked up.'

'And Jane too? Will she be staying?'

Joanna sensed the exclusion, heard frostiness in her voice and
hated herself for it. But however many times she told herself that
Matthew had left Jane to be with her, not the other way round, it
was always there. Any mention of Eloise Levin never failed to land
on a tender spot.

Matthew was looking at her, bemused. He flicked a lock of sandy
blond hair out of his eyes. 'I have no idea what Jane's doing,' he
said irritably. 'Or where she's staying. Why would I? But of course
she'll be there. She's Eloise's mother, for goodness' sake.'

She picked up on the rising note of impatience in his voice.

She's Eloise's mother, she thought, parroting the phrase to herself
– as if she didn't know. She managed to keep that comment to
herself, but still felt she and Jakob were being deliberately excluded.

'I-I just thought,' she stammered, and for once in her life, she
heartily wished Jakob would wake and let out one of his summoning
screams. But he remained silent. Today had been one of his days
at the nursery, and those days he was always flaked out by nine
thirty.

She tried again. 'What about your parents?'

'They're travelling back straight after the ceremony,' he said.
'Dad doesn't like driving at night. They don't want to go out for
dinner and stuff. So we're going out with some of Eloise's medical
school friends . . .'

'And Kenneth,' she finished brightly.

Too brightly. Matthew gave her a sharp look, but she managed to keep a neutral, innocent face while he was looking pleased with himself. He'd been so excited when Eloise had entered medical school. And it had all been working towards this special day when her degree would finally be conferred. That precious bit of paper that represented five and more years of hard work.

'And now,' he said, 'how about another glass of wine and we can watch another episode of that Korean drama you were so enjoying?'

'Perfect,' she said. 'Actually I'll just have a shower first, peep in on our little princeling and put something comfortable on.'

He was quiet for a moment before she asked him, 'So how was your day?'

'Not bad. Too many meetings and a nasty enquiry into a death that should have been preventable. Just a kid,' Matthew said. 'Too long a wait in A&E before he was assessed. By the time he was, sepsis had set in and he went into major organ failure. Tragedy. Shouldn't have happened, but you couldn't blame any one person. It was a succession of failures.'

'Heartbreaking.'

He nodded, and like parents up and down the country, they applied the circumstances to their own son, sleeping peacefully and safely, they hoped, upstairs.

Matthew got up with her. 'Think I'll just check on the little blighter.'

When they were both downstairs again, she continued the conversation. 'I was sort of involved with a death that should never have happened.' She told him then about the visit to the school, aware that her husband was watching her carefully.

'I did the post-mortem. Her arms were criss-crossed with scars. She must have been self-harming for years. And her parents hadn't realized. God . . . if I thought.'

Their eyes both drifted upwards.

She touched his hand, knowing that sometimes work took its toll on her husband.

'I think it's good the police are doing what they can to warn young people.' He paused. 'Think you got anywhere?'

His scrutiny forced her to be honest. 'Probably not. Fourteen-to-sixteen-year-olds aren't exactly the most responsive to police advice.'

He nodded, his face troubled, green eyes clouding.

They didn't have to express it, their dread of what might lie in the future for their son. They sipped their wine in silence until Joanna burst out with, 'The worst of it is that all the stupid texts were lies. They were malicious, but they weren't meant to have that result.'

She rested her head on her husband's shoulder.

Less than three miles away, Joseph Holden was staring up at the ceiling, trying to make sense of the events of the day. What did that cold, emotionless man have in store for him? What was he waiting for? Part of him wanted to test his captor's resolve. Would he really shoot? Was this a cruel bluff? It would be a long night, his mind churning through endless possibilities. He was dreading tomorrow.

And then he remembered. Tomorrow was Wednesday.

FOURTEEN

Wednesday 11 September, 6.45 a.m.

Jakob Rudyard Levin was an early waker. He always started with a noise – somewhere between a chatter and a howl depending on his mood – just to give his parents a chance to come and pick him up. If they didn't respond quickly enough, he upped the howl and stopped the chatter. Jakob Rudyard Levin meant business. Always. But his father was already framed in the doorway, and for a moment, father and son just looked at each other and smiled.

Joanna had been dreaming. She'd revisited the school and had been facing one of the girls who'd been laughing in her face. As she switched the kettle on for their morning coffee, she was still frowning. That girl, she thought, the one with the red hair, had been the instigator. Had the school visit achieved anything? Had she got her message home? Would the girl stop her trolling now she knew where it could lead? Or would she continue, revelling in the power? And if that was her response, where would it lead? She handed a cup to Matthew and a mug of milk to Jakob. From long practice, they knew they had ten minutes' grace.

The day had begun.

'So today?' Matthew asked.

'More of the same, I expect. And you?'

'Same here. Work, routine. Slides, pathology, histology, maybe a couple of routine PMs in the afternoon.' He turned to her. 'We need to plan our next holiday, I think. Something to look forward to always perks up the cooler months. I think maybe early October before we head to the ski slopes.'

'Where were you thinking of?'

'One of the Mediterranean islands probably. Rhodes?'

'Yeah. Sounds nice.'

They both eyed their son warily. He'd almost finished his beaker of milk. 'You first in the shower?'

'Uh-huh.'

7 a.m.

'Get up.'

He hadn't heard the door being unlocked or his captor entering. Exhausted, he'd finally dropped off into a deep and, thankfully, dreamless sleep. The first he knew of the morning was the command and the stranger bending over him, the gun in his hand.

He sat up, still groggy, and looked into the man's face, which showed no hint of a sleepless night. It was still granite hard, expressionless, giving no clue of what he had planned for the day ahead.

Nothing good, Joseph was sure.

The stranger jerked his head towards the bathroom, and Joseph took the hint, shuffling out of the room in slippers and pyjamas. He'd changed in the hope that the familiar night attire would help him sleep. And to an extent they had.

When he returned ten minutes later, the first thing he noticed was that his bed had been made, pillows squared up, duvet folded back, last night's clothes set out ready to wear. He raised his eyes to meet the stranger's and they almost exchanged a nod – one military man to another.

But he still held the gun.

However, Joseph had taken heart in the fact that today was Wednesday. Wednesday was the day Clarice called. Clarice had arrived a few months before, recommended by Doreen Caputo. Doreen had seen a card in the window of the newsagent's advertising her services as a cleaner and had drawn Joseph's attention to it.

Persuaded, he'd met the girl. Young, black, shy and quiet. He'd liked her and agreed to a trial period which had extended to a permanent position.

She lived somewhere in Leek, caught the bus into Rudyard village and tramped up through the woods.

But his optimism was dampened by a sudden, horrible thought. Was that what his captor had been waiting for? Clarice?

7.15 a.m.

Doreen Caputo was also taking comfort in the fact that today was Wednesday.

Helping her husband wash and dress in the morning was always a challenge – always exhausting – but ultimately rewarding when she saw the twinkle in his dark eyes. It was one of the few expressions he still had because Parkinson's made his face a blank mask. He managed to nod in response, and for a moment she paused, saddened by the cruel passage of time.

She'd met him on holiday, nearly sixty years ago, when she'd been a wild and adventurous teenager and Luca the most handsome waiter in the entire resort – let alone their hotel – in Brindisi. Since then her devotion to him had never wavered. Before they'd met, Luca had been a fisherman, until his boat had needed expensive repairs and the fish had stopped biting, and so he'd turned his hand to being a waiter. Which was when he'd met the young sea nymph Doreen Weston. She'd struck him as a bit of a live wire, and when their eyes had met, both had felt an instant attraction. Somehow, Doreen had persuaded him to follow her back to land-locked Staffordshire, and there they'd set up a business renting out sailing boats on the lake as well as teaching sailing, canoeing, paddle boarding and windsurfing. Doreen had handled the paperwork and advertising, and Luca had done everything else – until he'd developed Parkinson's ten years ago.

His faculties were unaffected, but his coordination and motor reflexes had been badly hit, and he'd recently developed drop-eye as well as a constant dribble.

But he was still the love of Doreen's life as well as her mentor, even though his articulation was sometimes difficult to understand. He'd had numerous medications from both his GP and a specialist unit, but they were simply slowing the progression of the inevitable. Nothing could take the disease away.

Luca Caputo, the retired sailor, sat in a chair, facing the water, and she knew he was reading the ripples and waves as though they whispered to him, interpreting the action of the wind and imagining himself reefing the sails when it was particularly blustery. He moved little and with difficulty, but the watery scene transported him back to happier, healthier days, calming him. Particularly when, like today, the waves were whipped up into activity. Not quite the ocean he remembered, but he could dream.

And though his speech wasn't great, his wife consulted him on all matters as though he was an authority.

She sat him in his chair facing the lake and helped him with his breakfast – porridge spooned in by her and coffee, drunk through a straw, his clothes protected by a bib, like a toddler. As he dribbled, she tried to superimpose his face with the lively, good-looking waiter who'd caught her eye and captured her heart forty years ago. But she still loved him because deep inside, that sexy young waiter with the flashing eyes and flattering attention was still there. Simply buried too deep, hidden behind the involuntary, uncontrollable, constant movements.

She winked at him. 'Time I took Stevie Wonder for his walk,' she said. 'And hopefully Joseph will be a bit more communicative today. But at least Clarice will be there later. She can check up on him – make sure he's all right.'

Luca managed a ghost of a smile, and his hand quivered as though he wanted to pat her.

7.30 a.m.

Joseph was back in the hated chair, the carvings torturing his back, his wrists tethered as before. He watched the stranger finger his phone.

He was still trying to guess exactly where the stranger was from, trying to place him far away from his very worst fear. Joseph studied him, ticking off each feature. He had short black hair. He gave off a slightly sweaty scent. He was muscular, a little under six feet, his eyes very dark. Dressed neatly in the almost universal uniform of black jeans, a leather jacket and a white, open-necked shirt, his clothes gave no clue, except for his shoes which were smart, expensive, Italian leather – and squeaked as he moved.

Oddly enough, it was those shoes which frightened Joseph more than the gun. Because they spelled money. Joseph had already worked out this was no casual thug out to rob him of ready cash, empty his bank account or load a lorry (which had yet to arrive) with some or all of his treasure. And far from being a potential relief, it was possible that Clarice was an accomplice.

Joseph felt a pang at this possible betrayal. Had he been duped by her quiet manners and downcast eyes? The girl was black. He'd never asked about her heritage, but he'd guessed it involved somewhere in Africa. It was even possible she was an illegal immigrant. He'd never asked for paperwork. He'd never checked anything. He paid her in cash. Again, he felt that shadow of the unknown creeping up behind him, stealthy as a panther. If there was a connection with Clarice, at least he would have certain answers and maybe a glimpse into his own fate.

He risked a glance across at his captor, who, sensing his interest, lifted his head, watchful. Joseph was tempted to challenge him again even though he knew it would be futile. But the inactivity was driving him mad. He was desperate to provoke some sort of response.

The stranger continued fingering the keypad on Joseph's phone. Maybe his captor was searching through his contacts. The atmosphere in the room was dead; the quiet was oppressive. Even the two men's breathing was muted.

8.50 a.m.

Doreen clipped Stevie Wonder's lead to his collar. She would let him loose once they'd reached the track that led up to Cloud Mansion. There he could sniff around the tree roots, do his business, which she buried under a pile of leaves, and generally run riot. He was a happy, curious dog. But she was worried. She only hoped that Joseph would come to the window, they could chat as normal and she would see, for herself, that he was all right. Then she, like Stevie Wonder, could run free and happy.

9 a.m.

This time the stranger was prepared. Through the tiny gap in the curtains, he watched as the woman and the dog tramped up the muddy track.

He kept his eye on her as she approached, positioning herself just outside the study window, no more than a few inches away from him.

'Joseph?' She was unaware she was being watched.

Without a word, the captor had cut the ties and motioned Joseph towards the front door.

'Doreen?' He'd forgotten his plan to call her Mrs Caputo.

He heard her footsteps rounding the house.

'Hello? Joseph?' She had a sing-song voice that reverberated around the whole house, as powerful as an opera singer.

Joseph reached the door and stood behind it, wondering how he could convey the situation when the man had a gun pressed to his head and had reminded him. 'You, her and the dog. You know how many bullets this can pump out in less than a minute.'

Joseph nodded.

'Joseph? Hello.'

He picked up on her concern, but his throat was too dry to respond.

'You all right there?' This time he could hear a note of suspicion.

He tried to muster up his normal voice. '*Mrs* Caputo. Yes. I'm fine, thank you.'

But even he realized his voice was quavery, as did she. 'You don't sound it.'

The gun was right up against his lumbar spine now. He tried again, heartily. 'Yes, really, *Mrs* Caputo. I'm fine. Really.'

He knew she'd got the message when she responded, 'Are you ill? Is it your heart again? Would you like me to call a doctor?'

The gun was jabbed harder into his spine. 'No. No, Mrs Caputo. Really no.' He was speaking quickly. 'No. I don't need a doctor.' *Yet*, he added to himself.

'Is someone there with you? Why aren't you opening the door?'

Joseph didn't know how to answer this, but the silence sounded even more awkward. The stranger was shaking his head slowly. He hadn't allowed for this prolonged interruption. Joseph heard a soft click; braced himself.

'No.' Alarmed, Joseph repeated, 'No.'

There was another silence before Doreen Caputo spoke again. 'Joseph,' she asked in a soft, suspicious tone that was curiously intimate, shutting out the intruder, 'what's wrong? Why aren't you opening the door?'

The silence that followed clanged like a fire alarm in his head while he stitched together the knowledge that the smallest thing – the silliest, tiniest little detail – and his captor's plan, whatever it was, would fail. So he too was waiting for Joseph to improvise and send this unwelcome intruder away.

You, her and the dog.

'It's fine.' Joseph finally managed to force his voice to sound firm. 'I'm really fine. But I'm not dressed, and I'm not up to seeing anyone. Not today.'

'OK.' Doreen's response was slow, dragging and unconvinced. 'Joseph, is someone with you?'

Curse the woman. 'No.' He knew he'd responded too quickly. And there had been a note of panic in his response.

'Well.' She did sound mollified. 'It's Wednesday. Clarice will be with you later.'

He heard his own intake of breath at the same time as his captor. As Doreen Caputo retreated, Stevie Wonder trotting obediently beside her, he didn't know whether to feel relieved or disappointed.

9.30 a.m.

Joanna was watching Jakob feed himself clumsily with a plastic spoon. Luckily, he was also wearing a shaped plastic bib which was catching anything that missed his mouth – which was plenty. Today's feast was mashed banana, which was one of his favourites. What he lacked in skill, he made up for in enthusiasm and a lobbing skill that might, one day, see him in the cricket team alongside his father. She was tempted to help him out but that would have resulted in a howl of protest. Her son, like his parents, was very independent.

Matthew chuckled. 'Maybe you should just dress him in banana-coloured clothes all the time.' He laughed at his own joke.

'And maybe redecorate the kitchen in a nice shade of banana?'

As though he was joining in the joke, Jakob laughed heartily with his parents.

Joanna looked from father to son. There was no mistaking the resemblance when comparing the colour of their hair and eyes, whereas Eloise looked more like her mother with almost Icelandic colouring: hair so blonde it was almost white, pale blue eyes and Jane's stick-like thinness.

Today Matthew was dressed casually in beige chinos and an open-necked pale green shirt. He kept a suit and tie strictly for court appearances and today wasn't one of them. 'Expect I'll spend most of the day peering down a microscope,' he said. 'My life isn't as exciting as yours.'

'Huh,' she retorted. 'Spending hours filling in forms, "collating"' – she scratched the air – 'evidence, information, gathering statistics, running the gauntlet of the general public's complaints. Hardly ever putting a hand on a collar.' She grinned and kissed his mouth. 'Policin' ain't what it used to be.'

'Such is life, Jo,' he said, returning the kiss before wiping Jakob's face, lifting him out of the high chair and planting a kiss on the top of his son's head.

'Come on, little man,' he said. 'Time to drop you off at your grandpa and grandma's.'

Peter and Charlotte, Matthew's parents, had bought a bungalow near Briarswood, specifically so they could help with childcare as both Matthew's and Joanna's hours could be erratic. But he was an energetic toddler, almost two now; watching him every day had proved too taxing, so these days young Jakob Rudyard Levin divided his time between a small nursery and his grandparents and was equally happy with both. It gave Peter and Charlotte some time to themselves and a chance to enjoy their retirement as well as having plenty of contact with their young grandson.

Joanna's mother had no input into her grandson's day-to-day life. She had never been particularly maternal, and besides, she had a full-time job as an assistant at a large accountancy firm in Wolverhampton.

10 a.m.

Doreen was back at The Lake House and, as was her habit, she came to sit by her husband's side. 'Something's up,' she said.

Her husband watched her, his face, as always, expressionless.

'Luca,' she said, 'I took a look round the back. There was a car there.'

Her husband moved his mouth. And, as though she'd understood, she added, 'No, not Joseph's little van. It was a car. He said he didn't have a visitor.'

She paused, thoughtful. 'Why would he lie?' She didn't try to answer her question but continued. 'Anyway – I took down the number plate. There's something else that struck me as strange. The study curtains. He never closes them. Why would he? He's not overlooked. That's not all. He always calls me Doreen. Has done for years. So why did he call me Mrs Caputo both yesterday and today? Is he trying to tell me something?'

Her husband made a noise.

She came to a conclusion, patting his hand. 'That's what I think. Luca, I'm going to ring the police.'

FIFTEEN

11 a.m.

Detective Constable Lilian Tadesse arrived bang on time for her shift. She was a thirty-year-old Mancunian who ran marathons in her spare time so was as fit as a flea. The partner she worked with couldn't have been more of a contrast. DS Bethany Hughes was from a village in North Wales, with, according to her colleagues, an unpronounceable name. Quiet and prone to plumpness, she was a perfect foil to her colleagues' rumbustiousness. The pair of them worked well as a team.

'Well,' Lilian commented, when Jason and Paul asked them to look into the neighbour's concern, 'as they serve the best home-made cakes around and it's a nice day, a trip out to Staffordshire's seaside will be welcome. So give us the details, eh?'

'Dog walker,' PC Jason Spark said. 'Walking past Cloud Mansion. The big house overlooking Rudyard Lake.'

'That creepy old stone place? I know it. I've run past it many a time,' Lilian said. 'To be honest, I quicken my step. Don't tell me someone lives there? I thought it was derelict.'

'Yeah, an old guy apparently. Name Joseph Holden. Lives there on his own. Bit of a recluse. A neighbour called it in,' he continued. 'She walks her dog past it every single day and always stops by to have a word with the guy that lives there.'

'OK. So what's the problem? He didn't answer?'

'Well, that's the odd thing. He did. But two days running he's stayed behind the door, and the curtains to his study have been closed. She says those curtains are *never* closed. He spends most of his time in there so why would he keep the curtains closed in the daytime? They usually chat either through the open window or else he comes to the front door.'

The two women looked at each other. Bethany shrugged. 'He answers so it doesn't exactly seem like a blue-light job.' Both officers smirked. 'I take it he says he's all right?'

'She had the feeling someone was with him, but he denied it. She also said there was a strange car out the back.'

'But he answered,' Bethany said again. 'Said he was all right.'

'Yes. But he called her Mrs Caputo.'

'So?' Lilian this time.

'He hasn't called her that for years. They chat every day. He calls her Doreen.'

'Maybe he's sick of her calling every day and wants a bit of privacy,' Bethany suggested.

'Maybe,' Jason agreed. 'But why would he lie about having a visitor?'

Lilian shrugged.

Jason made another effort to persuade them. 'She had a feeling something weird was going on. Thing is, she said, the old guy who lives there seems to quite like her calling in. He beckons her through the window or comes to the front door and they exchange a few pleasantries. Every morning. Every – single – morning – without fail. Yesterday he calls out he's not up to seeing anyone. Today he says he's not dressed and still isn't up to seeing anyone. She says he's never been like that before. She seemed convinced something was wrong. Said he didn't sound right.'

Lilian offered up an explanation. 'Probably got a mate staying with him and they had a few too many last night. Hungover and embarrassed the morning after.'

'She seemed properly worried,' Jason pressed.

'He just didn't want some old biddy poking her nose in,' was Bethany's suggestion. 'But don't worry – we'll call in.' She knew PC Jason Spark was a literal fellow and if they didn't assure him they'd follow this up, he'd go home worried. Lilian already had her mobile phone out. 'She get the reg of this strange car? Should be easy enough to check.'

'Yep. NP64SET.'

'Nissan?'

'Yep.'

'It's a hire car.' Lilian jumped to the obvious conclusion. 'Probably friend or family.'

'Or a workman?' Bethany put in.

Jason was still frowning. 'So why not simply say he had a roofer or a tiler in?'

Lilian again sought to reassure Jason. 'Look, we'll go. OK?'

But Jason was still intent on convincing them of the potential seriousness. 'Thing is he's got a lot of valuable antiques in the place so she was a bit bothered. He's elderly and in poor health.'

Lilian gave one of her signature wide grins. 'OK, we'll put it first on the list. But you owe us one.'

'Thanks.' He was, at last, pacified.

Bethany held her hand out. 'Better give me the contact details of the neighbour too.'

'It's a Mrs Doreen Caputo. She and her husband live in The Lake House.'

'That the one that sticks right out over the lake?'

'Yep.'

'I love that place. OK, Jase, we're practically on our way already.'

'Thanks.' Jason paused, suddenly uncomfortable but for no apparent reason. 'I hope I'm not sending you on a wild goose chase.'

Lilian smiled again. 'Me too.'

'I wouldn't have made a fuss, but this lady was adamant something was wrong.'

'Except she couldn't put her finger on it.' Bethany was already heading towards the locker room to fetch her coat.

Lilian, following her, disagreed. 'Maybe she *has* put her finger right on it.'

They grumbled all the way to the car. 'So we're social workers now checking up on an old bloke who doesn't feel like engaging with his neighbour?'

Lilian handed the keys to her colleague. 'You drive, Beth. I feel like being a passenger.' She tapped the side of her nose and narrowed her eyes. 'Instinct,' she said, affecting an air of mystery.

But Bethany hadn't finished grumbling. 'About as trustworthy as a pack of tarot cards if you ask me.'

'Whatever.' Lilian couldn't be bothered to justify her own feeling of unease. In an hour, they would have solved this mini-mystery and be tucking in to a nice bit of cake. Carrot cake, she'd decided, already salivating. DC Lilian Tadesse was cursed with a very sweet tooth.

Bethany turned the car in the direction of Rudyard Lake.

11.18 a.m.

They were there in less than twenty minutes, even though the traffic was heavy.

As they intended speaking to the neighbourly Mrs Caputo *after* they'd spoken to Mr Holden, they parked as close as they could to Cloud Mansion and walked the rest of the way along the rough track of mud and stones, under the canopy of trees, to the house which loomed, like a fortress, ahead of them.

Ten minutes later, colder and muddier, Lilian Tadesse was knocking on the very stout front door. There was an iron knocker which she lifted a couple of times, but from within the house there was no response.

Inside, Joseph stiffened in his chair, a wary eye fixed on his captor, who looked irritated at this further intrusion. His hands gripped the gun, but he said nothing.

The two officers looked at each other, frowning. What had seemed like a neighbourly check was starting to seem possibly more troubling. Lilian called out, 'Mr Holden, it's Detective Constable Lilian Tadesse and Detective Sergeant Bethany Hughes here from Leek police. Your neighbour, Mrs Caputo, was worried about you.'

His captor gave Joseph a slow shake of his head. Lilian called out again. 'Mr Holden. Can you hear me?'

Joseph's eyes stayed on his captor's.

'Are you OK?'

The man was looking along the barrel of the pistol now, his finger ready to release the trigger. Which would not end well for the two detectives standing outside his door, so Joseph risked it and called out.

'Yes.'

Lilian glanced at Bethany. It was a reedy, soft voice that had replied.

'I'm fine.' This time Joseph had managed to inject just the right amount of irritation in his voice to see them off. He continued, ad-libbing, 'It's nice of Mrs Caputo to concern herself, but she's no need to worry. She caught me at a bad time this morning.' He averted his eyes from his captor's, tried to shut out the soft click that meant he'd released the safety trigger.

For a few seconds, nothing happened.

Joseph improvised, injecting an extra shot of irritation in his voice. 'I value my privacy.'

'We understand that,' Lilian said smoothly. But DS Bethany Hughes was frowning and shaking her head at her. 'Mr Holden, there's a car outside. A Nissan. Is someone with you?'

Joseph didn't know how to respond this time. Again, he improvised.

'A friend's left it with me for a couple of days.'

Now both Lilian and Bethany were frowning at each other. That didn't square with it being a hire car. One did not hire a car to dump it outside a friend's house.

Lilian repeated her question. '*Is* someone there with you?'

Yes, he wanted so much to say. *Someone is with me. I have an unwelcome guest.* But he knew he'd probably get no more than one word out before . . .

'N-No,' he stammered. 'I'm alone.'

All four of them waited silently, the two detectives aware that something was amiss while the two in the study, captor and captive, waited to see what their next move would be. All teetering on a precipice, like a house on the edge of a crumbling cliff. Bethany frowned at her colleague, giving a small shake of her head. Then she gave him a last chance. 'We-ell, if you're sure you're all right?'

They were going to leave, and Joseph didn't know whether he was glad or not. Somehow he managed a final dismissal. 'I'm sure. I'm absolutely sure. Please leave me alone.' Silently, he added: *To my fate.*

The two officers exchanged glances, both shaking their heads. They knew things weren't all right. But with the owner of Cloud Mansion dismissing them, they had no option but to leave the scene and no justification for pursuing the matter. Certainly they couldn't break in. But they could put the house on a watch.

Now they shared the neighbour's concern.

'Let's take a look round the back.'

They rounded the property, checking for any obvious sign of a break-in: a forced door, a broken window, pausing at the study window, the curtains tightly closed.

Round the back was a damp, mossy area with a flat yard containing two cars: the Nissan and a small white van, presumably Joseph Holden's. The Nissan was empty, with a sticker confirming the hire company. They took a picture of it. When they returned to the station, they would contact the company and get the details of this 'friend' who had hired it only to leave it outside a house.

On the surface it appeared nothing was wrong. And yet they shared an instinct that something was amiss. They simply had no idea what.

Inside, Joseph was waiting for the two officers' next steps. He'd heard them checking the back of the house and knew that later they would run checks on the car's owners. He shot a surreptitious glance at his captor, who seemed unperturbed now. His mind rumbled over his response. Had he been right to play along, send them on their way? Should he have tried to warn them? That might have resulted in a shoot-out. But sending them away had lost him a chance to put an end to his ordeal, albeit a slim one. Had they picked up that, whatever he said, he was very far from being 'fine'? So . . . what would happen next?

He imagined the alternatives. A Glock worked fast, with enough rounds in a magazine to have killed both him and the two officers standing on the other side of the door, who would have had little chance of escaping. They would have been unarmed apart from their Tasers and truncheons and completely unprepared. No match for a Glock in a well-trained hand.

Could the diversion have given him a chance to escape? He tested the zip ties. No.

He heard their footsteps return and pause outside the study window. Inside, the two men were still as waxworks. His captor trained his eye and his gun on him, the message clear as a bell. *You call out – you die first.* To Joseph's relief, they moved on. He heard them head back down the track, their voices low and fading.

His captor shifted his trigger finger and made a slight turn towards him.

Now the silence had returned, Joseph's relief became disappointment. They had, at least, been a hope. A possible lifeline. Now he had nothing. Joseph sensed both his captor's tension and the anger probably directed against the neighbour who'd raised the alarm and involved the police. His anger he understood. Unexpected occurrences could foil even the best-laid plans.

DC Lilian Tadesse and DS Bethany Hughes had worked together

long and close enough to communicate without words. Each knew the other was uneasy as they headed down towards Doreen Caputo's house.

The Lake House was a well-known feature, a stone cottage on a promontory which projected out into the lake with views across the water. Like Cloud Mansion, Lilian Tadesse had passed it numerous times on her runs and had often wondered about it, curious as to what it was like inside. She was about to find out.

The approach was guarded by tall wooden gates with a keypadded door lock. They pressed the intercom.

Doreen had been sitting by her husband, still fretting about her neighbour, when she heard Stevie Wonder give a few loud, throaty barks and then the sound of the door intercom. She glanced at Luca.

'Looks like they're here,' she said, still nervous she'd overreacted and would soon have a telling-off from some already overburdened police officers. Luca managed an encouraging nod, and she responded to the intercom.

Midday

'Right,' Joanna said brightly, folding her arms and pushing her chair back from the desk. She held her hand up and counted along her fingers. 'Finished. Crime figures up to date, numbers for Stop and Search broken down to ages, ethnicity and outcomes.' She couldn't resist a grin at Korpanski. 'Potential crimes and teenage trolling prevented, and thanks to Alan King, we have enough evidence to charge our thieving Romeo scammer. So now we have a cannabis farm nicely tucked away in a remote cottage on the moors and some cash stolen from retail premises.'

'Would have thought they'd have all switched to cashless,' he said grumpily.

'Not quite all,' she said. 'The stalls at the Wednesday market, including the ones inside the Butter Market, don't use contactless. But today we turn our attention to the unfortunate owner of an antiques shop who's been fleeced out of a few hundred quid which was sitting in the top drawer of his *unlocked* desk. Careless or what?' She stood up. 'Coming?'

He shoved his chair away from the desk. 'Wild horses wouldn't stop me,' he said, still grumpy. 'Can't bloody wait.'

'Good. Bit of enthusiasm, Korpanski. So nice to see,' she mocked.

At one time she'd have called it *pulling his leg,* but she thought she'd probably drop that one for good now. 'I'll drive.'

'OK.'

He followed her out of the door and she heard, in his lopsided footsteps, the result of the accident. His vulnerability made her wince and at the same time provoked a huge wave of affection. Detective Sergeant Mike Korpanski had always been her rock, bulky as a bodyguard, reassuringly strong and, she'd thought, invincible. Except now he wasn't. The accident had exposed his weak spot. And he knew it.

As he climbed awkwardly into the squad car, he gave her a rueful grin accompanied by a shrug. 'Probably need a bit more physio.'

She gave him a warm smile, saying again, 'I'm just glad you're back, Mike.' She followed that with a very truthful, 'It was shit without you.'

'Yeah, I know.' His spirit and confidence was, at least, getting back to normal. He slammed the passenger door shut and added to the tease. 'Surprised you managed so well without me, Inspector, actually staying out of trouble for once.' Then he deliberately changed the subject. 'Do anything interesting while I was off?'

'Besides getting a mute girl to talk?' She backed the car out of the station car park.

'Yeah, besides you, erm—' He caught up with her train of thought and gave a spurt of laughter. 'What? Are you calling it a miracle?'

'Sort of.'

Korpanski groaned. 'Besides that.'

'I told you about my hostage training.'

'So you passed with flying colours?'

'Yep. Apparently I have all the necessary qualities.'

'Like?'

'I'm calm . . .'

He burst out laughing. 'You? You'd be the sort to burst in and beat the hostage takers up. Not negotiate.' And again, he burst out laughing.

She laughed too. 'Well – you know – it looks good on my CV.'

'Not thinking of moving on, are you?'

She caught the tension behind the question.

'No, but you know how Rush, our favourite chief superintendent in the whole wide world, likes to collect courses and awards. I thought it would look good.' She glanced across. 'Give me a gold star anyway.'

He chortled. 'So how are things in the hierarchy?'

'Pretty much the same.'

'Thought it would be. Maybe I should have grabbed an extra six months' sick leave while I had the chance.'

'Maybe you should, except I know you were fed up with watching daytime TV.'

'Yeah. All funeral plans, incontinence pads and life insurance. So where's this careless antiques shop owner?'

'Just round the corner. But the guy wasn't a hundred per cent careless. He does have CCTV.'

SIXTEEN

12.10 p.m.

'Hello?'

The detectives identified themselves and the door buzzed for them to enter The Lake House. They were greeted by an excited dog and a lady.

She was somewhere in her late sixties, at a guess, short and plump in a pair of dark trousers and a thick brown cardigan. She had a slightly anxious-looking face and 'red' hair showing an inch or so of grey roots. She shushed the dog and held him by his collar but, wanting to warn the intruders that they were trespassing, he continued to growl, not even stopping when his owner tapped him on the nose and admonished him again. 'Quiet, Stevie.'

Lilian Tadesse spoke first. 'Mrs Caputo? You contacted us about your neighbour, Mr Joseph Holden?'

Doreen took a cursory look at Lilian's proffered ID card. 'Yes,' she said, eyes scanning them both before she backtracked. 'I didn't expect you to come out. Not so quickly, I mean. Not so soon. I thought . . .' And now she looked embarrassed.

'We were out and about,' Bethany said, 'so we thought we'd pop in. Just check up on Mr Holden. See if there was a problem.'

Doreen quickly backtracked. 'I – I'm not sure there is a problem. Not really,' she finished lamely.

She continued to look embarrassed, so Lilian tried to reassure her and put the woman at her ease. 'We were out and about anyway. And it's part of our job to check nothing is amiss when a report comes in about an elderly person. And he wasn't answering either his landline or his mobile.'

Doreen's face relaxed.

Bethany spoke next. 'We've just called into Cloud Mansion and spoken to Mr Holden. He assures us he's fine.'

But Lilian Tadesse wasn't convinced. 'Why don't we come in and you can fill in a few details?'

The woman led the way down a steeply descending pathway, on to the causeway, beyond which the lake shimmered, its surface peppered with sailboats, canoes and a couple of hardy paddle boarders in wet suits.

Doreen led them into a kitchen with dark blue units, white painted walls and sparkling grey granite worktops. The effect was somehow maritime, reminiscent of a cabin in a boat. One might almost have expected portholes instead of the huge picture window in the room beyond which they glimpsed through a half-open door. Facing out towards the lake, a man sat motionless, not even turning to greet the two officers.

Doreen didn't sit down but leaned, pointedly, against one of the pristine units. She seemed embarrassed at the attention her call had generated.

Bethany opened the questions. 'Tell us about Mr Holden.'

'What do you want to know?'

Bethany glanced at her notebook. 'You say you speak to him every day?'

'Every – single – day. He either comes to the study window, opens it and we chat for a few minutes, or else he comes to the front door. Without fail.'

'What do you talk about?'

Doreen laughed. 'Anything and everything. The news, the weather, Covid. Just general stuff. What does that have to do with anything?' she finished sharply, appearing slightly suspicious.

'How long has he lived there?' Lilian asked out of genuine curiosity, determined to fill in *some* detail on the house while she had the chance.

'A long time.' Her eyes drifted towards the other room as though her husband might have put an exact figure over her vagueness.

There was no response. 'Must be somewhere around fifteen years.'

Lilian made a note. 'How old is he?'

Now she laughed – a pretty, almost coquettish sound. 'I don't know exactly. Late seventies, I guess.'

'Is this the first time that he hasn't come to the front door or the window?'

She thought for a moment. 'Yes – apart from when he had surgery a few months ago.'

'Surgery?' Bethany asked, concerned.

'Yes, he was in hospital at the beginning of the year.'

'But since then he's seemed OK?'

'Yes,' Doreen insisted. 'I walk Stevie Wonder past Cloud Mansion every single day come rain or shine.' She glanced at the dog, who was resting on the floor, his head on his paws, eyes watching the intruders. 'He's got Alsatian blood in him so he needs plenty of exercise. Every single day come rain or shine.' She'd repeated the phrase both for clarity and emphasis. 'Joseph and I have a bit of a chat and then he goes back inside the house and I carry on with my walk round the lake. Well, Tuesday he didn't come to the window; nor did he open the front door. Just shouted through. And the same today. Previously – even after his op and when he's had the flu or something – he's still come to the window or the door. That's not all.' Her voice was gathering confidence. 'He always calls me Doreen. We've been on first-name terms for years. But yesterday and today he called me *Mrs* Caputo. Why?' She leaned forward. 'When he first moved here, I called in.' She looked flustered. 'You know – just to welcome him to the neighbourhood. He called me Mrs Caputo then, and I said, oh, for goodness' sake, call me Doreen. And ever since then he's *always* called me Doreen.' She looked from one officer to the other as though asking them to interpret this anomaly.

The two officers' faces stayed expressionless.

'And then there's the car,' Doreen continued. 'He does have friends over a few times a year, but why on earth would he say no one was there if someone *was* there?'

'He said a friend had left it with him.'

'So why wouldn't he say?'

She stopped for a moment before insisting, 'It doesn't make sense.' She was frowning now. 'He sounded strange. Strained.'

Lilian felt she had to prove they'd taken notice of all of her concerns. 'We've checked up on the car. It's from a hire company.'

Doreen's frown deepened.

Lilian continued, 'We've spoken to Mr Holden. He's assured us he's fine. I'm sorry, but we can't really do much more if—'

Bethany broke in. 'Does he have any family?'

Doreen shook her head. 'Not as far as I know. He's never mentioned any close family. I've never seen a visitor there apart from his few friends – a gang of roughnecks – that he says he used to work with. They come and stay a few times a year.'

'You know their names or where they're from?'

Doreen shook her head again. 'No.'

Lilian was curious now. 'Do you know what his work was?'

'No. I got the impression it was something abroad.'

'Why did you think that?'

'The stuff around the house. All sorts of foreign things. Clocks and suits of armour; swords and African masks. I've seen them through the study window and the couple of times I've been in the house. That's why he never closes the curtains – not the study curtains. He likes to keep watch,' she said, her head moving closer as she confided. 'Keep an eye on anyone coming up the path. He's careful – suspicious. I mean the place . . . it's a treasure trove. The stuff must be worth . . .' She couldn't find a figure to match it and gave up with a shrug.

Both Bethany and Lilian felt the slight frisson of unease they'd felt earlier compound.

Maybe it was the word cloud tossed into the air by a concerned neighbour . . . treasure trove . . . elderly person . . . surgery . . . alone . . . strange car. And there were their own observations: large, isolated house. Put together these were ingredients that could spell a situation.

But . . .

'OK, Mrs Caputo,' Lilian said, aware that these were feelings rather than facts. 'We'll keep an eye on him. Maybe call again. In the meantime, if you do have anything more to report, let us know, will you?'

'Sure. Yes. I will.' Doreen gave the first broad, reassured smile they'd seen. 'And thank you – for not just thinking I'm a nosey old neighbour.'

They couldn't look at each other. 'That's OK.'

Doreen Caputo watched them go before locking the door behind them. Then she walked back inside her house and sat beside her husband. 'That went better than expected,' she said. 'At least they listened.' And then she cursed. 'Damn,' she said. 'I forgot to tell them. It's Clarice's day today.' She looked at her watch. 'She should be there by now.'

With an effort, Luca managed to turn his head away from the water.

12.50 p.m.

'You've got to be joking.'

Joanna too was smirking. 'Yeah. Maybe calling the shop Noah's Ark wasn't such a great move.'

'Better than the *Titanic*,' Korpanski added.

They were in the car, heading back to the station, both laughing at the outcome of their encounter with a very crestfallen antiques dealer.

'Six hundred pounds,' he'd said and started to play back the CCTV.

They saw it all too clearly. A man gesticulating, demanding attention . . .

'He said he wanted a table,' the dealer had said grumpily. 'He didn't say what sort – dining, occasional, console. I showed him a couple. He wanted to look at one upstairs.' On the camera they'd watched the dealer stomping upstairs, resentment in every step. Which was when the two women with the man had slipped into the back office and, just as surreptitiously, slipped out again.

Korpanski and Joanna had looked at each other, bemused. Both women had been wearing face masks, peaked caps, pulled down low, and sunglasses.

Joanna had looked at the dealer incredulously while he grumbled. 'Well, we're told to keep people safe,' he'd said. 'I thought they were just being extra . . . Can't you make *any* sort of ID?'

She'd let him down gently. 'Not with just this,' she'd said. 'But we can put the word out. A man and two women using diversionary tactics. I'm sorry,' she'd tacked on. She'd watched how the man's face had drained and felt bound to scratch down a few details as well as copying the footage on to a USB stick.

'I don't suppose the man actually touched the table upstairs?'

The dealer had shaken his head and looked even more embarrassed. 'He was wearing gloves,' he'd responded moodily.

She wasn't cruel enough to extinguish all hope so had replied, 'We'll do our best.'

They'd managed to return to the car before bursting out laughing. 'How the hell—' Korpanski exploded. 'How the hell did he think we were going to get any useful description off that? The bloke had his back to the camera the entire time,' he next observed.

She labelled the memory stick. 'You never know,' she said. 'His footage was decent. And the cameras were placed at a sensible angle. We have some details from this. We can work out their height, body shape, walk. One of the girls was wearing what looked like White Company trainers. We have their clothes. We don't have nothing, Mike; we just don't have their faces. And one of the girls had a blonde ponytail. Let's get the forensic guys in and see if they can pick anything up, maybe a hair or something.'

'In a shop?'

'Which doesn't have that many customers. The girls weren't wearing gloves, and they had to put their hands in the drawer.'

'I see you haven't quite lost that optimism,' Korpanski commented drily.

She looked full at him then. 'You're back, aren't you,' she said softly. 'And on two legs. That's enough to feed my optimism for a few years yet.'

Even Korpanski couldn't think of a suitable response to this.

'So, are you glad to be back diluting my optimism?'

'I've missed it,' he admitted. 'And you.'

'And you're blushing, Detective Sergeant?'

'I am not,' he said indignantly. 'I never blush.'

She touched his face. 'So what's with the hot pink cheeks?'

'Maybe I have a fever,' he growled.

They both burst out laughing again. And, right on cue, Korpanski's personal phone buzzed. He took it out of his pocket and muttered, 'Better take this. It's Fran.'

He pressed the green icon. 'Hi, love.'

She could hear Fran's response and the sourness behind it. 'You sound awfully happy.'

'Just glad to be back at work, love.'

She missed Fran's next sentence, focussing on her driving. But Korpanski's response was loud and clear. 'Just checking up on someone who didn't take enough care of their money.'

They exchanged a few more pleasantries before he ended the call.

They chatted on the way back then spent the afternoon filling in statistics, which, no matter how hard they worked, always seemed to highlight failures. There had been a concerning rise in petty thefts – pickpockets, shoplifters and thefts from cars in the rural parking spaces where the county's hikers, climbers and cyclists left their vehicles. No matter how many warnings they posted, people still left valuable equipment in plain sight. Inviting a smashed window. When yet another theft was reported, it was tempting for the police to say, *Well, what did you expect?*

However, newly installed CCTV cameras cleverly concealed behind rocks and lodged in bushes by the side of the road were exposing car number plates which, in turn, were leading to some of the petty thieves, and arrests were imminent. Collating the information was cause for celebration. But no matter how many thieves they arrested and fined, more would always come to take their place.

Sometimes Joanna thought Canute had the easier job.

Though neither was going to win.

SEVENTEEN

1.30 p.m.

Joseph too had been thinking about Clarice. He'd heard her arrive at her usual time – an hour ago. He'd heard her open the kitchen door, and his captor had quickly disappeared, closing the study door behind him. He'd strained to hear voices, hoping to work out whether there was a connection, but he could make out nothing.

He reflected on the way she'd come into his life.

Doreen had seen a card in the window at the newsagent's near the traffic lights.

Honest, hardworking girl willing and able to do housework and shopping.

Underneath that had been a mobile phone number.

He'd never bothered much about housework, but Doreen had known he was about to have an operation. 'You won't be able to drive for months,' she'd said. 'If she just gets the shopping in, it'll be a help. With Luca the way he is, I can't help you out as much as I'd like.'

So, partly to salve her conscience, though he'd assured her he'd manage fine, he'd rung the number on the card.

Over the phone he'd realized the girl had a foreign accent. African at a guess. And, strangely enough, this had reassured him. He'd worked in Africa over the years and he'd found the people trustworthy as well as trusting. On occasions too trusting. Perhaps a little naive. But apart from the usual ruffians, he'd liked the people with their old-fashioned devotion to the church, their touching appreciation of even the smallest act done for them and their lack of entitlement, something he classed as a disease in today's wealthier nations.

He'd liked her even more when he'd met her. Petite, with hair cut so short, her head was practically shaven. She was quiet and polite, doing her work as softly and unobtrusively as a ghost. She brought the receipts of the shopping she'd done as though she expected not to be trusted. Most of the time he forgot she was there. If they met on the stairs, she lowered her eyes, pulled in and allowed him to pass.

They spoke hardly ten words a week.

She left him meals: home-made soups, sandwiches, salads. Simple items but set out with neat pride, covered with a damp tea towel and left in the kitchen. If he particularly enjoyed a meal, he'd tell her when next she came.

Really he could have let her go once he'd recovered from his operation, but she'd become a habit, part of his routine, like his daily chat with Doreen Caputo.

But now he wondered. Was Clarice a link in this chain?

His captor came back into the room, and Joseph studied him. Did he seem less watchful, more relaxed, now Clarice was here? Or did he have a second victim to guard? Joseph continued to worry at a possible connection between the girl, as quiet as a panther, and this man, whose motives and intentions remained a mystery.

He would continue to put on an act of compliance, hope to have an opportunity to put his captor off guard, pick up some clue as to what was going to happen next, maybe even make a break for it, although with his wrists so tightly bound, he'd never escape the chair. It would have to be at the few moments when he was released.

The pale hairs along his forearm shivered slightly and he recognized the reason: Clarice. Friend or foe? Could he trust her?

Or was she in danger of also becoming a victim of this hideous siege?

The stranger gave him no clue. He sat back in the chair by the window, eyes trained on the narrow view he had of the outside. He appeared mesmerized by the rain and deep in thought while he waited.

For what? Or for whom?

At one point during the afternoon, he left his watch at the window to walk around the room, stopping in front of a large mahogany cabinet filled with smaller pieces – his collection of trophies. His captor stood for a moment, scanning the contents shelf by shelf, piece by piece, giving each piece his whole attention. As his eyes passed over the objects, Joseph tuned in, recalling where and when he'd bought them, how much he'd paid for them, if he'd decided to pay. Their age and origins from tiny little Regency patch boxes to Japanese netsukes, okimonos, a fine piece of shibayama, a ship carved from the tooth of a sperm whale and a grotesque made from a beetle nut propped up by a tripod of three nails hammered long ago by a ship's blacksmith. A goblet formed from a coconut shell, a shrunken head. Sometimes he bought. Other times he just took.

His eyes moved up to the pale patch where another object had hung. Almost two feet long and curved. A piece which hadn't been bought on a whim but acquired by other means. Gone now.

Revisiting those memories provided an escape – to welcome places, to havens and other areas less comfortable. Despite his physical discomfort tethered to a chair never built for comfort, Joseph found himself smiling at the memory of the choreographed public presentations, the fiasco and obsequiousness of officials, who even as they clapped and sang were looking around them nervously, wondering which of them would survive this latest coup. Then he had been in control. Not a helpless victim. 'Ah well.' Joseph sighed, lost in that moment. All that fear and dread had had a particular stink about it. So how many of them were alive today? How many had died a violent death? Had any of them died in their own beds?

Unlikely, he thought.

The stranger gave a huff of anger and muttered something. '*Wase*.'

He recognized the word. It was a Somali swear word. It meant dog.

The tension in the room was mounting, vibrating like a violin string. Tiny beads of sweat were breaking out on the man's forehead, and his breathing had quickened. The waiting could soon be over.

And the stranger confirmed it, jerking his head in Joseph's direction. 'Not long now.'

Then he sat down again and resumed his study of the narrow view through the window, stroking the curtain with his free hand as though it was a woman's fine dress.

EIGHTEEN

4 p.m.

Joseph's mind was fixed on Clarice once more, trying to work out what her part was in this. She hadn't entered the study, but he'd heard no screams, only quiet voices. His captor could have been warning her, threatening her or colluding.

He pictured her, the first time she'd visited, asking . . . He frowned. No, *begging* for a job. It had been partly that desperation that had persuaded him. That and her quiet, submissive manner. 'All right,' he'd said, knowing his voice was gruff and unfriendly.

But then he was unused to hiring a cleaner. And, apart from his daily exchanges with Doreen, had had little to do with the opposite sex. He'd never been married, and the couple of girlfriends he'd had had been so long ago, he could hardly remember their names – or their faces.

Some mornings when she was due, he'd watched her through the study window, walking up the track in that recognizable steady, rhythmic lope, her pace not varying even when the path levelled up to pass his front door. It was as though she marched to an inner drum, in her cheap, plastic shoes which let the water in, so when she arrived, her socks were often muddy and sopping wet. He'd watched her strip them off to hang in front of the Aga and observed neat, bony feet.

He left the back door unlocked on a Wednesday so she could let herself into the kitchen without disturbing him, her presence only hinted at by a draught that swept through the house, wafting up the stairs and making the curtains billow as though they too were unsettled by an alien presence.

Had his captor been familiar with this routine? Had he too left the back door open because it was a Wednesday?

The air disturbance would be followed by unfamiliar occurrences:

the scent of cooking, the spitting sound of onions frying, the buzz of the vacuum cleaner, the lavender aroma of polish, or the scent of clean lemon wafting from the newly washed kitchen floor. Apart from the thrum of the vacuum cleaner, she never made a sound. Her walk was soft and soundless as though she made no contact with the floor but moved, like a hovercraft, on a cushion of air. She was like a little mouse, he sometimes thought – when he thought about her at all. And even then the thoughts had been fleeting. He'd never given her much attention – until now. He had never asked her personal questions: where she was from, where her parents were, did she have family, was she married? Children? And so they had passed wordlessly, if, by chance, they encountered each other in the hallway, on the stairs or in the rooms. She tended to avoid the study, but on the days he left the room empty to go into Leek Market, he returned to find the room cleaned and still smelling of furniture polish. They didn't even have much contact when he paid her. He simply left the money, dignified by being placed in an envelope, on the kitchen table.

Now he was thinking bad thoughts about her, suspecting her. Her unobtrusiveness could have been a ploy, a part of this sinister picture. And though their contact could hardly be described as close, the thought hurt him. He hadn't expected loyalty; but neither had he expected treachery.

His anger rose. It had been a deliberate ploy. Over the months she had been transforming the house, stealing away ghosts and vanishing cobwebs, she had been spying. He'd left the back door open not just physically but metaphorically. He realized now how vulnerable having her in the house had left him. She knew every inch of Cloud Mansion, the contents of every cupboard and drawer, the pieces that adorned the walls, trophies he had locked away trying to forget about, photographs of past times. She'd dusted pieces he hadn't seen clean for years, things he'd forgotten about. Others he wished he could forget about. She would hold them carefully as she wiped the dust from them, and sometimes it had seemed that, through her fingers as small as a child's, she could divine the stories that lay beneath them, some of them ugly as a scream. Sometimes she'd put them down abruptly, as though she'd picked up something hot. Only now was he realizing her inside knowledge of his past had given her power.

In frustration, he pulled at his wrists; tried to rock the chair. But the ties kept them tethered and the chair was too heavy, and all he achieved was making one wrist bleed. He tried to wriggle his back if only to relieve the sharp edges of the carvings that seemed to find the knobs and painful places of every vertebra, but he achieved nothing save a quick warning look from his captor, who turned away from the window for a brief moment before returning to his watch.

While Joseph's mind returned to Clarice.

If, heating up his tea, he was in the kitchen when she was due to leave and he handed the envelope to her she'd take it soundlessly, in both hands, with a slight bowing of her head, slipping her jacket on and disappearing back through the trees like a wood nymph. He'd watch her and think how well she blended in. How she vanished leaving behind intangible traces: the absence of dust, the money envelope gone. Not only did he not know her origins, he didn't know where she lived, and the only way he had of contacting her was by texting her mobile. He realized now he'd been uncurious.

So now his mind stumbled over the question. What then was the relationship between Clarice and his captor?

Ethnically they seemed different. He was lighter skinned; his nose was different, as was his build and general demeanour. So who was he? What was the connection? Was Clarice even now bound and terrified in the kitchen?

And still he tried to work out what was in his captor's mind. What had brought him here? Why hadn't he simply robbed him and escaped? Why this rigmarole of keeping him tethered to a chair – while doing nothing? He could have filled a lorry and been far away before anyone – even the ever-vigilant Doreen – had raised the alarm. He'd brought a gun – to intimidate a frail man he could easily have overpowered without it. Joseph drummed his foot on the floor. What *was* his purpose?

And to those questions repeatedly buzzing around in his head he added his new, chilling question about Clarice's involvement. If his captor hadn't simply been waiting for her, as an accomplice, what *was* he waiting for?

NINETEEN

K orpanski stood up and stretched. 'I am shattered.'

Joanna looked over at him, concerned. 'You should go home, Mike. No point overdoing it. Light duties, remember?'

'I'll take you up on that,' he said. 'By the way, Jo . . .'

She looked up.

'Thanks for the welcome back. Truth? I was looking forward to it and dreading it in equal measures. Now I've actually come back, apart from one leg still being a bit thinner, it's as if it never happened.'

'Good. That's even better than I'd hoped. It's great to have you back. The place was empty without you. No one to chew stuff over with. Just crap really.'

Korpanski's face warmed. 'Nice of you to say.'

She put a hand on his arm. 'I mean it.'

Korpanski couldn't stop the grin from spreading right across his face. 'And as an added bonus, I've put the details of the antiques shop robbers on the PNC. Maybe one of the other forces will pick them up. Or at least warn retailers to be extra careful.' He slung his jacket over his shoulders. 'Advise them not to keep large amounts of cash around.'

'Good. See you tomorrow then. I'll just have a word with the team and see if anything's cropped up. Then I'll tackle the real challenge of the day.'

Korpanski looked across, eyebrows raised.

'Jakob,' she explained. 'Jakob who can now walk and since learning words never shuts up. He babbles and talks all the time.'

'Still a daddy's boy?'

'Not so much. He appears to have noticed he also has a mother. Particularly when he wants something. Matthew is the sterner of us.' How could she describe the way her heart melted when Jakob Rudyard Levin fixed her with those guileless green eyes or climbed on to her lap so she could stroke his flaxen curls? The way her will was sucked out of her.

'Has he started at a nursery?'

'Part-time.'

'Matthew's parents still having him the rest of the week?'

'A couple of days.' On the occasions Matthew was the on-call pathologist and Joanna was working over the weekend, they had no option but to depend on Matthew's parents. They were still happy to pick him up from nursery when neither parent was available. They would give him tea and play with him until a parent came to pick him up. Now Peter, a retired doctor, had time for his golf, and Charlotte had joined a local book club as well as the Women's Institute. Both looked better for it. When Joanna and Matthew planned a night out, they either employed a babysitter or Peter and Charlotte hosted their small grandson in their bungalow overnight. They had a bedroom prepared and a large, white cot which was just about Jakob Levin-proof. He was proving quite an escapologist.

'Just like his dad,' Charlotte had said fondly.

What really warmed Joanna's heart was the way Jakob held his arms out to his grandparents, giggling at them. And seeing his delight mirrored in their faces.

'See you later then. You following on soon?'

'Yeah. But before I go, I'll have a quick word with Lilian and Bethany. See what they've been up to.'

She found DC Lilian Tadesse and DS Bethany Hughes catching up on their items for the day. Lilian had originally been seconded from Manchester to the Staffordshire Police, but she'd liked the town of Leek so much – and being a keen long-distance runner, the surrounding moorlands providing ample space to enjoy her hobby – she'd asked to stay.

The Moorlands weren't short of officers, but Lilian had spent some time talking to CS Gabriel Rush and had come out triumphant, her smile as wide as the Mersey. 'Knew I could pull it off,' she'd crowed. 'Only had to point out the lack of diversity in the Staffordshire Police and I was home and dry.'

'There's a lack of diversity in the whole local moorlands population,' Jason had pointed out with his native pedantry, but Lilian had responded with a soft punch on his arm. 'Sometimes,' she'd said, with one of her loud belly laughs, 'it's a good idea to play the race card.' She'd winked at Joanna. 'Opens plenty of doors.'

Bright, optimistic and funny, she was a welcome addition to the 'family'.

'Anything interesting turn up today?' she asked almost casually.

'Same old, same old,' Bethany began. 'Some evil greedy worm supplying poisonous fake vapes to the kids outside school.'

'Any ideas?'

'Working on it,' Bethany said while Lilian was quiet.

'Lilian?'

'It's nothing,' she said. 'Nothing.'

Joanna sat down. 'So tell me about this . . . nothing.'

'Some old biddy rang in earlier to say she hadn't seen her elderly neighbour.'

'For how long?'

'Today was the second morning. She said she talks to him every day, but this morning for the second time he responded from behind a closed door.'

'That doesn't sound very alarming.' Joanna waited, looking from one to the other, sensing unease. 'Presumably he assured her he was OK?'

'Yeah. Yeah. But she got the impression someone else was there. She said his voice sounded strange.'

'Sounds a bit fanciful. But you went out there. Right?'

'Same with us,' Lilian said. 'Spoke from behind the door.'

'You didn't insist he open it?'

'Well, no.' Lilian sounded awkward. 'We just said his neighbour had been concerned.'

Bethany had remembered something else that the neighbour had thought significant. 'She said he called her Mrs Caputo when normally he calls her Doreen. She felt he was trying to tell her something.'

Joanna thought about this, still puzzled.

Lilian took up the narrative. 'And she reported a strange car there.'

Joanna tracked along the same path the two detectives had. 'Friend staying? Relative?'

'He said no. He said a friend had left it there.'

'You run the number plate through ANPR?'

'It's a hire car,' Lilian said quietly.

Joanna frowned. 'That doesn't make a lot of sense.'

'That's what we thought.'

'Where does this guy live? Doesn't he have other neighbours who keep an eye out for him?'

'No. It's an isolated place. Tricky vehicular access. The old guy doesn't have many visitors and no casual visitors. There's something else, Joanna.'

'He's got some valuable antiques there. Loads of them,' Lilian said. 'And the old guy isn't in the best of health. He's only been out of hospital a few months.'

Joanna sensed an underlying concern. 'Where does this guy live?'

'A place called Cloud Mansion. It overlooks Rudyard Lake.'

That was when Joanna's pulse quickened.

'I know the place,' she said, disturbed. 'Matt and I have walked past there hundreds of times. I didn't know anyone lived there. I thought it was derelict. Wonder what sort of person he is to live out there instead of in the town,' she said. 'Well, if he responded, I guess it doesn't sound immediately concerning, but keep an eye on it, will you? I'll be heading home in a bit.'

'Yeah.'

She was acutely aware of the time. Nursery hours were fixed, not moveable, and her little boy would be waiting anxiously.

TWENTY

She reached the nursery just before five and parked up, walking quickly towards the main entrance and spotting him straight away. She could pick him out from all the others by his bright yellow curls, and the minute he spotted her, he yelled – or rather screeched. 'Mummy. Mummy.' He ran towards her, and she buried her head in his hair. 'Well, young man. What have you been up to today?'

He produced a picture – or rather a scribble – and handed it proudly to her.

It was the best moment of her day, the moment when she questioned nothing but felt the warm glow of motherhood, the world of crime fast receding. She strapped him into his car seat and took him home.

A child could bring such happiness, she reflected as she drove. She understood now how proud Mike was of his two clever children: Ricky, currently at university, majoring in rugby, it seemed, though his actual course was modern languages, and Jocelyn – 'Jossy' – who was studying for her A levels and already had offers from three universities.

A text came in from Matthew while she was driving. She pulled over to read it then smiled and turned to the back. 'Daddy says he'll be home for bathtime.'

Jakob's grin broadened, and he started rocking in his car seat.

She'd hardly got him out of the car before Matthew's BMW pulled up behind them. She felt a moment of pride looking at her husband and son.

Matthew unstrapped his son and then dropped his arm around her. 'So,' he said teasingly, 'how did the day go? How's Korpanski? Still living up to expectations?'

'Uh-huh. He's still not quite back to normal, but he's nearly there.'

'Good.'

The issue about Cloud Mansion lay dormant for now. It would be later that something Lilian had said troubled Joanna.

Now she wanted to ask Matthew about houses and atmospheres and, knowing her husband, he would listen and at least consider, though Matthew was a literalist, not prone to believing in the supernatural or fantastic. His natural response would be to pooh-pooh the idea that a house could contain menace within its walls. But he would, at least, discuss this most far-fetched of subjects.

Which was what it was, she decided. Far-fetched.

But for now bath time had to take precedence while she made a light Caesar salad. Upstairs, she could hear Matthew's voice and Jakob's excited shrieks. All felt good in the world.

And then the phone rang.

She recognized the number from caller ID but still answered it, knowing it – or rather she – wouldn't give up.

'He's upstairs bathing Jakob, Eloise.' She hadn't waited for the girl to announce herself. She always knew who it was and that her stepdaughter wouldn't want to talk to her. Eloise Levin never had *anything* to say to her.

The girl's sharp little voice cut in. 'I just wanted to remind him about the twenty-first. Mummy says they can meet with Grandpa and Grandma and Kenneth outside the Great Hall. Eleven o'clock. She says for him *not* to be late. *And* to be tidily dressed.'

'I'll tell him.'

'No. Don't bother. I'll ring later.'

So the sour pall would hang over the evening – there would be no chance for a light-hearted conversation with her husband teasing her for her superstitions about houses and atmospheres. Joanna knew any contact with his daughter brought everything flooding back. His mood would be reflective, his guilt still tangible, for having abandoned his wife for his lover. Her.

And the call was ended.

They both kissed their son goodnight and left him to sleep, his mobile tinkling out Brahms' 'Lullaby'. On the way downstairs, Joanna told Matthew that his daughter had rung and that she'd said she would be ringing back and watched his face take on that oh-so-familiar guilty, unhappy expression.

He picked at his salad before disappearing into his study where she knew he would immediately ring his daughter and try to reassure her that all was well, that he wouldn't be late for her graduation ceremony, that he would wear his best suit and tie for the proud moment when she was handed her degree, and he would also promise he would meet her mother, with his parents, outside the Great Hall, bang on time. Joanna didn't have to listen in. She could have recited the entire conversation herself and knew it would be mirrored many times in the future, at all family occasions: engagements, weddings, christenings. One might divorce one's wife, but you could never divorce your child – particularly one as persistent as Eloise Levin, who never missed an opportunity to drive a wedge between Joanna and her father.

Oh well. Joanna took a large glass of wine into the sitting room and switched the TV on.

10 p.m.

The routine followed the same as last night. The gun trained on him, he was escorted to the bathroom and then locked in the bedroom. But there was one difference. He sensed his captor was gearing up to something. He moved quicker, breathed quicker, was suppressing something. There was a strange excitement in his movements; tension was building. As he'd followed him up the stairs, Joseph had felt his eyes resting on him.

Tomorrow?

Of Clarice there was no sign. Had she gone home as usual? He'd heard whispering between them, and the food that had been provided had her pretty little touches – sliced tomatoes framing a cheese sandwich. His tea was already sugared and served by his captor, and a chocolate biscuit had been placed on the side of the plate. He couldn't see her or hear her. There were none of the usual signs of her presence – no scent of polish, no sound of the vacuum cleaner, nothing.

But he sensed she was still there.

TWENTY-ONE

10.40 p.m.

Joanna had been right about the evening being spoiled. When Matthew rejoined her, it was with that familiar hangdog expression. He dropped on to the sofa next to her with a heavy sigh. 'Eloise,' he said. He didn't need to say more. Actually, he hadn't even needed to say that.

When they went to bed, the distance was as wide as ever, Matthew, his arms folded under his head, staring up at the ceiling, while she, who had given up pointing out that Jane was remarried with two sons and seemed happy with her new life, closed her eyes and tried to direct her thoughts elsewhere. It was only Eloise, his daughter, who refused to move on but dropped back into spoiled little princess/Daddy's girl mode whenever she was around her father.

The strange thing was that she sensed that Kenneth, Eloise's long-term boyfriend, also a medic, sympathized with her.

She'd read warmth in his eyes, almost hidden by large, thick glasses, and knew he hated seeing the way Eloise treated her step-mother with concentrated disdain. Joanna sensed that Kenneth had tried to reason with Eloise. But it obviously hadn't worked. If anything, it had made Eloise even more overtly spiteful. Joanna rolled over in bed. Maybe when Eloise had a child of her own, she would, finally, move on.

Or not.

11 p.m.

He was trying to derive some comfort from the fact that the police had called. Doreen must have alerted them so his subtle clues must have worked. He tried to imagine what they might do next. Would they call again? Or had his assurance from behind a closed door been enough to keep them away? How long was this going to go on? Days? Weeks? And he still hadn't worked out what side of the fence Clarice sat on.

Finally . . . he slept.

2 a.m.

Joanna woke in the middle of the night and sat bolt upright, sleep abandoned. While she'd slept, her mind must have been tussling with an anomaly, a problem, a feeling of something unfinished, unsatisfactory from the day before. Carelessness, perhaps, because she'd still been so excited by having Korpanski back at her side and in a hurry to collect Jakob from his nursery.

A hire car. A vulnerable elderly man unseen for two days, assuring from behind a closed door that he was 'fine'. Valuable antiques. And most sinister of all, playing its part as a backdrop, Cloud Mansion.

'They didn't see him,' she said out loud – to no one, as Matthew was still an unconscious lump beside her. 'No one's *seen* him.'

And now she began to wonder. Who was this man? Where had he come from? Why had he chosen to live out there? She should have checked, worked on finding more detail and she hadn't. She hadn't asked questions, delved into the man's past and identity. They hadn't followed up the number plate on the car, spoken to the hire company, found out who had driven the car and where it had been picked up.

Her omission. And now she was paying the penalty of a sloppy job: sleeplessness.

She was annoyed with herself. 'You're better than that, Piercy,' she muttered under her breath.

But maybe Matthew hadn't been quite so deeply asleep. 'Levin,' he muttered, his arm reaching out for her. She snuggled into him and let the self-castigation go.

Joseph wasn't asleep for long either. When he closed his eyes, he could see too much, the past rising against him, finger pointing, accusing him. Nightmare memories intruded: men, women, children, the sound of screaming, the scent of fear. Homes destroyed, villages burning, men murdered for trying to defend them. He hadn't felt emotions then, not fear, dread or guilt. He had a job to do and that was what he'd focussed on. He could even recall the exhilaration; feel his heart rate increase as though he was striding through a battlefield, directing men, feeling the weight of the machine gun he'd hefted on to his shoulder, the *rat-tat-tat* of gunfire all around.

He'd felt strong – then.

And now he knew he was weak.

4 a.m.

She woke again and pressed the dial on her watch. It was too early to do anything to rectify her slipshod omissions of yesterday, but she knew she wouldn't get back to sleep. She wrapped a dressing gown around her and went to make a cup of tea.

By her side, Matthew was deeply asleep and she didn't want to disturb him.

The silence in the house was thick and soft as velvet as she padded downstairs into the kitchen. And even though her mind was uneasy, she couldn't help but feel some pleasure as she flicked on the lights over the granite counter they'd had installed in the spring.

Briarswood, one of the larger houses that lined the Buxton Road, had been built in the 1880s and had all the welcome features of a Victorian house: fireplaces: ceiling roses, high ceilings that could accommodate Matthew's height. But in common with other houses of the era, the kitchen had purely been a place to cook. Not eat, watch television, lounge on a comfortable sofa. And so, earlier this year, they'd extended into the garden, making the room thoroughly modern.

They practically lived there, in this one family room, watching Jakob play on the swing, his blond hair flying out behind him. When he was older they would cut it short, but for now Joanna loved his flaxen curls. (Matthew's parents had told her their son had had the same beautiful blond curls until he was four.) In fine weather, they opened the patio doors and Jakob played, running in and out. The garden was filled with his toys – a car, a plastic tractor with trailer, a slide and a paddling pool when the weather was fine.

They still had a formal dining room, seldom used except when friends, Matthew's parents or, on rarer occasions, Eloise and Kenneth came to dine. They also had a formal sitting room, complete with log burner, but basically she, Matthew and Jakob lived in this room.

She boiled the kettle and sat at the kitchen table, trying to work out why exactly she felt so disturbed and guilty. Trying to convince herself that this was just an old man who didn't want to be bothered making small talk with a nosey neighbour. There was nothing in it.

But as she sat drinking her tea, she could afford to be honest with herself and face the real source of her anxiety, which was less logical. It was the house, that great grey mausoleum – isolated, difficult to reach and menacing. Put that with the other things that had bothered her during the night – an elderly man, living alone; a mention of frail health; the presence of valuable antiques – and you had a recipe for a situation . . . or at least the potential for one.

She formulated a plan. First thing, visit Cloud Mansion, see the old man for herself, speak to him and check that all really was well. And then she would be able to focus on her other work.

Decision made, she should have felt calmed. But she still felt a tingling in her toes.

They didn't see him, the voice persisted. *No one* has *seen* him.

'Jo?' Matthew was standing in the doorway, his eyes almost closed with sleep. He was in pyjama bottoms, but his chest was bare, his hair a tousled mop. 'What the hell?'

'It's all right,' she reassured him. 'I'm coming back to bed. I was just making mental notes. Ready for the morning. To remind myself. Something I didn't quite finish today. Something left undone or at least not done properly.'

He made no comment but held out his arms and folded her into them. 'Come on,' he said, leading her towards the stairs. 'Bedtime.'

They climbed the stairs together.

He didn't ask for details. Matthew knew her methods only too well. Knew she hated unfinished business.

His arm still around her, they tiptoed past Jakob's room, resisting the temptation to peep in on him. Their son was a light sleeper and ready to play at any time, day or night, once he was roused. And soon, their darling little boy, the son Matthew had so desperately wanted, Jakob Rudyard Levin, would be an incredible two years old. A walking, talking flaxen-haired person with a mind of his own.

They tumbled back into bed.

TWENTY-TWO

T he first thing Joanna did on reaching the station was to start her checks, working through a list which, in the cold light of day, she could consolidate, trying to push aside the personal feelings she had about Cloud Mansion. Her first observation was that they had never been called out there. Yes, they'd attended various fracases in and around Rudyard Lake, mostly connected with youngsters and alcohol, as well as an incident of fairly violent road rage, but they'd never attended Cloud Mansion. However sinister she personally found it, in this case her instincts were wrong.

Her second observation was that this was the first time Mrs Caputo had ever called the police. She ran through the anomalies Doreen had picked up on.

The apparent reluctance for Mr Holden to engage with her.

The hire car apparently left outside.

That was the first task of the day. Speak to the hire company and find out who'd hired the car and from which depot.

There was the added bonus of the focus. 'Neighbourhood policing' was one of the chief constable's 'areas for concern', though what he thought they'd been doing ever since the formation of the police force, they couldn't even dream up. At the time, she and her colleagues had greeted the directive with an eye roll. But now it served a purpose.

She and Mike would take a trip out to Staffordshire's seaside, speak to and reassure the neighbour, check up on the old man, answer these awkward questions that scrabbled around at the back of her mind and then, mirroring Lilian Tadesse's plan, treat themselves to a coffee and a piece of cake at the tea shop.

At almost the same time, Joseph was being tethered to the chair again, and he and his captor waited for Doreen's usual cheery greeting. Of Clarice there was still no sign.

Was it his imagination or was Doreen being less persistent than usual, almost as though she didn't even expect him to open either the curtains or the front door? She called out and he responded, feeling despair when she left with a bland wish that he would soon 'feel better'.

'Thank you.' He heard the sound of hopelessness even in the two words of his response and felt a flash of anger. Surely she realized something was up? Or, having handed her concerns over to the police, possibly aware they'd called yesterday, was she now backing off, leaving it to them?

He focussed on his captor and sensed the drama was about to begin. Joseph recognized the drill he'd performed many times himself: checking the gun, slotting the magazine in and out, rehearsing silent lines, his face screwed up in concentration, his fingers playing with the keypad on Joseph's phone, which it seemed he was going to use rather than his own. Perhaps he was trying to keep his identity a secret, although the car would prove an easy lead for the police.

He watched his captor flex his muscles. Was he expecting another visit from the police? Was his plan to lure officers here – and then shoot them? Had that been his plan all along, and Joseph's role was to act as bait?

He could have shot the two detectives who'd called yesterday, but perhaps he was playing a different game.

Tethered to the uncomfortable chair, Joseph continued to wonder while he watched the hostage taker fiddle with his gun and silently rehearse his plan, while his dark eyes stared far, far into the distance.

10 a.m.

Once she'd set DC Alan King on to extracting detail from the car hire firm, Joanna and Korpanski headed out towards Rudyard Lake. She'd shared her list of concerns with him, and he'd listened, but she could read his scepticism all too well in the pursing of his mouth and his small grunts of disagreement. She sort of agreed with his silent protest. They did have plenty of other things to be focussing on, and this didn't seem top priority.

'It's a short drive,' she said, trying to placate him, 'just to put my mind at ease.' She tried out her charm offensive. 'I won't be able to focus on anything else until I've set my mind at rest and *seen* this man for myself. Besides,' she tried to console him with an encouraging smile, 'it's a lovely drive. If we speak to Mrs Caputo first and get a bit of background, we can walk up the track to Cloud Mansion. It'll be good for your leg,' she teased. 'Get it back in shape.'

'Hey, hold on.' Korpanski was indignant. 'That's a bit personal.'

She held her forefinger up. 'Merely reiterating what the physios must have told you. Exercise will soon restore it.' She stopped there.

'OK.' His good humour had returned.

She drove the four miles out to Rudyard and parked in front of a pair of double doors that marked the entrance to The Lake House, a place she and Matthew had often admired. From the other side of the tall wooden door, they could hear a dog barking out a warning.

But she stood for a moment, taking time to look around. Today, in her opinion, Rudyard Lake had never looked more peaceful or innocent. The sun beamed down, turning the surface of the water golden.

They loitered in front of the gates before ringing the bell. She could have stayed there all day, watching the reflections ripple and re-form, Canada geese flying overhead, their shape reflected, calls amplified by the water. Trees dipped into the lake on the far side, completing the picture of an idyll. Even the human sounds of early-bird canoeists and dog walkers only added to the picture of rural peace and tranquillity. Pennants on the masts of the sailing dinghies rattled, fluttered and dropped, fluttered and dropped, the scent of damp leaves completing the sensory image.

She could have turned her head and observed, in the opposite direction, the tall grey house, looming large, looking down on them, forbidding and sinister, but she didn't want to lose the peaceful image. Not yet.

Then she drew in a deep breath and pressed the bell again. They had a job to do.

They were speaking in low voices, just outside the door. Joseph strained to listen.

Clarice's voice was soft but firm. 'I'm not coming back, Abdi. You have what you want.'

Joseph listened. *They knew each other.* He had a name: Abdi.

'You intend to stay here?' He sounded puzzled rather than angry. 'Why?'

She said something in a dialect he couldn't understand.

She reverted to English. 'I have my reasons.'

'Abdi' must still be holding the gun and yet her voice was unafraid.

Joseph's mind sifted through these few words. If they were in collusion, Clarice must have led him here. Maybe told him about the antiques, described the isolated location. But it still didn't answer the many questions. If robbery was their aim, why didn't they just get on with it? Load up the car and leave. If murder was their ultimate aim, again – why didn't they just get on with it? Pull the trigger.

He tried again to free his wrists, still trying to puzzle it out. Why was this Abdi taking such care with him, keeping him prisoner by day, locking him in a bedroom by night? What did they want? And now he wanted to know how Clarice knew Abdi. Why this shy woman wasn't intimidated by either the gun or its carrier.

Outside, Abdi thumped the door, making it shiver. 'I tell you, girl. You are coming back with me . . . afterwards.'

After what? Joseph thought.

10.15 a.m.

As the door opened, a brief shower started, and a pale rainbow arced over the head of the lake.

A woman stood there, her hand restraining an enthusiastic dog. She was plump, somewhere in her sixties, wearing loose trousers and a navy sweater.

'Mrs Caputo?'

She smiled at them with a hint of embarrassment, and Joanna and Mike displayed their ID.

'Oh,' the woman said, looking flustered now, 'an inspector. I didn't expect . . .' She shifted her glance to Korpanski; flashed him a smile. 'Two of you. I didn't think— Again?'

Even the dog was tilting his head to one side, as though imitating the question.

'May we come in?'

'Sure – yes. Do.' She stood back, and they entered a small yard, following her along a path to the front door.

'We will be calling on Mr Holden, but I wanted to speak to you first.'

'OK.' Doreen Caputo still seemed a little embarrassed but led them into a sitting room which had bow windows overlooking the lake. A man was sitting facing the water. He didn't turn round to greet them.

'My husband,' Doreen explained, 'Luca. He has Parkinson's so doesn't move much, do you, love?'

The man in the chair grunted and lifted a shaking hand.

Mike and Joanna sat side by side on a soft sofa, also facing the water, which was now subjected to a sudden squall.

Doreen was smiling, starting to relax. 'My husband was a sailor,' she said proudly. 'So he loves to watch the water. Takes him back to his fisherman days. He . . . we don't get out much.' Now she looked a little sad.

Joanna smiled a response. 'So, Mrs Caputo, how long have you and Mr Holden lived in close proximity?' She could hardly call them neighbours when Cloud Mansion was a few hundred yards from The Lake House.

'Fifteen years, round about.' She gave a nervous smile. 'You think something's wrong?'

It was Mike who corrected her. '*You* think something's wrong.'

Now Doreen looked flustered. 'Well . . . I don't *know*. It's just a feeling. You see – I walk Stevie Wonder . . .'

Both detectives looked up.

'My dog. His name's . . .'

'OK.' They both smothered a smile. *Got it.*

'I walk him every day. Every – single – day. I never miss a day whatever the weather. He's part Alsatian, and he needs his exercise. Obviously Luca can't take him.' Her eyes drifted across the room. 'Anyway . . .' She hurried past this. 'I have a chat with Mr Holden every day. Sometimes we speak at the front door. At other times, when the weather's nice, he leaves the study window open.' She looked from one to the other. 'We *always* talk. And he *always* calls me Doreen. Has done ever since I told him that was my name.' She was firm about this.

'What do you chat about?' Joanna asked.

Doreen drew in her chin. She clearly hadn't expected this. 'Just trivia,' she said. 'The weather usually. Things that happened in the news. Anything really.'

'Has he ever mentioned family?'

Doreen shook her head. 'I don't think he's got any. He's never mentioned any relatives.'

'So no visitors?'

'I didn't say that. A few times a year, some of his friends come to visit.'

'Friends? What are they like?'

Doreen made a disapproving face. 'Roughnecks,' she said. 'Three of them. One has an artificial leg, I think. He's got a funny walk. They come together every few months and stay a night or two.'

'When you say roughnecks, what do you mean?'

'Just that. Bad language, drink a lot, loud voices. They sound rough. Don't care who hears their raucous noises. No manners. Except' – her face softened for an instant – 'they really took to Stevie Wonder. And he took to them,' she tacked on.

'Is Mr Holden what you'd call rough?'

'No.' She was quick to defend him. 'He's quite a gentleman. Nicely spoken, polite. Keeps himself to himself. Seems to enjoy his privacy.'

'Can you be more specific about these guys?'

Doreen shrugged and turned towards her husband, who was mumbling something. 'Yeah.' Obviously understanding him perfectly, she nodded in agreement. 'They were like ex-army.'

Which gave both Joanna and Korpanski a lead, something else. 'And is that how you'd describe Mr Holden?' Joanna continued.

That made Doreen thoughtful. 'No, I wouldn't have thought so. He seemed different.' She thought for a moment before adding, 'But they are his friends. I can tell.'

'OK.'

Her husband's hand had started shaking again, and he tried to say something.

'There's something I forgot to tell your colleagues who came the other day.'

'Oh?'

'He has a cleaner. That's one of the reasons why I stopped worrying so much . . .' Her voice trailed away.

'A cleaner?'

Her words came out then in a quick babble. 'She put a card in the window, and I saw it. He rang her, and he seemed to like her. She comes on a Wednesday.'

'*Every* Wednesday? So she would have come yesterday?'

Joanna and Korpanski looked at each other. Now it seemed this whole trip had been a waste of time. Joanna tried not to convey that emotion, but she knew Korpanski would have noted the drop in her shoulders.

Doreen obviously hadn't cottoned on as she continued blithely. 'She catches the bus up from Leek.'

'So did she come and go yesterday?'

'I don't know. But . . .' Now the words dragged out reluctantly as she realized the implication. She looked from Korpanski to Joanna, embarrassed.

Joanna stood up. 'OK. Well, we're here now so we may as well call in and put your mind at rest.'

'Thank you. I'm so sorry.' She tried to turn it into a joke. 'I won't be charged with wasting police time, will I?'

Joanna reassured her, forcing out a weak laugh, and they left.

She waited until they were outside before turning to Korpanski. 'Don't rub it in. Don't say I told you so. But it seems you were right. What a bloody waste of time.'

TWENTY-THREE

10.45 a.m.

B ut Korpanski couldn't stop himself as they started walking up the track. 'Well' – he clapped Joanna on the back – 'we're here now and we may as well enjoy it.' He gave a mischievous chuckle. 'Hey, Jo,' he said, looking down at a couple of paddle boarders making heavy weather of crossing the lake. 'Once we've checked up on the old man, how about we play hooky for the day?'

She joined in his good humour. 'Tempting, I admit. Well, we're not in a great hurry. Maybe the old man did resent his nosey neighbour checking up on him every day. Maybe he just fancied a couple of days off for a change. You're right. We can afford to dawdle. It'll be good exercise for your leg,' she teased. 'And the cake's on me.'

Korpanski gave her a long look, his face soft and warm with affection. This was what she'd missed for over a year. His sense of humour, the companionship, the knowledge that he always had her back.

His grin widened. 'As long as you don't say *race you to the top*.'

'Would I ever?' But an unexpected memory had welled up: she and her father, Christopher 'Kit' Piercy, running alongside the little train that ran at the far side of the lake, him urging her on to run faster and faster. '*Race you, Joey. Race you. Beat that train.*'

The memory brought in its wake that familiar twinge of grief. Kit, in the end, had run too fast, life with the younger woman he'd left her mother – and her – for ultimately responsible for the heart attack that had finally killed him. Or so her mother never tired of insisting.

And as though the little train shared that distant memory, it gave a little toot, warning the walkers not to stray on to the track.

Swamped with the painful memory and sense of loss, of a void that could never be filled – not by Korpanski, not by Matthew and not even by Jakob, she looked ahead, through the dark tunnel formed by the trees bending inwards, towards the square, grey outline of Cloud Mansion, which loomed ahead of them, blocking their route like a king's guardsman.

She stopped and turned to Korpanski. 'You know, even when I was a kid, it had a bad reputation,' she said, 'way before the present owner bought it. It used to be called Cliff Park Hall, but I guess Mr Holden changed the name back to its original title. A mad "hermit" lived there, or at least that's the story I was told. Probably one of many legends about the place. I guess it is the sort of place that would always attract stories, tales of strange old men, wizards, vampires and child killers.'

'Tell me more,' Korpanski said, striding ahead of her with hardly a limp as she watched. Day by day, he was growing stronger.

'The story Dad told me was that that an old man lived there with a fierce dog, who occasionally took a child, because he resented anyone trespassing his castle grounds, which would have been a bit difficult as the footpath goes right past his front door. I was frightened, used to scuttle past the door really fast, terrified I'd be snatched either by him or – even worse – the dog.' She was trying to laugh now, tossing her hair back. 'None of us ever actually saw him of course, but we did hear a dog barking, and it did sound pretty ferocious. Not one of us would have ventured up here after dark. They said' – she gave a thin laugh that still held a twang of nervousness in it – 'that any children found trespassing after dark would be fed to his dog, who had a taste for such delicacies, and then they would be turned into zombies.' She could still taste her childhood fear at the back of her throat and slowed her pace.

'I have no idea where all these stories originated from,' she lied.

Korpanski's eyes were fixed on the horizon. 'I can guess,' he said softly. 'Your dad?'

'Yeah. He was good at playing tricks and making up stories.' That had been part of the problem. Her dad had seen himself as eternally young. Full of fun and fond of jokes and tricks mixing practical jokes with genuine tomfoolery. A court jester. He didn't stick to the truth but built his own Neverland so she was constantly unsure whether the versions he gave her were a truth or an untruth. Maybe that was one of the reasons she'd joined the police. She valued the truth because, even as a child, she'd recognized that to play with the truth had led her precious father to the well-worn path of all fantasists – neglect of real responsibilities, the pursuit of a youth-giving younger woman. Like all Peter Pans, he'd been hugely charismatic. Joanna still mourned him, privately, while recognizing that there had been times when his tricks had bordered on cruelty, making her anxious and doubtful of the truth, searching for pitfalls in solid ground. Yet they'd also taught her to value that solid ground when she found it, more than anything else. Matthew was, to her, solid ground.

'I never knew when he was making something up and when it was the truth,' she confirmed, looking suddenly vulnerable.

Korpanski glanced over as if he was tempted to put an arm around her. But he didn't.

The day was an early autumn heaven, the trees just starting their final colour splash. Tinges of browns and greens, oranges and reds dappling the sunshine lifted their spirits as they continued up the muddy track, drawing nearer to the house which, had Joanna been just a tinge more fanciful, seemed to be warning them to keep their distance.

They strode on, and she replaced the discomfort with another, happier thought.

She and Matthew, latterly with Jakob in a baby carrier, must have walked this way hundreds of times, skirting right the way round the lake, passing the two tumbledown chalets – scenes of another case – then a field of cows and, along the railway track, finishing at the coffee shop where they'd indulged in mugs of hot chocolate topped with marshmallows and a blob of cream together with well-earned home-made cakes.

A splash of rain landed on her cheek, and she wiped it away. The wind was rising, and the thin arms of the trees joined the chorus to stay away. As she looked up, through the trees, towards a hostile sky overshadowed by the darker, geometric shape of Cloud Mansion, she lectured herself. This was no time for superstition, fear or fantasy. She was a police officer, for goodness' sake. A pedantic plod, Matthew always called her, a wide grin robbing the phrase of any insult.

She lectured herself.

Get a grip, Piercy. A well-meaning neighbour has reported concerns for an old man, who was probably fussed over all day yesterday by his cleaner, who hasn't reported any problem. So get on with the job. Stop searching for ghosts.

Korpanski had sensed her unease and was looking at her in a funny way. 'You all right there, Jo?'

Her, 'Yeah,' failed to convince him.

He gave her a questioning look but said nothing, and they continued up the track, towards the house. A stone rolled down the track towards the lake. Either they or the rain must have loosened it and sent it on its way.

'God, Jo,' Mike said, pausing to look back at her. 'You look as though you've seen a ghost.'

Which was exactly how she felt, the past having returned to taunt her. And even now it had the power to unsettle her.

Again, she was drawn back to one particular day. She would have been about seven. Her father must have hidden, running ahead and dodging behind a tree, while she and her mother negotiated the cattle grid and reached the top of the incline. She'd shivered, clinging to her mother – not from cold but because the place frightened her. She'd wanted to walk quickly past it, but a stone had rattled at her feet, just like now. But then another and another had joined them while she'd heard a sort of babble like a witch's incantation. She'd wanted to hurry past the door, but her father had lifted the iron knocker, shaped like a devil's grinning face, complete with projecting horns, and banged on it, shouting, 'Come on out, you devil.'

She'd heard it echo inside what they'd thought was an empty house.

But Kit Piercy had turned, looking pale and shocked. 'There's someone in there.' For once the trickster had been tricked.

They had all turned towards the door before they'd run, helter-skelter down towards the meadow and the cows, who'd simply looked up before continuing to chew the cud.

So now was she about to face the monster inside the house? *Come on out, you devil*. She smiled. Maybe that would stir the old man into answering the door.

At the bottom, her mother, always the pedant, had scolded him. 'Nonsense, Christopher.' She'd never bought in to the 'Kit' business. 'The place is derelict.' She'd added, in a low voice, meant only for her husband, 'The old man died. It's empty. It's up for sale.' And she indicated the For Sale sign, which had blown down so it lay, lifeless, on the ground.

But her father had shaken his head, and even to Joanna's seven-year-old eyes, he'd seemed upset. She'd looked from one parent to the other, not knowing which to believe.

In the end, she'd grabbed both their hands and forced them to run away further, towards the little steam train and the crowds of people who walked along the railway line.

The phrase rang in her ears again. *The old man died*.

Maybe Korpanski had picked up on her mood. 'Come on, Jo,' he said kindly. 'It's just an old man who lives in an old house.'

'Yeah,' she said.

And then her mobile phone rang.

TWENTY-FOUR

11 a.m.

It was PC Jason Spark, and he sounded worried. In fact, Joanna reflected later, he sounded panicky.

'Where are you?' His voice was shaking.

'Just climbing up towards Cloud Mansion . . .' She'd been about to say they were checking up on the old guy the neighbour had been concerned about, but she never got to finish the sentence because she'd picked up on something in his voice. 'Jason. What's the matter?'

'You need to back off.'

'What?' Joanna looked around her. Apart from the tiniest shiver of the curtain in the long window which lay only a hundred yards ahead of them, all was peaceful.

Jason spoke quickly, his voice rising. 'Some guy called in, says he's holding Joseph Holden and a young lady named Clarice Hani hostage.' Jason paused and added in a stunned voice, 'He says he has a gun.'

'What?' Joanna said again, knowing she'd heard it all the first time.

Jason repeated the two sentences. Shocked, Joanna stared at Korpanski then up at the house. Which looked deserted. She seemed to hear her mother's voice, speaking low as she hadn't wanted to be overheard.

The old man died.

'That's not all. He's using Mr Holden's mobile phone, and he wants to talk to you.'

'What? Me?'

For a moment, she was paralysed. Unable to process this new situation which seemed to have barged into a routine follow-up. Korpanski was watching her, having picked up on at least part of the conversation. And he too seemed in a state of suspended animation, his mouth having dropped open. A ping told her that Jason had texted her the number of Joseph Holden's mobile phone.

'You need to back off.'

She looked at Korpanski then at the grey walls that rose ahead of them, before instinctively grabbing his hand and taking cover behind some trees, her gaze fixed on the house.

'Jo?'

'Did you hear that? Mr Holden has been taken hostage by a man with a gun.'

Korpanski nodded.

She needed to process the information. The words floated in front of her – *hostage, gun* and the *hostage taker* who wanted to speak to her. She eyed the mobile number displayed on her screen and knew before she spoke to this man she needed to retrieve at least some of the lessons from the course she'd attended and which she and Korpanski had so recently been joking about.

First lesson? *Keep calm.*

Easier in a classroom mock-up than in this situation, but the tutor's words flooded back randomly.

Ask open-ended questions.

Encourage the hostage taker to talk – and talk – and talk.

Focus less on the why, always on the how. Let them be the ones to work out the mechanics of their demands.

Stall – but not in an obvious way.

Separate the person from the emotion. They will be on heightened alert. You suppress any sign of impatience, anger, anxiety.

Don't get wrapped up in what they want but why they want it.

Safety of the hostage is paramount.

Keeping her eyes focussed on Korpanski's and tucking herself well out of sight, she steadied her breathing, opened the message with Joseph's number and pressed call.

TWENTY-FIVE

I t was picked up right away.

Breathe. Robbie Callaghan's voice was ringing in her ears.

She kept her voice crisp and business-like. 'This is Detective Inspector Joanna Piercy, Leek police. I understand you want to talk to me.' She had a hundred questions she wanted to ask but restricted herself to one. 'Who am I speaking to, please?'

'My name is Abdi Daud.'

A foreign voice, maybe North African? And he sounded calm. She tucked the facts away.

'Have we met, Mr Daud?'

He didn't answer so she waited.

Use silence as a weapon.

He broke the silence. 'You have questions you wish to ask me?'

She smiled, and Korpanski gave her a surprised look. *They will be able to hear that smile in your voice.*

'I understand you have Mr Joseph Holden and a lady called Clarice Hani with you.'

No answer.

And so again, she waited, as though she had all the time in the world, though in reality her mind was in turmoil. And a small part was already preparing for the logistics of dealing with this drama.

Korpanski was watching, his dark eyes showing his shock, confusion and a tinge of respect.

He glanced towards the house. Korpanski was an action man. She knew he was itching to seal off the area and summon armed response, as well as find somewhere they could use as a safe base, somewhere safer than simply ducking behind a tree.

She held a hand up to him. *Press pause, Korpanski.*

Again, she let the silence seep upwards, towards the house, while she glanced down to the lake and watched the clouds drift across the water's surface, grey on blue.

Abdi Daud finally spoke again. 'I have them. Yes.'

'Are they safe?'

'For now.' He tucked the threat in between those two short words.

Obtain proof of life before you start any negotiations.

'I need to know they're all right.'

This time he was the one who weaponized silence, so she was forced to repeat her request.

'I need to know that both Miss Hani and Mr Holden are alive and well.'

Silence.

And then: 'You will have your proof of life, don't worry, and neither has been harmed . . . yet.'

Joanna digested this information. 'I understand you have a gun.'

This time she heard the smile in *his* voice. 'For your information, Inspector, I have a Glock 17 and plenty of bullets, though I suspect you are not particularly familiar with firearms.'

She guessed he would be aware his confirmation of being armed would trigger a response.

She nodded across at Korpanski, sensed his impatience.

Next, Joanna expected Daud would state his demands. But he didn't. She'd expected heightened emotion and again he was confounding her. He sounded calm, unemotional and fully in control. She felt as though the scales were tilting in his favour. He wasn't conforming to the textbook step-by-step description of a typical hostage taker. Which could mean he wanted to play a long game.

She waited, her mind still questioning how Daud, whose name was unfamiliar to her, knew her name. It destabilized her even more given this exchange wasn't following the expected route. But she couldn't accede to or deny his demand unless she knew what it was.

So still she waited.

And so did he.

Don't be impatient. She could hear Robbie Callaghan warning her against one of her abiding faults. She was always in too much of a hurry. Impatient to see events through to the end.

Breathe.

Then Daud laughed, a strangely happy sound. Which in the context sounded mad.

Then he picked up the narrative, tossing the challenge to her as carelessly as though he was discarding litter. 'You had better go now, Inspector Piercy – or is it Inspector Levin? Or simply Joanna?'

Linking her married name to her job title chilled Joanna even more. She put her hand on the tree to steady herself, gaping at Korpanski and slowly shaking her head with incredulity. Who was this guy? And how did he know so much about her? Not just the DI Piercy part but her actual married name. That chilled her beyond words. Colleagues called her Piercy. Friends called her Levin.

'Yes, you had better go, Inspector,' he repeated. 'I think you have much to do. Keep your phone with you. I shall call you on this number later. I will keep your hostages safe. But, Inspector, I will talk only to you. No one else. You understand?'

'Yes.' She'd responded automatically. It was only after the call had ended that she realized how badly she'd failed this first test. Mr Daud was the one with the upper hand. She clung on to the assurance. *I will keep your hostages safe.*

By her side, Korpanski was increasingly agitated. They both knew the drill. Mention firearms and they had to follow protocol: secure the area, put an armed response unit in place. Keep the public at bay and the phone lines open.

She started to process the conversation, recalling the role play they'd indulged in on the course, giggling at the time until Robbie Callaghan had stopped them with a sobering warning. 'Lives depended on your skills as a negotiator.'

Which was when she fully understood. She was now responsible for the lives of two people: the old man and the cleaner.

She echoed his words, adding a warning of her own. *Mess it up, Piercy, and that Glock 17 will do its dirty work.*

TWENTY-SIX

11.15 a.m.

For a moment, she couldn't think. Her mind was paralysed, unable to formulate any plan while Korpanski watched her, allowing her a few moments to recover herself. She peered around the tree trunk at the house, picking out the two tall sash windows in the side which faced them. She thought she detected a tiny movement in the curtains. He was watching her.

Dodging between trees, the two officers backed down the track.

Daud moved away from the window, smiling to himself. He'd anticipated this encounter, imagined it time after time. And Joanna's responses had been exactly as he'd predicted. The phrases the inspector had used were familiar, the attempt at turning the control away from him clumsy. A sudden fury rose up inside him as he remembered. '*Aabahaa was!*' he cursed, crossing the room to kick the chair. '*Aabahaa was!*'

Joseph recognized the curse as well as the fury in his captor's voice. He closed his eyes, felt the gun jabbed into his neck and knew he was in for a rough time now the 'party' had begun.

Abdi spoke into his ear, the spittle forming in his mouth making the words sound as if they came from underwater. 'I pull this trigger, Mr Holden, and you die. Make no mistake – you die.'

Joseph closed his eyes.

As they'd retreated down the track, Joanna's mind had freed itself from the feeling of panic and she started to plan.

First: seal off the area.

Inform Chief Superintendent Gabriel Rush, who would have to be kept up to date with the situation.

An armed response team surrounding the house would have to be put in place and an incident room set up nearby.

Korpanski waited for instructions. Finally, she turned to him and gave him the ghost of a smile. 'Well, Mike, this is what you wanted. Real policing.'

His return grin was lopsided, his dark eyes reaching towards her. Concerned.

She looked around her. 'Right let's get started. Seal off the area. I don't want anyone wandering in and "having a go". We need to keep this under wraps as far as possible. Facts leaked on a need-to-know basis. And see if you can find somewhere suitable where we can set up an incident room.'

'Got it.'

He pulled out his mobile phone, ready to set the wheels in motion.

'It's possible the whole thing will blow over,' she mused. 'This Mr Daud might be bluffing.' But the next moment she recalled Abdi Daud's calm, controlled voice and doubted this would be the case. 'I'll have to let Rush know, and we need to find out who this guy is. He sounded foreign. See what Alan King's dug up from the hire company.'

Korpanski was already working on her instructions while she spoke to Chief Superintendent Gabriel Rush, explaining the situation as best she could. As she spoke, she pictured his prim mouth and humourless face, and hoped that for once she would find a glimmer of empathy in his response.

Give Rush his due. He listened without comment, letting Joanna convey the situation, starting with the alert from the neighbour, detailing the presence of a cleaner as well as the owner of Cloud Mansion, and finishing with her reading of it. She articulated it all, even sharing the fact that the hostage taker had used her married name as well as her work title and appeared familiar with the work-ings of hostage negotiation. When she'd relayed all that, there was a brief silence before he spoke. His voice was dry and raspy as sand so she couldn't fix on his underlying thoughts. Then he said just one word. 'So . . .?'

She outlined her plan and told him DS Korpanski was already putting together an armed response team and the area was being sealed off.

When he did finally offer an opinion, she had a surprise. 'You sure you're up to this, Piercy, after just a four-day course?' He actually sounded sympathetic.

The short answer was no. Four days' teaching hadn't equipped her for this, but she had no choice. 'He specifically asked for me, sir. I'm not sure he would deal with anyone else. And I plan to ask Robbie Callaghan, my lecturer, if he'll advise me as I go along. It's the best I can do, sir.'

That resulted in silence. She was about to speak again when he cleared his throat. 'What do you know about the hostage?'

'He's a bit of a recluse, in his late seventies, and he had major surgery around eight months ago.'

'And the hostage taker, this Mr Daud?'

She dredged up some long-ago stored fact. 'I believe Daud is an Arabic name. DC King is following up the lead from the hire company.'

'You think this is terrorism related?' She could hear alarm in his voice.

'I don't know, sir, but it isn't the way they work surely?'

'And the cleaner? What do you know about her?'

Again, she wanted to use the phrase *early days* but had to satisfy herself with, 'We're working on it, sir.'

He paused. 'Phone?'

'He's using the hostage's phone, sir.'

There was a brief silence and then Rush made his decision.

'Best get on then, Piercy. I'll expect a report as soon as you have any developments.'

'Yes, sir.'

'Set up an incident room close by. Out of range of this person's firearm.'

Was she imagining a smile on that thin scar of a mouth?

'Yes, sir.'

'And stay on board. You won't be going home for a little while yet. We'll get an officer to keep an eye on your family.'

'I don't want them involved, sir.'

He simply sighed while she read his mind: that she might not have a choice.

She ended the call with a feeling of trepidation as well as one of relief. That was the worst job over. And he'd given her a free hand as well as not even mentioning the word *budget*.

Korpanski was still speaking to someone so she waited until he gave her a thumbs up and ended the call.

'There's an old boat house,' he said, 'just a little way down the track. It used to belong to the yachting club, but they haven't used it for years. They have new premises. King is in charge of setting up computers there. We already have the entire area surrounded with armed police.'

'Nice work.'

As though to confirm his claim, through the trees they could see camouflaged figures crouching, eyes on the house, and there was the sound of cars moving. The lake had been emptied of the water sports participants. They walked down the track towards the boat house, whose tall doors were already swinging open.

It had been abandoned years ago and had the damp, chill atmosphere of a derelict building. But, on the plus side, it had large arched windows to the front, with views over the track that led to Cloud Mansion, while a smaller side window held a perfect view of the place. And, according to the firearms expert, it was out of range of Daud's Glock.

Tables were being set up, and a single light bulb illuminated the room, which had all the ambience of a wartime 'ops' room. In one corner, a ladder stood against the wall leading to some sort of upstairs, and on the side opposite Cloud Mansion, a sanilav stood.

Joanna looked around without enthusiasm. This, she realized, would be her home for the foreseeable.

Her next job was to try and contact Robbie, her lecturer, who was based at Staffordshire University. When Rush had voiced his doubts that a four-day course in hostage negotiation would equip her for the task ahead, he'd echoed her own misgivings. She needed her lecturer's professional guidance. His secretary said he was teaching but would call her back.

She knew his first suggestion would be that she learn all she could about the three people involved in this situation: the two hostages as well as the hostage taker.

Although, for the moment, she placed the cleaner, Clarice, somewhere in the middle. She didn't yet know which side she was on.

Neither did Joseph. He strained to listen to the whispered conversations between the cleaner he'd trusted and Abdi Daud. And his mind was tracking along the same path Joanna and Chief Superintendent Rush's were. Was this a terrorist-related incident? Or was it a personal vendetta?

3 p.m.

Joanna was bent over DC Alan King's shoulder, studying his screen, which held the details the car hire company had sent over.

Name: Abdi Daud.

Age: 37.

It was the nationality that disturbed her most. Somali.

Somalia was, to her, a troubled region in the horn of Africa with a history of extreme violence.

She drew back. This wasn't looking good.

She tried to focus. 'These may not be our hostage taker's real name and contact details so can you check with someone from the Somali Embassy? And we need to find out everything we can about Mr Holden, in particular if there's any past connection with Somalia. And then there's Clarice,' she said, almost to herself. 'The unknown quantity. She could be part of the whole thing or an innocent caught up in the drama. Wrong place. Wrong time. She could even be the original target if she's Somali too. But there's a possibility that she's a confederate.'

She was beginning to realize this wasn't a simple hostage situation but something tangled up in a past she didn't yet know and might have difficulty understanding. She needed Robbie Callaghan's help more than ever.

She moved over to PCs Kitty Sandworth and Jason Spark. 'We need a warrant for phone taps on Joseph Holden's mobile and landline.' She stepped towards the opposite wall where a whiteboard was being hoisted up. 'I need a detailed map of the area in case there are other routes out.' She looked around her, assessing access points. Lake in front, open areas to the sides and that steep track down from Horton Road at the rear, ending at a rusting gate left permanently ajar. Another memory flashed in her mind – she and Matthew had once commented on it while cycling past, Jakob in a baby seat behind her.

She took a deep breath.

Gradually her mind was clearing, her thoughts clarifying, and her direction as easy to see as a straight road ahead on a bright day. In the end, it all came down to the tried and tested methods Robbie Callaghan had drummed into them on that four-day course.

Standing in the doorway of the boat house, she scanned the lake, currently sulking underneath a scowling sky, devoid of paddle boarders, flapping pennants or canoeists. To her left stood the house, its granite walls as threatening as an enemy. Down the track, two officers clad in stab vests were turning away a couple who looked as though they'd dressed for a jog around the lake and were indignant at being turned away, gesticulating furiously. Eventually, realizing they weren't going to be let through, they left, patently disgruntled judging by the set of their shoulders and the stamp of angry footsteps.

Sealing off the area was going to prove both difficult and unpopular. But it could have been worse. It could have been a warm day in the school holidays when the businesses that relied on the lake – the tea rooms, yachts, canoe and paddle board hire – would have been even more affected.

Her eyes roved over the whole area, assessing it as a combat zone. The wooded areas would provide both a challenge and a blessing. Plenty of trees for the armed response officers to take aim from while keeping cover. But the same was true of the hostage taker. Was it possible he too could slip through the trees, dodging their surveillance and escape? But, again, there was a silver lining. Here, where there were few people around, fewer people at risk, had to be a safer background than a crowded street or restaurant. But apart from the *drip, drip* of rain falling from leaves, despite the drama playing out, the scene still appeared tranquil. She stopped and tried to console herself with one of Robbie's end-of-day summaries, where he'd tried to inject some humour into the final half hour by showing them footage of the aftermath.

Most 'dramas' end up with a hostage taker giving himself up out of boredom. He'd smiled. *While the hostage is released without harm.*

She'd never felt less like smiling. It wouldn't take long for the local media to sniff out a 'situation' and start asking questions, which meant Matthew would guess she'd be involved and start to worry. But Daud had insisted she be the sole officer to handle this.

I will talk only to you. No one else. You understand?

Alongside that was Rush's warning that she wouldn't be going home for a while.

Through the window, beyond the house, though she couldn't see it, she knew the path dipped down to some cows grazing behind an electric fence. Despite the gravity of the situation, Joanna smiled. They wouldn't be evacuating the cows.

On the other side of the lake, the small train still puffed along its track, back to its shed, its last trip until the situation was resolved one way or another. According to their firearms expert, if Daud was telling the truth about the weapon he held, the other side of the lake was out of range. But it might all be a lie. Why should she trust him? He could have been deliberately misleading her, armed with a long-range sniper rifle rather than a pistol. And if access to the far side of the lake wasn't closed, there was another weapon that might be used to compound the risk to Joseph Holden. The long lens of a camera in the hands of a vigilant hack could reveal the whereabouts of their incident room as well as the positions of the road blocks. And if they were shared through social media, the information could provide valuable information to the hostage taker.

Another risk she couldn't take.

Like most police, she was anxious to keep reporters at bay – unless, by informing the general public, they could aid an investigation.

The rain had stopped now, but the leaves still dripped. She could hear the steady sound as the water droplets fell. *Tap . . . tap . . . tap*. Rivulets trickled down the track to the lake, drawing her eye towards the neighbour's house, which reminded her to send a couple of officers to speak to Doreen Caputo again. Maybe there was some detail she hadn't mentioned which might help them find a link between the owner of Cloud Mansion and someone who appeared to have travelled all the way from Somalia with the sole purpose of taking him hostage.

She turned back into the hive of activity that marked an ongoing police investigation.

Korpanski crossed the room towards her. 'Good job you did that training course then,' he said gruffly.

She gave a huff of agreement and tried to laugh. 'Tempted fate, didn't I?'

And then he put an arm around her, patting her shoulder, before tapping on his phone and opening up the picture of the car that Lilian and Bethany had taken the previous day.

It was nothing remarkable – a mud-spattered blue Nissan with 2014 plates. No one and nothing visible inside it. 'Hired at Manchester airport late on Monday evening.'

'So if this all started on Tuesday morning, as Mrs Caputo believes, he hired the car and more or less drove straight here.'

'Seems like it.'

She spoke to DC King again. 'Any luck with Interpol?'

'Not yet.'

'And Mr Holden?'

'Ah,' he said and pressed a few keys. But there was little to see.

Her phone was ringing and, recognizing the number, she felt a stab of concern. It wasn't a great time for Rush to call. She relayed their findings so far and waited.

'Have you found out anything more about the hostage?'

'We're having a bit of difficulty there.'

'As in?' Rush was also a man of few words.

'The lot. Employment. National Insurance number. He was in the military but left some time ago. Since then, on paper, he doesn't seem to exist.'

'Hmm.' He was silent for a moment before pursuing yet another angle. 'You'd better go home, Piercy. Get some sleep. Put someone else in charge for the night.'

'Thank you, sir, I will head home. I need my family to know what's up, and I'm going to need some clothes. I'll keep the phone on me and come straight back.'

'Is that really—?'

She cut him off. 'Daud insists he will only speak to me.' She'd remembered one of the many facts she'd picked up on the course and drew in a long breath. 'He could call any time day or night. It's the practice, apparently, for the hostage taker to try and catch the negotiator out by ringing at odd times. I need to be here – on site – in case anything happens. I'll get the guys to rig up some sort of bed here.'

'Where exactly is "here"?'

'We're set up at the boat house, the old sailing club. It's within a few hundred yards of Cloud Mansion. In fact,' she added, 'if I look out the side window, I can just about make out its walls.'

'Right.' He paused. 'Korpanski's back from sick leave, isn't he?'

'Yes, sir.'

'Don't work him too hard, Piercy. Don't want him going off sick again.'

She couldn't decide if that was Rush's idea of a joke. She decided to play it straight. 'No, sir.'

'I shall expect you to report developments to me tomorrow. First thing.'

He rang off before hearing her final, 'Yes, sir.'

TWENTY-SEVEN

Friday 13 September, 6 a.m.

The date seemed like a portent. As though now the action had begun and Daud was determined to punish him. Joseph had spent an uncomfortable night tied to the chair, Daud propped up in the corner, apparently neither awake nor asleep, the gun loose on his lap. He couldn't see or hear Clarice so didn't know whether she was still around or had left, had been similarly restrained or was free to come – and go – as she pleased, and he didn't ask. It was the one shred of dignity he could hang on to. She'd only worked for him for a few months, but he felt betrayed and a little foolish. He'd let his guard down, and now he was paying the price.

At six o'clock, he'd finally spoken up. 'I'm uncomfortable. I need to move. I need to go to the toilet. I need something to eat. I'm hungry.' Even he despised the whiny, brattish sound of his voice. Particularly the wavering undertone of fright he hoped only he could detect.

Daud glanced across briefly before sinking back into that state of suspended animation.

He wondered when Daud was going to ring the detective again.

6.05 a.m.

Joanna, also uncomfortable, was lying on a rigged-up camp bed covered with a sleeping bag.

She was watching the minutes slip by on the digital display of her work mobile. When was he going to ring? she wondered, then wished Robbie Callaghan would contact her. She'd passed on her personal mobile; she couldn't risk the line being engaged if Daud did ring.

She'd been driven home last night, the driver waiting outside while she'd bagged up some clothes and toiletries. She'd given Matthew only the barest details – that she was snarled up in a major case and might not be home until it had been cleared up.

He'd been silent for a moment until his emotions had spilled out. 'Are you in any danger, Jo?'

She'd tried to reassure him. 'No.'

He hadn't believed her.

She'd tried again. 'No, Matt, I'm not in any personal danger, but this is a situation I can't abandon.' She'd known she was leaving out the most worrying fact: that the hostage taker was armed and appeared to have her in his sights. Instead, she'd skirted around it. 'I'm the one who has to deal with this. I don't really have a choice.'

She'd known he couldn't understand. And she didn't want him to understand.

What could she tell him that would reassure him? As she'd left, perhaps sensing his father's mood, Jakob had been crying and Matthew's face had been twisted in concern. He'd kissed her, hugged her tightly and finally let her go.

7 a.m.

Clarice stood in the doorway. 'We need to eat, Abdi,' she said, keeping her head in profile, avoiding looking in Joseph's direction. He tried to catch her eye by shifting forward in the chair, but it was as though he'd become invisible. He watched her, realizing she wasn't a prisoner – unlike him, she was free. The realization upset him partly because he'd been fooled and partly because he knew he had two adversaries now – not one.

'I will make something.' She turned round, and then she did glance at Joseph, blinked a couple of times and frowned, giving her head a very slight shake. He couldn't work out what the gesture meant. Disdain? Dislike? Amity? Were *they* the co-conspirators? He pondered this until she returned, carrying a plate of sandwiches.

As Daud sliced through the ties so he could eat, he kept his eye on her and tried to interpret her body language. Had she *disliked,* even *despised* him from the start? How far back did it go? Had she targeted him? When she'd put the card in the window, had it been the equivalent of a fishing fly, wriggling on the end of a hook? When he'd engaged her, had she realized she had the fish on the end of the line and she simply needed to reel him in? Each time they'd passed on the stairs or in the passageway, had she been gloating as the line grew shorter and shorter, the landing moving nearer?

Apart from her name, Clarice Hani, he'd known nothing about her. Had she been acting, adopting that submissive, down-at-heel demeanour, which was effective as a disguise because it had made her invisible?

Again, as he watched her leave the room, he felt that strange prick of recognition. That same old memory reawakened in the way she walked, swaying, erect, proud. Quite different from her previous persona. The memory brought in its wake a troubling consciousness, a sick feeling of guilt that crept over him, and another biblical reference, from Deuteronomy this time – vengeance is mine – but Daud interrupted his thoughts, pushing him with the barrel of the gun.

'Move,' he said. 'Bathroom.'

While he walked, the gun was pressed against his spine. He looked up and his eyes picked out the pale patch above the Chinese cabinet.

And his mind hopped from A to B.

7.30 a.m.

Finally, the call that she'd been hoping for came through.

He began with an apology.

'Sorry I didn't ring earlier, Joanna.' The relief that she now would have the backing of her lecturer was immense. 'I was teaching, and I thought you could handle the first twenty-four hours on your own. Do some fact-finding. Build up a relationship with the hostage taker. So where are you?'

'Robbie,' she started to say, 'I don't feel up to—'

But he cut her off short.

'Don't let's waste time on doubt. Give me the facts – so far.' His voice was brisk and business-like.

He listened without comment as she related the scenario, telling him the neighbour's concerns, the hostage taker's name and apparent ethnic origins. She gave him a description of Joseph Holden and detailed the mystery of his whereabouts since leaving the armed forces. She also shared the presumed presence of the cleaner, whose origins were, so far, unknown. She described Cloud Mansion with its collection of objects, apparently collected worldwide. Finally, she finished with the hostage taker's insistence that she be the sole person he would deal with.

He listened, still saying nothing, but she knew he would be absorbing all the facts. In the four days he'd spent lecturing them, she'd observed an almost hawk-like intensity in his eyes. She'd also realized he didn't waste words. Which made her listen hard as he spoke.

'Have you proof of life?'

'Not yet.'

'That's step one. You can't progress until you know Mr Holden is alive.'

She felt chastened.

'Has he made any demands?'

'No.' Joanna paused. 'That's what's bothering me. I'm floundering, Robbie. I don't know what he wants. How can I even begin to negotiate,' she blurted out, 'when I don't have that basic premise?'

She could hear the frustration in her voice.

So could Robbie Callaghan, whose response came back instantly. 'Patience,' he said, scolding her. 'What was I constantly telling you, Piercy? Currently you feel he's the one dictating the rhythm and pace of this situation, not you. But you have to regain control. And you can't do that if you're trying to force the pace. Don't forget you have him surrounded. He can't escape, so whatever you might think, whatever priorities you're setting yourself, you have the upper hand, not him. You have time.'

'But Mr Holden is in poor health.'

'Right.' Even the sound of his voice calmed her. 'So first of all ascertain what state he's in. You must have proof of life. If possible, talk to him. Get an idea of his mental state as well as his physical one.'

'Should I ring?'

He responded quickly and forcefully. 'Absolutely not. It would make you look weak. He'll ring at some point. It's the only way he can gain his objectives. In the meantime, what was the word I got you all to repeat?'

'Background.'

'That's it. Find out all you can about the three major players.'

'Three?'

'Your hostage, the hostage taker and Clarice Hani, the cleaner. It's no coincidence that she appears to be Somali as well as Mr Daud. Treat her as his accomplice.

'There is a possibility,' he added thoughtfully, 'that *Clarice Hani* is Daud's target, but it doesn't seem likely. In my opinion, she led him to Joseph Holden and Cloud Mansion. Lovely name by the way.'

'Not a particularly lovely house.'

'No,' he said drily. 'I saw a picture of it on the Internet. It's quite forbidding, isn't it?'

'Yes.'

'Difficult area to seal off.'

'We've done our best.'

'OK.' His voice suddenly became brisk. 'Although these situations are unpredictable, it doesn't seem that there's an imminent threat to his hostage's life.'

'You think not?'

'Why else wouldn't he have just murdered him and left? You say this siege began on Tuesday, and you weren't involved until yesterday, so he had a couple of days to make his escape. No . . . his reason for being there isn't simply to shoot his hostage. He wants something.'

Joanna didn't know whether to be relieved or even more worried.

'Does he sound balanced?'

'Yes.'

'So we assume he does have a plan.'

She listened hard as he continued.

'My guess is, considering what you've told me about Mr Holden, that this is connected with his past somehow. You say he was a military man?'

'Until the late eighties. We don't know what he's done since then.' She wanted to ask him if she could continue to consult him, but he hadn't finished.

He summed up. 'It's a game of poker, Piercy. A bluff. A waiting game with a terrible penalty if you play your hand wrong.' He paused. 'There are two – three – lives at risk. You have to give Mr Daud the illusion of control while you hold on and wait for events to unfold.'

She finally moved to the angle that had been gnawing away inside her head. 'How does he know me, Robbie? My rank and title as well as my married name. He called me Joanna,' she blurted out.

Her lecturer took her concern seriously. 'I agree. This is something specific, deeply personal. You say you don't know him?'

'No.'

'Have never met him?'

'No. I looked at his passport photograph. He's a stranger.'

There was a pause as her lecturer chewed over this concern, and then he responded briskly. 'Leave it with me. And, Joanna, have faith in yourself. You can do this.'

With you holding my hand, she thought.

'Let Daud dictate the rhythm and pace of these negotiations because, in the end, you hold the ace. Send me an email detailing the whole scenario as well as a map of the area and Daud's passport details.'

'Should I try and obtain the release of Clarice Hani?'

'I don't think so. It seems pretty obvious to me that she led the hostage taker to Cloud Mansion, so for now, focus on your main target.'

'Which is?'

'Ah . . .' She heard a smile in his voice. 'Interesting that you ask that. And I'm glad you see the wider picture. Your main target is, of course, the safe release of Joseph Holden. But behind that is the task of finding out what links a Somali national to Joseph Holden because that, in the end, will be your lynchpin. Find the reason behind this drama and you have a better chance of solving it. Background, Joanna. Background.'

'Is Joseph Holden's life in danger?'

Robbie Callaghan paused, and then he spoke in a sober voice. 'Hostages' lives are always in danger. You have a criminal of uncertain motives as well as a precarious mental state, a gun, which doesn't take much effort to fire, an elderly man in poor health who's probably frightened and tied to a bed or a chair or something. Certainly not free to leave. There's the unknown status and vulnerability of a second person. We can assume our hostage taker is in a state of heightened tension.'

'He doesn't sound it.'

Robbie countered that. 'He's bound to be. He knows as well as we do that his actions are illegal. And yet he probably planned this months ago.'

'Months?'

'Didn't you say that Miss Hani has worked at Cloud Mansion for a number of months?'

She fell silent, and Robbie Callaghan continued. 'But he decided to go ahead. Why? That's the real question. Why? What does he want?'

Neither of them attempted to answer.

Robbie gave a huge sigh. 'I'm here. Keep in touch. If you want more guidance, call this number. It's personal and doesn't go through my secretary.'

'Thank you.'

He laughed. 'I'd like to say my pleasure, but when I run these courses I hope . . . I pray, sincerely, that none of my attendees will have to experience the role of negotiator.' He paused. 'It's stressful and – whatever the outcome – you invariably feel you could have done it better.'

She appreciated his honesty as well as the support he was offering her.

She repeated her thanks, and they both ended the call.

Which was when the questions started to pile up. When should she authorize the armed response team to storm the house?

What were the truce breakers?

How would she know?

Background, Robbie had advised. *Background*.

And there lay the puzzle.

8.15 a.m.

It was time to give CS Rush his daily report. But she had little to pass on that sounded positive, and she knew her self-doubt would be picked up by her sharp, intuitive superintendent.

However, he listened without comment, apart from saying that he was glad her lecturer would be available for advice. And he repeated one of Robbie's key questions.

'Have you proof of life yet?'

'No, sir.' She added that Robbie Callaghan had told her to prioritize that demand.

'Well,' Chief Superintendent Rush said, 'I'm glad he's watching your back. Keep me informed of any changes.'

'I will, sir.'

'You have your work phone with you?'

'At all times.' She didn't add, *even on the toilet and while I'm having a shower*. He wouldn't appreciate such intimate detail. Or the levity behind it.

'Good.' And then the chief superintendent surprised her. 'I have full confidence in you, Piercy. There isn't anyone I'd rather see handle this.' But then he couldn't resist giving *himself* a pat on the back. 'Seems it was a good decision to send you on that course.'

And he hung up before she could think of a response.

Half an hour, later a text came through from Matthew.

Just got the detail over the radio about the 'incident' around Rudyard. An armed man understood to be holding a member of the public hostage! I should have locked you in the house last night. But I didn't. Keep safe, my darling M X

PS Jakob and I love you X

She felt like texting back to say *she* wasn't the one in danger, but something stopped her. The fact that Daud had asked for her not only by her professional title but also her married name. Again, she searched her memory for a Somali national named Abdi Daud, but he wasn't there. Even if he'd used fake ID, he still wasn't there. She didn't know him. So why was he insisting he deal only with her?

She marked Matthew's text as read but couldn't find a suitable, honest response. Her husband could sniff through empty platitudes like a trained bloodhound.

She descended the ladder.

The map had been pinned to the wall next to the ubiquitous whiteboard which was, apart from the names of the three protagonists, depressingly blank. All the officers knew they were waiting for the next call from Daud.

Which didn't come.

DC Alan King had searched for Clarice Hani – and come up with nothing. She remained an enigma, her status uncertain. What seemed probable was that she wasn't in the country legally. But having no background information on Joseph's cleaner meant they had no idea what had brought Clarice Hani to Cloud Mansion in the first place.

Background. Robbie had driven the point home. So she decided to meet up with Doreen Caputo again, the start of it all. She was the only one who knew their hostage.

Korpanski had appeared just after eight, as bleary eyed as if he was the one who'd worked through the night and slept on site.

'Didn't get much sleep,' he confessed, yawning. 'Might as well have stopped here with you. My mind was going round and round. Can't make much sense of it.'

She patted his shoulder. 'You wouldn't have got *any* sleep if you'd stayed here. The lines were buzzing all night long.'

'Yeah.' He bounced back with a grin as wide as the Mersey. 'You do look like shit this morning.'

'Thanks.'

'Anything interesting turn up?'

'No.'

Maybe Korpanski had picked up on her lack of confidence. 'You all right?'

'Robbie rang.'

'And?'

'He seems to have a misplaced trust in me.' She had to confide in someone. 'To be honest, Mike, I'm not up to this.' She managed a grin, but it was accompanied by her biting her lip. 'I really wish I could pass this one on to someone who actually does have the experience and expertise. I don't.'

'Hey.' He tried to boost her confidence with a reassuring grin, but she shook her head.

'I'm in free fall, making it up as I go along.' She managed a smile. 'Like an actress, on stage, who doesn't have a script, ad-libbing. I'm not in control. He is.'

Korpanski shrugged. 'You're doing your best, and he won't talk to anyone else.' He made an attempt at pulling her leg. 'Even you have to be better than no one.'

'Thanks.'

He nodded.

'Come on,' she said. 'I need to get out of here. Let's take a walk.'

TWENTY-EIGHT

9 a.m.

But the walkdown to The Lake House wasn't long enough. Ten minutes later, her head still filled with doubts, they were there, having passed through the cordon of armed personnel in camouflage, their faces similarly decorated. Even if they'd been officers she'd known, Joanna wasn't sure she'd have recognized them, they looked so menacing.

Doreen Caputo came to the door as soon as Stevie Wonder started barking, launching into her concerns even before she'd led them back into the house.

'What's going on, Inspector? We've been told to stay inside. But Stevie needs his walk. I need groceries. And Luca his medication. They mentioned evacuating. But where would we go?' Joanna could hear the panic in her voice. 'Luca needs special equipment. We can't just . . .'

She looked quite distraught.

Joanna tried to calm the anxious woman down. 'Let's go inside and we can talk about it.'

They followed her into the house, to the same room overlooking the lake and the still, silent man who sat facing it.

They gave Doreen a sanitized and heavily edited version of the events at Cloud Mansion, adding the fact that it wouldn't be safe for her to walk her dog through the woods.

She looked from one to the other. She wasn't fooled. 'Is Mr Holden in any danger?'

They couldn't duck this one. 'I'm afraid he is, Mrs Caputo,' Mike returned gently. 'He's being held against his will.' He didn't mention either the words *hostage* or *gun*. The word *gun* in particular had a panicking effect on the British public, who weren't used to them.

Surprisingly, Doreen quickly divined the reason behind their visit. 'And Clarice?'

They waited. Doreen's face was questioning, her head tilted to one side. 'Does *she* have anything to do with this?'

Joanna sensed the guilt behind the question. She was the one, after all, who'd introduced Clarice Hani to Joseph Holden.

Joanna knew from experience that involving the general public in decisions and even quandaries in investigations could bear fruit. And it hadn't slipped her notice that Luca Caputo's mouth had moved as though he was trying to speak.

'Clarice is one of the reasons we've called in today, Mrs Caputo. You're the one who brought Clarice to Mr Holden's attention. Tell me about her.'

'I met her on her first day,' she said defensively, 'to show her the way.'

Joanna nodded, her face encouraging. 'How old is she?'

'I don't know exactly. Mid-twenties?'

Although Joanna knew the answer to this one, she feigned ignorance. 'A local girl?'

Doreen spluttered. 'No. She's . . .' She hesitated before saying in a soft, conspiratorial voice, though there was no one apart from her husband who might have heard and objected, 'She's black.'

'From Leek?'

Doreen shook her head, frowning.

Mike interrupted. 'Just because she's black doesn't mean she's not from Leek.' He was smiling, obviously picturing Lilian Tadesse fending off questions about her origins – her usual response being a peal of mocking laughter. *Moss Side actually.*

Korpanski's comment had put Doreen on the back foot. 'She doesn't have a local accent.'

According to their computer search, Clarice Hani didn't even exist in this country.

'Did she mention where she'd lived before?'

Doreen looked from one to the other. 'All I did was see her card in the window, and because Joseph said he could do with some help after his operation, he agreed to meet her. I met her bus and walked her up to Cloud Mansion. That's all I did, Inspector.'

'But you were the one who brought her to Mr Holden's attention.' Korpanski was playing devil's advocate.

Joanna took over. 'Had Mr Holden actually said he wanted a cleaner?'

Doreen looked even guiltier. Even her immobile husband seemed to have shrunk into his chair. 'No,' she began, 'but when I chatted to him, I couldn't help but see—' She stopped herself then adjusted whatever she'd been planning to say. 'I thought he could do with a bit of help. Particularly as he'd had that operation.'

'Oh . . . what operation?'

Doreen looked embarrassed. 'They called it a cabbage,' she said. 'I know it was something to do with his heart. Quite a big operation, I understand.' She looked from one to the other, smiling now, obviously pleased with herself for bearing this knowledge. 'Anyway, he met up with her.'

'She came to the house?'

'Yes. I suggested they meet up. I took her up there. They seemed to hit it off. Is she in danger? I'd feel awful if . . .' She stopped there.

'What *do* you know about her? Do you know where she lives?'

'Somewhere in the town, but I don't know where. Oh, wait a minute. She said that she rents a room somewhere in Barngate Street.'

'You know the number?'

Doreen shook her head. Then: 'No.' She thought for a moment before adding. 'She said something about the girl she rents it off. Claudia someone or other. Shannon, I think.' Her voice tailed off, and she looked miserable.

Joanna felt she must say something. 'This isn't your fault, Mrs Caputo.'

'But I—'

Joanna shook her head. 'No,' she said. 'We don't know the full circumstances, but I think you just happened to be the go-between who connected Mr Holden with Clarice Hani. It was chance.'

She didn't appear mollified.

And then she cottoned on. 'What's she got to do with this?'

'It appears that the man holding Mr Holden hostage and Clarice Hani might be from the same part of the world.' Joanna was skirting delicately around their suspicions.

Doreen looked alarmed. 'You mean—' She stopped. 'Is she still in there? Is she a hostage too?'

'We don't know her exact role. Whether she's working with the hostage taker or an innocent victim. We're keeping an open mind.'

It was Korpanski who turned the conversation into something useful. 'Does she work for anyone else, do you know?'

'I – I think she helps out at the antiques shop sometimes.'

It was the tiniest sliver of light shining through. 'Noah's Ark?' Korpanski and Joanna exchanged glances.

'Well, there isn't another antiques shop in Leek anymore, is there? Years ago . . .'

She was about to lapse into reminiscence.

Joanna stood up. It was time to go.

They left with the usual request that if she remembered anything to get back in touch.

But she was still looking miserable when they left.

As they made their way back to the boat house, Joanna's personal mobile rang. It was Matthew.

'Hey,' he said. 'You OK?'

'Yeah. Nothing to report. Jakob?'

'He's good. With Mum and Dad today. Thought they might settle him. He's missing his mum.'

'His mum's missing him. Matthew – what's a cabbage?'

He laughed. 'I believe,' he said seriously, 'it's a brassica.'

'No. Not that. The op.'

'Ah. I thought for a minute you'd flipped your lid.' Then his medical training took over and he changed his tone. 'Coronary artery bypass graft. They replace clogged-up arteries with a healthy vein or artery from the leg, chest or arm. It's quite a big op. They have to do something called a sternal split, but it has good results. Why?'

'Our hostage had one.'

'Ouch.'

Korpanski was watching.

'I'd better go, Matt,' she said. 'Thanks for the information. Kiss Jakob for me and . . .' She knew she couldn't hide behind empty promises. 'I'll be home as soon as I can.'

'OK.'

And the call ended.

TWENTY-NINE

2 p.m.

There was still no word from Daud. Which intensified the tension. Joanna was looking at her phone constantly, waiting for the call, trying to work out a strategy, anticipate his demands. She repeated Robbie's mantras over and over again. The first rule was proof of life. She couldn't open any rapport unless she knew she was fighting for the freedom of a person who was still alive.

But Abdi kept quiet, and the afternoon wore on.

When Chief Superintendent Rush asked for an update, she had little to tell him except that they were detailing the background of Clarice Hani as well as waiting for the Somali Embassy to update them on Abdi Daud. Rush rang off with a disgruntled reminder to keep him informed.

Once or twice, Joanna stepped outside the boat house and looked up at Cloud Mansion. Whatever drama was happening inside, from the outside, the house looked deserted, lifeless.

Unlike the boat house, which was a hive of activity.

At some point, she and Mike would head back to Noah's Ark and see what Mr Pargeter could tell them about Clarice Hani, but for now they worked inside. It was strange that Clarice worked for two people who both had connections with antiques. Could there be a link?

2.15 p.m.

DC Lilian Tadesse and PC Gilbert Young had found Claudia's address and were heading round to Barngate Street where Clarice apparently lived.

Number twenty-six was a mid-terraced house, a neat place, with UPVC windows and a front door which opened straight out on to the pavement, the street lined with parked cars.

Claudia Shannon proved to be an attractive woman in her early forties with a trim figure and energetic look. She had a blonde ponytail which bounced as she talked, and was dressed in yoga leggings and a loose top which hinted at a sporty lifestyle. She'd looked half excited, half apprehensive at the sight of two police officers knocking at her front door and glanced up and down the street before letting them in.

Her house smelled of air fresheners and the scent of cakes baking.

She led them into a kitchen with a view through bi-fold doors of a neat garden, with glazed blue flowerpots filled with scarlet geraniums around a square lawn, and they sat down with a mug of coffee around a varnished pine table.

They approached the subject obliquely.

'We understand you rent a room out to a lady called Clarice Hani?'

Claudia looked from one to the other before she spoke and began to defend herself. 'There's no law against—'

Lilian broke in. 'No, no, of course there isn't. That isn't why we're here.'

Claudia looked from one to the other before nodding. 'I separated from my husband two years ago,' she said. 'I struggled to pay the mortgage on my own, particularly since the interest rate went up.'

She waited apprehensively for their next question.

'Do you let rooms out to any other tenants?' Lilian asked the question conversationally, as though she was genuinely interested, but Claudia responded sharply. 'I do not. I don't like sharing my house, but it's my home, and I don't want to lose it.' She pressed her lips hard together, frowning, looking from one to the other as though challenging them to find another way to deal with a hefty mortgage-rate interest rise.

Finally she asked, 'Is there a problem?'

Gilbert and Lilian looked at each other but didn't answer the question straight away.

'How long has she been here?'

'Almost a year.' She repeated her question. 'Is there a problem?'

'No.' It was a lie, and Claudia Shannon obviously sensed it but waited for their next question.

'Tell me about her,' Gilbert invited.

Claudia frowned. 'I'm not sure what you want to know.'

'In general,' Lilian said.

'Well . . . she's a model tenant actually. Clean, tidy, doesn't make a noise. She's like a little ghost around the place. I forget she's here most of the time. Pays her rent on time.'

'In cash?'

This time they sensed evasion before Claudia nodded.

'Did you see any paperwork when she came?'

'Sorry?'

'Did you check her passport, for instance?'

'No.'

'Does she have any visitors?'

That drew a shake of her head.

'Has she mentioned family?'

'I think she has an older brother who's quite bossy.'

'Don't we all?' Lilian was laughing while PC Gilbert Young looked affronted.

'I've heard her arguing with him on the phone a few times.'

She waited before asking. 'Do you mind telling me what this is all about?'

When neither of the two officers answered, she continued, her eyes narrowing with suspicion. 'She works out at Rudyard on a Wednesday, and she's usually home by six o'clock. But on Wednesday she didn't come back, and I haven't seen her since.'

When both Lilian and Gilbert still failed to respond, she continued. 'She's never stayed out before.'

The two officers looked at each other. It'd be all over the papers in no time at all. And Ms Shannon was more likely to cooperate if she was involved.

'I'm afraid she's involved in an ongoing incident,' Lilian said gently. 'You understand we can't give you any more details.'

'Will she be back?'

'We can't answer that,' Lilian said. 'And we'd be grateful if you kept this to yourself for the moment.'

'Yeah.'

Lilian got up. 'Do you mind if we take a look around her room?'

'No. No, of course not.' She led them up the stairs, along a narrow landing into a small, tidy room containing a three-quarter-sized bed and a fitted wardrobe. Inside were few clothes: one dress and some jeans, with T-shirts and sweaters folded on the shelf. Below was a pair of trainers, a rucksack and one pair of low-heeled black shoes. A small TV stood on a chest of drawers underneath the window. There were no books or other papers.

Lilian slipped on an examination glove and pulled open the top drawer of the chest of drawers. Inside was a wad of twenty-pound notes and a hairbrush.

There were no official documents or personal possessions, nothing that gave any clue as to who Clarice Hani really was – her citizen status, family, friends or other links; nothing to tell them what had brought her to Leek at the beginning of the year.

4.30 p.m.

Back at the boat house, they made their report to Joanna. 'Claudia Shannon said she received her rent in cash.'

'We put in at a couple of the nearby shops where she bought her groceries,' Gilbert Young added. 'They said the same. Cash.'

'So . . .' Joanna mused. 'She's been here since the beginning of the year. Plotting this siege at Cloud Mansion? Mention of an older brother did you say?'

'Yeah.'

'I wonder . . .'

Following their visit, a couple of forensic officers had visited Barngate Street and collected samples – fingerprints and hair, etc. – before sealing the room and asking the obliging Ms Shannon not to admit anyone.

Joanna passed the information on, which met with both Lilian and Gilbert's approval. 'Had the feeling,' PC Gilbert Young said, grinning, 'that she had the idea she could show people round – for a price.'

'Nothing like turning a problem into cash,' Lilian added with a broad smile and a wink.

Joanna heaved out a big sigh. 'Even if Daud is Clarice's brother, it doesn't really help us.'

The question was always the same. If this had been a pre-planned, pre-organized exercise why . . . why . . . why?

What did they still not know?

And as Daud still hadn't called, they were still missing answers.

Joseph hadn't known whether to be pleased, furious or frightened that he'd been locked in the bedroom all day. From somewhere they'd hauled a bucket.

'Use this,' Daud had said. 'Today' – he'd grinned at him –'you have a rest day. We will bring food. Relax.'

Joseph had shot him a furious look. He was feeling unwell. Tired, anxious and frightened. The situation was taking its toll.

He lay on the bed and stared up at the ceiling then out through the window, which had been sealed up long ago. He could see movement between here and the lake, but it was an impression. He couldn't make out actual figures. The entire area looked deserted. But he knew better. He knew they were being watched, that decisions were being made. But why had Daud wanted him out of the way today? Still, he was relieved to be having a day away from the chair. He wondered why Daud was stretching this out. What did he have to gain from it? The police were involved. Whatever it was, he may as well make his demands and get it over with.

He heard their raised voices echoing up from the hall. They seemed to be arguing over something.

'Enough.' He made out the word because Clarice had shouted it.

And Daud's response? Calm and controlled. 'Not yet.'

THIRTY

The surprises kept coming. Abdi Daud, it seemed, was bona fide. He'd flown in from Mogadishu Airport into Manchester four days ago. His occupation was down as a professor of political sciences at Mogadishu University.

Joanna stared at the screen. Daud was a professor? She looked at Korpanski, confused. 'So why would a university professor come all the way to the UK, presumably having followed his sister, and taken an elderly man hostage?'

The answer, they both knew, must lie with Joseph Holden, who'd buried himself in the Staffordshire countryside for the past fifteen years and whose past remained an enigma.

She set Alan King to work again, this time focussing on their hostage. If Daud was a professor, then the answer for this situation *must* lie in his hostage. There must be something in Joseph Holden's past, some connection to Daud, but it was proving elusive.

Joseph had spent the day threading facts together and was cursing himself because he knew he'd been careless. And he'd been careless because he'd needed money. He gave a wry smile and looked up at a stain on the ceiling. Cloud Mansion took some considerable upkeep. It was a large, old house lying in an exposed situation and repairs were expensive. One day, a little over a year ago, skirting the side of the house most exposed to the elements, a lead gutter had detached and almost dropped on his head. While repairing it, the builder had found a leak in the roof and the cost had mounted, so he'd been forced to sell some of his possessions. It had been hard choosing which one, and he'd finally picked out the Jile. A souvenir of his eventful time in Somalia.

As African artefacts were currently in vogue, it had fetched a good price – easily enough to cover the cost of the roof repairs. In some ways he hadn't been sorry to see it go. It represented a black hole in his past, something better buried than remembered. It was distinctive, unique and would attract attention given its handle was formed from a carved rhinoceros horn.

But there was a downside. Attracting attention meant he would have to state its provenance. A heroic past could put a few noughts on the end of an estimated price, but not his past, he'd thought, handing it over after sanitizing its true provenance and hiding its bloody story. When he'd narrated *his version* of the way the Jile had come into his possession, he'd seen the antiques dealer's eyes light up and watched him fondle it, knowing the dealer would likely embellish the story with little touches of his own, as they'd discussed value and the best market to sell it.

The dealer had made a face and met his eyes. 'Not going to cheat you, mate, but I can't afford to make an offer on this. Not outright. I don't have the capital. Not for this.' His eyes had turned shifty, lighting with an avaricious gleam as he'd fingered the carving. Then he'd looked up and made a suggestion. 'If we try it out in a London saleroom, it could hit the heights.' He'd paused before offering another tempter. 'Could attract international interest.'

He should have been warned. Joseph had wanted the sale to be completed quietly, tucked away in some provincial saleroom, with little fuss and no publicity. A quick money exchange. But he'd wavered, remembering the leaky roof and the estimated cost of repairs, and reluctantly he'd agreed.

And that had led to this.

The only thing Joseph still couldn't work out was why the hostage situation? Why the drama?

Was it publicity they wanted? Did they have a political statement to make?

Were they planning to take him back . . . somehow? Punish him? Make him face his fate? They wouldn't get away with it. They wouldn't be able to prove anything. There was no extradition treaty between the UK and Somalia. No legal system to get him on a plane. Or to prevent it.

Revenge he could understand but not this drawn-out process.

He had a secondary puzzle. He'd heard, one-sided, the conversation Abdi had had with the detective in charge, using her Christian name, as well as her title and, presumably, her married name. How did he know a local police inspector? Where had he got her name from? Why insist on her? Was it because otherwise a professional, more experienced negotiator might have been called in? In fact, why involve the police at all? He came full circle. He might know part of this scenario, but he didn't know it all.

And then he faced the possibility of what they would, ultimately, do with him. He closed his eyes and saw nothing but the black of oblivion.

7.30 p.m.

Joanna was sitting quietly, Korpanski watching her, as she too was tossing around theory after theory. 'If they have come specifically after Joseph Holden, why, and how did they find him?'

Both were silent before she followed on with, 'I think we should make another visit to Noah's Ark. Clarice worked there before she came to work for Joseph.'

She looked at her watch. 'It's too late now, but I'll make a note to visit tomorrow. If I've time.'

She'd let the stakeout guys sort out their own shifts, suggesting they report to her at each changeover, but every four hours all she got was: 'No movement.'

She knew it was boring, tedious, cold work. And as her phone remained stubbornly silent, she continued to fact-find but knew she was missing vital points. And the wait was frustrating. But she kept in mind Robbie Callaghan's advice.

Never approach the hostage taker unless you have a clearly stated purpose that benefits the hostage, such as bringing food or water.

Otherwise, you looked weak.

But the waiting was the hard part, her mind constantly turning over the reason behind the delay. Perhaps it was simply that Daud was toying with her, drawing out her anxiety for no specific purpose other than to test her.

She called a team meeting for eight o'clock where PC Gilbert Young suggested he could try and interview Doreen Caputo again to see if they'd missed anything vital about either Clarice or Mr Holden.

'Maybe,' he suggested tentatively, 'she's had a chance to think about things, see if she remembers . . . anything else.'

Joanna studied the young PC. Although in his thirties, he looked much older – balding, with a faintly anxious expression and a crooked grin. She'd met his girlfriend, Silvia, a media student, who was usually mistaken for his daughter. But Gilbert was a literal person whose ability to delve into the depths of a case had impressed her before, and he would often turn up to briefings with intelligent suggestions. And perhaps Doreen would be more relaxed under his interrogation.

'Go for it,' she said. 'You might be right.'

He shot her one of his rare grins.

8.30 p.m.

Indeed, Doreen Caputo immediately warmed to the officer with his crooked grin and polite, formal manner. 'Come on in,' she said, warmly welcoming. 'Would you like a cup of tea?'

'Nothing I'd like more,' Gilbert said, tucking his headgear under his arm.

He was ushered into a sitting room with a panoramic view across the lake. Staring out across it sat a man with a frozen expression. 'Mr Caputo?'

Luca turned, and Gilbert held out his hand. 'How do you do, sir?' He was rewarded with an attempt at a smile and a slight nod before Luca turned to face the lake again.

Mrs Caputo ('call me Doreen') bustled back in holding a steaming mug of tea. 'Biscuit?' she asked brightly.

Gilbert refused. His doctor had advised him to go easy on the sweet stuff.

He sat on the edge of the settee and opened the conversation. 'What can you tell me about Mr Holden?'

'I don't know much.' She seemed flustered as well as anxious. 'He's not a hugely sociable character. We just exchange a few words when I pass with Stevie Wonder.' She paused. 'Is he all right?'

'At the moment, he's still being held.'

'And Clarice?'

'She's OK as far as we know.' He leaned forward as though about to share a confidence, and Doreen responded, eyes bird-bright. 'To be honest, it's kind of hard to know exactly what's going on in this sort of situation.' He didn't mention that this was his first.

She gave him a hard look for a moment, and Gilbert felt he should prompt her.

'So . . .? How long has he lived in Cloud Mansion?'

'He came around about fifteen years ago. I know because Luca was still working then.' She sent a fond glance at her husband, who continued to stare out across the water.

Gilbert followed his gaze and wondered what he saw out there, what he thought, when he watched rain sweep across the lake or the wind whip its surface into frothy waves, sailing pennants indicating which sails to reef and which to hoist or the quick rhythmic smack of the canoeists' paddles. Perhaps his mind still sailed, still felt the rocking of water beneath his chair, as though he stood on the deck of a boat.

He turned his attention back to Doreen, who was also watching her husband.

'Where did he come from?'

Doreen turned back to him, frowning. 'I don't know. I never asked him. I think he said he'd worked abroad. He had a deep tan when he arrived.'

'Didn't he say where he'd come from?'

'No.' She altered that to, 'I'm sure he *didn't*. I'd have remembered.'

Somewhere hot, Gilbert thought. 'Does he have many visitors?'

'A few of his friends come a couple or so times a year. They seem like roughnecks. Not quietly spoken like Joseph. Maybe ex-army,' she added. 'That's just a guess. I told your colleague who came the same.'

Gilbert made a note. 'Ex-army?'

'Something about them. Roughnecks but polite. I think I saw one of them give a sort of salute. One of them called him Captain – but I took it that that was just, you know, a bit of banter.'

'How many of these friends?'

'Three. One of them looks as though he's lost part of his leg. He walks stiffly. You know, from the hip?'

'They travel together or separately?'

'All in one car.'

Gilbert changed tack. 'Does Mr Holden go out much?'

She shook her head. 'Takes his van into Leek a couple of times a week. He keeps it in the backyard.' She smiled. 'It's a bit of an old banger.'

'Does anyone call at the house apart from you?'

'Clarice. Just Clarice.' She covered her mouth. 'Is she safe?'

Gilbert hid behind formality. 'I'm sorry, I can't divulge . . .'

She gave him a sympathetic smile.

Gilbert stood up. 'Thank you, Doreen. We appreciate your help.' He tried out a broad smile. 'I'm sure he'll be all right.'

But the anxiety on her face didn't fade.

Gilbert made a last effort to placate her. 'If it hadn't been for you, we wouldn't have been involved so soon.'

She still looked downcast.

Gilbert turned to go but hesitated. 'You speak *every* morning?'

'Yes. Always says good morning. He either comes to the study window if he's working or to the front door.'

Gilbert had picked up on a word. *What work?* he wondered.

'We have a few words, like. Exchange pleasantries about the weather and the sailing.'

Gilbert snatched at that. 'Sailing? He was a sailor?'

'Not that I know for certain, but I think he had a love of the water.'

Another dead end.

'Anything else?'

Doreen shook her head, but her husband seemed agitated. His right hand, which had been resting quietly on his lap, started to shake. His wife watched him, startled, then asked him tenderly, 'What is it, love?'

Which led Gilbert to wonder. One day, when he was old and frail, like Mr Caputo, if he and Silvia stayed together, would she greet him with equal tenderness? He was so absorbed in this reflection that he almost missed Doreen's interpretation of her husband's excitement.

'Oh yes,' she said, drawing her face conspiratorially closer. 'I saw his van parked outside the antiques shop on the Stone Road one day. I took particular notice because the dealer who owns the shop gets really cross about people parking there because he says it blocks the windows. And it does, I suppose,' she finished up, throwing a grateful glance in her husband's direction. He managed a return smile.

'So I came to the conclusion that he was either loading something up that he'd bought there or else' – she paused to give her conclusion dramatic effect – 'I wondered if he was selling one or other of those antiques he has lying around.'

9.15 p.m.

Joanna had been trying to convince herself that she was up to this, that she would live up to CS Rush's belief that she could manage this situation, but she felt stuck in a mire.

However, when PC Gilbert Young relayed the result of his interview with Doreen and Luca Caputo, she knew he'd given her some extra leads. 'Well done, Gilbert. Nice work.'

She wondered whether Joseph Holden and his mates had continued with their military careers after they'd left the forces, and now a small strand linked him to the antiques shop – the same shop where Clarice Hani had worked. It was another little thread.

And still they waited for another phone call.

THIRTY-ONE

10 p.m.

The phone rang, sparking life into the incident room, which had been increasingly subdued as it played the waiting game.

She'd anticipated he would ring late, hope to catch her off guard after a day of silence so, in a way, she was prepared. But the sound made her instantly tense, a tone she could hear in her voice, even in one word.

'Hello.'

She wondered if he'd picked up that she sounded tentative, guarded and weary.

His response – cold, calm and unmistakably in control –was chilling.

'Detective Inspector Piercy.' It was almost a mockery. 'Or would you prefer me to address you as Mrs Levin? Or simply . . . Joanna?'

Again, the fact he'd done his homework on her touched a nerve, and again she wondered if they'd had some previous contact. But she knew no Somalis.

She waited for him to proceed, aware that it was time for him to state his demands, if he was to follow the rules of the game.

What game? This had never felt less like one.

Impatience, Robbie had said. *You need to guard against that, Piercy. The hostage taker will sense that impatience and use it to his or her advantage. Don't give them that gift.*

She smiled. *They can hear that smile in your voice.* She schooled her voice to sound light. 'You can call me what you like, Mr Daud.' She decided to aim a barb of her own. 'Or should I call you *Professor* Daud?'

If she'd hoped to knock him off his perch, she was about to be disappointed. He simply laughed. 'I see you've been doing your homework, Joanna.'

Her mouth was too dry to respond. All eyes in the incident room were on her.

He continued, 'You want continuing proof of life.'

And suddenly the whole scenario felt like a game of chess, the exchanges following set moves, each skirting around the other, wary as wrestlers after the opening bell rings. If this was a game, she had to make her next move wisely.

'Of course.'

In the background, she heard some shuffling then the sound of a chair scraping across a wooden floor. There was a pause. She heard breathing. Then a thin voice. 'Hello?'

'Mr Holden?'

'Yes.' He sounded weak, the voice of a frightened old man. 'This is Mr Joseph Holden speaking.' His voice was gathering strength. When he'd been hauled from the bedroom only minutes ago, he'd thought this was it.

The end.

The police, possibly even the wider general public, would witness his execution.

Instead, he'd simply been bound again to the chair to listen to the exchange over the telephone.

He sounded older and frailer than Joanna had hoped. But then this was the fourth day he'd been held captive. Who knew how he'd been restrained, whether he'd sustained any injury, quite apart from the sheer terror of his situation. And he'd had surgery, major surgery according to Matthew, a few months ago.

She felt rising concern and anger. If Daud wanted something from this guy who'd buried himself in the Staffordshire countryside, why hadn't he gone through legal routes? He was an intelligent man. Hostages did die, and even if he wasn't held directly responsible, there would be no doubt he would have contributed to Joseph Holden's demise. Just the stress of the situation could be enough to trigger a health crisis. And Daud had arrived at Cloud Mansion with a gun, which would lose him the sympathy of the British courts and lengthen any jail sentence. Why was he risking so much?

'Am I speaking to the detective in charge?'

'You are.' Joanna was overwhelmed with sympathy. 'I'm Detective Inspector Joanna Piercy of the Leek police. I don't think we've actually met.'

'No.' He made an attempt at levity. 'I'm pretty law abiding . . . on the whole.'

'Mr Holden, are you injured?'

He started to speak. 'I've—'

Daud's voice cut in. 'He's been better.'

'Does he need a doctor?'

'Not at the moment.'

He was toying with her, which made her angry as well as apprehensive. 'And Clarice Hani?'

That resulted in silence. She realized, with a little skip of optimism, that he'd been unprepared for the question and had no response to hand. Was she ahead of him?

She waited.

Silence.

The call had been ended.

And after a minute or two, she stopped staring at the display.

But they were back on script. She'd had proof of life. Joseph was alive.

And Clarice?

Clarice was something different, off-piste. A possible reluctant participant.

Her thoughts turned sideways. To Daud's familiarity with her name. Attendees to the hostage negotiation course had come to Staffordshire University from all over the world, attracted by Robbie's international reputation. He'd written books on the subject, detailing the management of various real-life hostage situations. Now the question she was asking herself was: had Daud been one of the course delegates? Because if he had, it would explain his familiarity with her name, both professional and personal. And if he'd received the same training as she, he would have the same level of expertise. He would be able to anticipate her movements because they'd been trained by the same person. He would anticipate her bargaining moves, the levers she might use to persuade him to free Joseph Holden. But there was something else. If Daud had attended the course, Robbie would have his details. And he might be able to advise her how best to use Clarice Hani's position to her advantage.

She spent a moment trying to visualize the others on the course, but there had been too many, the lecture theatre crowded with people from all over the world – all shapes, sizes, ethnic origins and ages. And she'd been so firmly focussed on trying to learn new skills, taking notes and making clear references, that she'd given little attention to the others and spent the evenings back home with Matthew and Jakob, and revising the day's lessons, rather than socializing. But if Daud *had* been one of the other attendees, it posed a real problem. He'd recognize the track she'd take, be familiar with its tricks and turns, anticipate her demands and sense her weaknesses. He'd be immune to her posturing and possess the skills to sideswipe it like an expert batsman. He had deliberately come here and asked for her by name to flush her out, which made her wonder. Had *she* had something to do with his arrival here? When/ if he'd attended the course in Stoke, had he come out here one day, to Rudyard, and looked around, planning his moves?

If Robbie confirmed that Abdi Daud *had* attended his course, it would, at least, remove the mysticism from his familiarity with her name, rank and status and might present her with more information.

THIRTY-TWO

Saturday 14 September, 7 a.m.

She'd tried Robbie's number after the phone call last night, but it had been late and the call had gone straight through to his answerphone. No surprise there. Even lecturers on hostage crisis duty need their downtime, she supposed. Then she'd thought over some of the details PC Gilbert Young had told her and focussed her mind and plans on their next step.

Find the narrative had been one of Robbie's mantras. *Buried in the narrative is the path that led to this situation. Find it and you have an idea how best to handle the negotiations. And don't forget to search for the golden nugget – the explanation that leads right back to your hostage taker's vulnerability and hands you an advantage.*

The fact that Mr Holden had visited Noah's Ark and possibly bought or sold something was a link, and any link was a potential gold nugget. And this felt like one. A link between Clarice Hani, her two places of work – Cloud Mansion and Noah's Ark – and their hostage. It had to be significant.

She'd texted Matthew asking him to kiss Jakob goodnight for her. But although she saw from the double ticks that the message had gone through, he hadn't responded. At a guess, his mother would be cooking them all a late meal, phones banned from the table. It had been too late to give Chief Superintendent Rush her evening report – he wouldn't thank her for disturbing his downtime – and Korpanski had clocked off earlier, looking drawn after the day's work. So she had, eventually, suppressed her thoughts and tried to grab a few hours' sleep, phone in hand.

But her thoughts had chewed endlessly over the case, Cloud Mansion looming large as a sinister backdrop to the vulnerability of Joseph Holden. The path which had led Daud to Holden's door, as well as the mystery of Clarice Hani's involvement, had tossed around in her mind, as choppy and unpredictable as the waters of Rudyard Lake. And so, instead of a restful night's sleep, her mind had continued to work, the night hours spent somewhere between a doze and a dream. Or rather a doze and a nightmare. She'd left instructions to the night team to rouse her if there was any movement around, but the woods had remained still, Cloud Mansion wrapping its granite arms around its secrets.

It was unhelpful to focus too much on the hostage's situation she knew. She couldn't afford to lose her detachment, but he had remained centre stage as she imagined how he must feel – frightened, uncomfortable, hungry? Thirsty? Possibly in physical pain from a beating. And the worst part was that Abdi Daud was outsmarting her. So she'd drifted, rudderless, through incomplete, disturbing thoughts.

And then Korpanski was bending over her, gently shaking her shoulder, smiling as she opened her eyes, initially confused as to where she was, wondering why it was Korpanski who was rousing her and not Matthew. Then, as she came to, all the anguish of the situation flooded right back, threatening to engulf her.

She met her sergeant's dark eyes and knew he could read her complete apprehension.

'I'll wait while you clean your teeth,' he said, grinning at her as she pushed her hair out of her eyes.

'God, Mike,' she said. 'What time is it?'

'Early. It's OK,' he said. 'Nothing doing. I just thought you'd like to tidy yourself up.' The grin broadened. 'Make yourself glamorous, ready to face the day. Have a wash. I'll keep an eye on the phone for you,' he added. 'Give you a shout if he rings.'

'Yeah. Thanks.'

Once she'd had a quick shower in the dingy back room of the boat house, cleaned her teeth and changed her T-shirt into a clean one, she started to feel halfway to human and planned her day.

'I need to talk to Mrs Caputo again – follow up on what she told Gilbert about Joseph visiting the antiques shop.'

Find the narrative.

'I think there's a connection that might prove interesting, and I want more details if she has them.'

He put a hand on her shoulder. 'Sounds like a good plan, but it's too early yet, Jo. Have some breakfast. Get yourself sorted out. She has an invalid husband to get up in the mornings, a dog to walk . . . somewhere. She won't appreciate your barging in at just past seven o'clock on a Saturday morning.'

'It's that early?'

He nodded.

'Then granted. Any bacon butties?'

In the end, it was half past nine when they headed down the track in the direction of The Lake House. As they tramped through the woods, along the still muddy path, Joanna reflected how much had changed since their initial visit just two days ago. And the contrast was even greater to the last time she, Matthew and Jakob had passed this way.

The road blocks were in place, flashing blue lights illuminating the scene in short bursts, a few personnel in fluorescent green jackets manning their posts, while the camouflaged team moved, like ghosts amongst the trees, so stealthy that if you tried to pin your look on one, they vanished, blending in with their surrounds. There was a strange sense of drama so suppressed it felt imagined, a stage set. Plenty of people were ready to act – but as yet there was no script.

She and Korpanski didn't speak as they traversed the scene, moving quietly, periodically turning back to glance up through the trees at Cloud Mansion, but there was no sign of activity. The grey walls were as silent as a tombstone. No lights, no sound. And yet she had the feeling he was watching. She studied each window in turn, hoping for a glimpse of him. But the house kept its secrets, the curtains closed at the long windows which overlooked the track.

As they stood outside the gates to The Lake House, they heard Stevie Wonder barking out a warning and Doreen's voice telling him to be quiet.

When she opened the door, she looked anxiously from Joanna to Korpanski but led them into the house without a word. Not even a greeting. Her mouth was tense and disapproving as though she blamed them for failing to release her neighbour, restore the lakeside to its tranquil peace and put an end to this violent, alien drama.

Joanna felt she should apologize.

'I'm sorry,' she began, but when Doreen's head whipped round as though she was about to ask what for, Joanna fell silent. What *was* she sorry for? What *should* she be sorry for? This might be her job, her career, but she hadn't orchestrated this situation.

It wasn't her fault. She was simply dealing with it as best she could. The negotiations were delicate. One wrong move and it could end in tragedy – the deaths of not only Doreen's neighbour but others as well. She'd had a short briefing on the capabilities of a Glock 17, but it might not be Daud's only firearm. At no time had he claimed that. What if Clarice was also armed and hostile? In that case, more people could die. Not just Joseph Holden and the hostage takers, but personnel for whom she was ultimately responsible.

She wasn't frightened for herself. There were armed personnel who would protect her, and she'd been fitted with a bulletproof Kevlar jacket – although fitted wasn't quite the right description. At a guess it had been made for a man not a female with a full bust. But she was frightened for that frail, elderly man imprisoned in his own home. Daud might be a professor in his homeland, but he was here now, threatening a local. Clarice was an unknown quantity. She might share Daud's violent tendencies, or she might be his second chosen victim or a non-combatant.

Robbie's advice about the narrative rang true and clear as a church bell. The reason Daud was here at all was key. And Joseph Holden's neighbour might hold a vital clue.

All these thoughts raced through her head as she and Mike followed Doreen into the sitting room. This morning, the chair facing the water was empty – Luca Caputo had yet to make an appearance.

Joanna opened her mouth to speak, but Doreen forestalled her, her voice bitter and angry. 'They stopped me,' she said. 'I tried to go up there for my usual walk.'

Stevie Wonder, who'd been sitting silently, started wagging his tail at the familiar word, his brown eyes beseeching.

Doreen continued, 'I've been walking my dogs that way for years,' she said, her mouth still tight and bitter. 'Even in the foot-and-mouth outbreak I never been stopped. Through Covid it was a bit quieter, but still Stevie Wonder and I had our daily walk. And now? They won't let me pass.'

Joanna opened her mouth to speak, but Doreen got there first. 'Why don't you do something? Storm the place. Get Joseph out of there and . . .' Here she stopped, at a loss to find a fate bad enough for the hostage taker. She fell back on: 'Arrest him or something.'

'It isn't as easy as all that,' Joanna said, proud of the way she'd kept her voice calm when her primary emotion was anger. 'It would actually put Mr Holden in even greater danger.'

Doreen's mouth snapped shut.

'We all want a return to the norm,' Korpanski said, trying to help.

Both women turned their heads to stare at him.

Doreen's face changed. 'Well, I haven't seen an ambulance so I suppose he's still in there.' She too was clearly trying to suppress her frustration. 'Where there's life, there's hope.'

Joanna nodded.

Cloud Mansion wasn't visible from this room, which faced the lake, but all three of them turned their heads in its direction, towards the door, as though they could peer through walls.

'How long's it going to take?'

Joanna caught Korpanski's eye and knew they could both answer that with the analogy of a piece of string, but it would have appeared insulting to this woman, angry at her day-to-day life being disrupted.

'We don't know.' Inwardly Joanna knew the drama would probably increase rather than die down.

News was already leaking out. Day-trippers had been replaced by the emergency services, water sports enthusiasts by the media and, as Doreen had intimated, family days out had stopped. Television vans would make Rudyard Lake famous . . . for a time. And perhaps someone watching, somewhere, would make the connection, not with the Kipling of Victorian writings but with a man whose past appeared murky, from a foreign land, who'd arrived at this location with a purpose.

As she absorbed not only the detective's words but also her cautious demeanour, Doreen's eyes focussed on Joanna. And her petty concerns were replaced by apprehension bordering on fright.

'Is he in . . .?' She sniffed and replaced that with: 'Are *we* in danger?'

'No,' Joanna said. 'If we thought you were, we would have moved you and your husband out.'

'He doesn't like change.' Doreen's response had shot out of her. A reflex.

'Our priority,' Joanna said, 'is keeping *everyone* safe – including your neighbour.'

Doreen said, cross now, 'What does this man want?'

'We don't know.'

'Then what's the point?'

Joanna was tempted to smile. Doreen was voicing the same questions she had.

Doreen was silent, then she looked up, first at Korpanski and then back at Joanna. 'You think the person who's holding him hostage is somebody from his past?' Her voice was low and worried.

'It's one of the possibilities we're considering,' Joanna said carefully. 'That's why we're here. You're one of the few people who had contact with Mr Holden. So anything you know . . .?'

Doreen nodded, as though this made sense.

'Well,' she began, 'we were already living here when he came. It was a surprise to us. We'd thought Cloud Mansion would either be sold as a wedding venue or else to some big property millionaire. So when he came, this man who lived on his own and had boxes and boxes of stuff. Well . . . it was a surprise.'

'What sort of stuff?'

Doreen looked flustered. 'Foreign things. Elephant tusks and a rhino head. Pictures, Chinese stuff. Some of those ugly African masks. Spooky, I call them.' She gave a mock shudder. 'Scary eyes. Knives. A sword. Daggers and stuff.' She was frowning. 'Lethal-looking weapons, old guns.'

Joanna gave Korpanski a swift glance. This, she felt sure, was where the origins of this siege lay. Buried deep, somewhere, in those boxes and boxes of 'stuff'.

Korpanski framed the next question, his hands resting on his knees. 'Did he say anything about this collection of pieces?'

'Huh.' Doreen's eyes turned towards the sergeant. 'He did. One day – a few years ago now – I was looking around his study and he said, "Every piece has a story to tell".' She looked thoughtful. 'I said something about an interest in folk tales and stuff, but he picked up something and said, "You wouldn't want to know the stories that lie behind some of these pieces".'

'What did you make of that?' Joanna was genuinely interested.

'I felt . . . frightened. I wanted to get out of there. His face when he said those things. He looked . . . different. Nasty.'

They heard a sound from one of the other rooms. Luca was stirring.

But Doreen continued with her narrative. 'Before his operation and then Clarice coming, I used to do some shopping for him – sometimes. I used to put it away for him in the kitchen cupboards. But after that, I just left it outside the back door. I've never been inside Cloud Mansion since. I saw a different side of Joseph that day.'

Joanna and Korpanski exchanged glances. 'What was the piece he'd picked up when he said those things?'

'A sort of dagger thing. Big with a carved handle. Hung on the wall over the Chinese cabinet.'

'Did he say where it came from?'

She shook her head. 'No. But what with his very dark, suntanned skin – which looked darker against his hair – and the look of it, I guessed it was somewhere in Africa. I don't know where,' she added quickly. 'Me and Luca – we've never been to Africa.'

Joanna and Mike exchanged glances. *Somalia?*

They changed the subject. 'Any family?'

'Not that I know of.'

'You mentioned that he has three friends that stay maybe once or twice a year.'

Doreen nodded.

'Do you still not remember any of their names? Where they're from?' Joanna asked gently.

Doreen shook her head. 'Sorry.'

They moved on. 'Does he leave Cloud Mansion?'

'Not really.' She smiled, perhaps momentarily forgetting the circumstances. 'He toddles into Leek maybe once or twice a week.'

'PC Young said you saw him visit the antiques shop.'

'Once – I just happened to be passing and saw he was parked outside the antiques shop, but I don't know whether he was buying or selling something.'

'You mean the shop on the Stone Road?'

'Yes. That's the one.' Her eyes were bright with curiosity. 'I have no idea what he was doing there. Maybe the owner's a friend.'

And Clarice 'cleans' for both.

Joanna's instincts prickled.

Her gut was telling her to tug at this thread and see where it led.

'Did he say anything else about his past?'

'No.'

Joanna hesitated before asking her next question. 'What ethnic origin is Mr Holden?'

Doreen looked slightly shocked at the question. 'Why, he's just like you and me,' she said indignantly.

Which Joanna took as meaning he was white. So where was the connection with Abdi Daud? Who was, according to his passport, Somali, as was Clarice Hani?

'Did he come from round here . . . originally?'

Doreen made an attempt to answer. 'I don't know. It is a local name. There's plenty of folks named Holden round here, but I don't know as he was Staffordshire born.'

'OK.' Joanna was searching for another clue. 'Did he ever mention Somalia? Or any other part of Africa?'

'It was just the masks,' Doreen said. 'And maybe that dagger thing.'

Which returned Joanna to step one again. 'These friends,' she hit on finally. 'What did they seem like?'

'A bit rough and ready. Seemed like a bit of a rogue gang to me.'

'You used the word ex-army to PC Young.'

Doreen nodded.

'And Mr Holden?'

'He was a bit more . . . no, a bit less gentlemanly when they were here, if you know what I mean. They were using bad language – and so did he when they were there. He seemed a different person. Normally he's quiet, polite. Reserved, I'd say.' She gave a shadow of a smile. 'There was another side to him when he was with those friends.'

'Another side?' Korpanski asked.

Doreen turned her head to look at him, her mouth bent into a smile. He had that effect on women – of any age. They warmed to her detective sergeant. It wasn't just his build; there was something undeniably masculine about him – and, Joanna admitted, but only to herself, attractive. DS Mike Korpanski had undoubted sex appeal. His effect on the opposite sex was one of the things Joanna had frequently used to her advantage – and it was one of the things she'd missed during his long absence.

'Yes. They'd arrive full of noise on the Thursday or Friday and leave a right mess behind them, Clarice said.'

Ah yes, Joanna thought. Clarice, whose precise role in all this was still unclear, though they could hazard a guess.

It seemed Doreen was reading her thoughts. 'I like her,' she said almost defensively. 'Sometimes if I was walking the dog a bit later than usual on a Wednesday, we'd walk up together, chat a bit. Anyway, it was her what told me the beer cans would pile up after one of these . . . visits.'

The three of them fell silent, and Joanna turned thoughtful, trying to build up a picture of their hostage and the people around him, who seemed limited to his neighbour, the cleaner and these three uncouth friends. Although now there was the question of the antiques dealer, who might or might not also be a friend. How had he arrived at Cloud Mansion and lived quietly for fifteen years until Abdi Daud had followed a woman who might be his sister and travelled from Somalia with the sole purpose of . . . what? That was where she got stuck.

They thanked Doreen Caputo and left, but as they returned to the boat house, Joanna remained deep in thought, remembering Robbie Callaghan's words.

Each has something the other wants.

You want the hostage free; they want money, impunity, freedom, a platform. Wait for their demands before you negotiate.

She knew what she wanted: the safe release of Joseph Holden

and, possibly, Clarice Hani. But what did Daud want? He was here legally. He was educated, intelligent and, according to the Somali police, had a clean record. So what was he doing here threatening an elderly man with a gun?

What had brought him here?

Until she knew that, she had no leverage against him. Robbie was right – it was all buried in the narrative.

THIRTY-THREE

11 a.m.

They were about to step back inside the boat house when Joanna's phone rang. She made it through the door, indicating to Gilbert Young to record the conversation while telling the others to keep quiet and listen. *Listen.* It was another of Robbie's mantras that he'd drummed into them. Get *everyone* to listen. Who knows what extra details or impressions might be picked up by the extra sets of ears? Gilbert nodded and switched on the recording equipment at the same time as Joanna put the phone on speaker mode.

'Professor Daud.' She had the instinct that using his title needled him.

'Inspector,' he responded, mirroring her tone with an added note of mockery. 'I expect you wondered when I would make contact again.'

She restricted her response to one word. 'Naturally.'

'I expect you are also waiting to hear my – shall we call them – requests?'

Her chest tightened. 'Go on.'

In the study in Cloud Mansion, Daud had set the phone to speaker mode and was holding it in front of Joseph's mouth. 'Speak,' he ordered.

'What do you want me to say?'

'The facts.'

The facts, Joseph mused. Where to begin and where to stop? He didn't know.

'Mr Holden? Joseph?'

He recognized the brisk voice with its hint of anxiety and found he couldn't speak.

'It's DI Joanna Piercy here.' Her voice was gentle now. 'Hello?'

A moment passed.

'Hello?'

He still couldn't speak.

His mouth was dry, his lips cracked, his pulse racing and he recognized the dull ache in his chest like an old friend. He was sweating even though he was ice cold.

'Hello,' he finally managed.

'Mr Holden?' Her voice had dropped and now she sounded even more anxious. 'Are you all right?'

The gun pressed harder into the side of his head. One flick of his captor's fingers and he would be dead. He knew, from experience, that the end could be quick – or slow – depending on the skill and intent of the person holding that gun.

'Yes,' he managed.

'I take it Mr Daud is with you?'

'Yes,' he managed again. 'He's holding the phone.'

'I want you to know we are doing everything – everything,' she repeated, 'that we can to secure your release.'

'Thank—'

'Is there anything you—?'

But Daud was back on the line. 'I am here, Inspector,' he said. 'So tell me, what exactly are you doing to secure Mr Holden's safe release?'

'Well . . .' She was tempted to respond, *Talking to you, you bastard*, but she kept her cool and her tone conversational. *Late night Classic FM tone*, Robbie had advised.

'You know Mr Holden is alive. As he seems unable to tell you the facts, that is enough for now.'

'What facts? Daud, what do you want?'

'Not yet. In time we will talk. But now is not the time.'

'Do you need anything? Food?'

'There is enough food in the house.'

'Professor Daud, Mr Holden is elderly and had major surgery recently. I don't need to spell out to you that his condition might deteriorate if he's detained much longer.'

Daud didn't respond.

'And you will be held responsible.'

'Quite.'

Joanna took a stab at it. 'And your sister—'

She didn't get to finish the sentence.

'My sister?'

Joanna ignored the interruption and continued smoothly, as though he hadn't responded. 'She will be treated as a co-conspirator.'

Daud was silent while Joanna felt a little skip of delight. She'd got one over on him. And now she could hear Robbie Callaghan's voice ringing in her ear, urging her on.

Find out what his demands are. That will give you a clue as to the backstory.

The line was silent as both she and Daud realized they were at an impasse.

Joanna kept her voice steady. 'However, I do want to know that Miss Hani is also safe.'

That resulted in silence.

'Professor,' she said, 'you're an intelligent man with a good job. What on earth has led you to fly all this way to hold an elderly man hostage?'

'You will find out.' His voice remained steady.

After a brief pause, he spoke again, still moving along a pathway of his own choosing and ignoring her previous request. 'I expect you are wondering why I asked for you specifically.'

'Of course.'

Daud gave a soft laugh. 'We've met,' he said, and the call was ended.

Now it was even more imperative that she speak to Robbie. She tried his number again, and this time he picked up.

'Your hunch was right,' he said. 'Professor Daud was on the course at the same time as you.'

'Who sent him?'

'You mean who sponsored him? He came as a freelance.'

'What does that mean?'

'He paid for himself.'

Robbie drew in a deep, considering breath. 'You looked at the course purely from a police/crime perspective. But negotiation can be used in all sorts of scenarios. Businessmen need it, employees need it. It can be used against all sorts of backdrops. Not simply in hostage negotiation. I don't vet the people who book into the course. I don't ask how they're going to use those skills. Very often,' he said, almost regretfully, 'they're setting up some sort of consultancy business.'

'Have they ever been used as criminal research?'

'How would I know that?'

'You don't do any follow-up?'

'Have you any idea how many students pass through my courses in a year?'

Something prickled at the back of Joanna's neck. 'So you possibly train people how to act as hostage *takers*, to anticipate the moves a negotiator's likely to make.'

Robbie Callaghan had picked up on her outrage. 'I'm freelance,' he said. 'I train anyone who wants to learn about negotiation. Many of my attendees are business people who need to negotiate either with colleagues, potential customers, employees or even rivals. I can't afford to be picky.'

She took her mind back to the lecture hall, crowded with students milling around, a few outside drinking coffee, chatting, some impassioned, others apathetic and she quiet, sitting in a corner, revising her notes. She'd taken little notice of the other students but realized they'd come from all four corners of the earth, with all skin colours present. She'd sat next to a pair of Korean detectives whose noisy chatter had, at times, been distracting, while, at the same time, she'd envied them their energetic enthusiasm. She'd identified Dutch being spoken, German too, as well as a variety of accents speaking English: South African, American, Australian. Hostage crises as well as business conflicts were a worldwide problem, and Robbie Callaghan was a renowned expert who'd dealt with many situations, resolving almost all of them successfully.

She tried to visualize a guy with the same features and skin colour she'd seen in Daud's passport photograph. Calm, good looking, with a steady stare, but all she saw was a string of faces. Unable to pick anyone out. Sure, there *had* been a good contingent of Africans, Caribbeans, even a few Native Americans and African Americans, but she hadn't really socialized with anyone beyond lunch breaks and coffee queues, and couldn't remember Daud, though he had, obviously, remembered her.

'Joanna.' Robbie hadn't finished. 'I should warn you. On Professor Daud's résumé it mentioned some military training. Before his post at the university, he was a soldier.'

THIRTY-FOUR

2 p.m.

Mid-afternoon she received a text from Matthew and almost laughed at the glimpse into a normal world.

Hi Jo, darling. Hoping all is going well and you're not in any danger. Sorry I missed your text last night. Was having dinner with Mum&Dad. I'm guessing Eloise's graduation is far from your mind but it's a week today and now I'm getting nervous you won't have wound up the case before then. Obviously it's hugely important to us all. Eloise's big moment. I'll try and make alternative arrangements for Jakob if you're still tied up. Otherwise, I'll just have to hope he'll keep quiet through the ceremony conferring that precious certificate on his half-sister.

Half-sister, she mused. She'd never thought of Eloise Levin as being Jakob's half-sister. But now it hit her. That was what she was. Same father, different mothers.

She read on.

Darling, keep safe. Don't take risks, and I'm proud of you and the work you do.

I love you, Matt X

There followed a heart emoji.

She sent him back a message assuring him she was well and doing her best. But when it came to showing some enthusiasm for Eloise's graduation, she couldn't quite find the words.

2.30 p.m.

Memories pricked their way into the light. He was exhausted. Sometimes he wasn't sure what was real and what wasn't as memories punched their way out. Images grew between spaces like weeds through the cracks in paving stones. Something scratched inside his head, a rat trapped behind the skirting board, gnawing its way through. It would emerge.

A memory that should have faded years ago was surfacing, finding prominence, pushing to the fore, finding light and horrid clarity. Had his arms been free he would have pushed it away, pushed *her* away, freed himself from the tangle of her legs, which were trapping him. *Go*, he said. *Now go. Leave me.* But she wouldn't. She was stuck to him, and the best he could do was rock in this wretched chair.

His mind was meandering, and the further away he drifted from reality, the more vivid was the memory. But through it all, one point disturbed him more than all the others. Something he couldn't put into words.

They were whispering outside the door, speaking in some foreign dialect he didn't recognize. She sounded angry. And then her voice dropped and he realized she was indeed a conspirator. He pictured them outside his door, huddled together, plotting. She never entered the study; he hadn't actually seen her except when she'd brought a sandwich, refusing to look him in the eye, but he knew she hovered outside. He heard her soft steps hesitate just outside the door before backing away. And he wasn't sure whether he wanted to see her or not because he knew that once he searched those black eyes, he would read her role in all this. He would read treachery, duplicity which would add to his suffering. And now he wasn't making sense even to himself. He felt dizzy and sick – possibly a side effect of the blow he'd received on his temple. Since Abdi had arrived, he'd had little to eat and probably not enough to drink either. How many days had it been? He didn't know. He'd lost count.

At times he opened his eyes to see Abdi planted in front of his chair, scrutinizing him. His dark eyes were searching for something, but he didn't know what. He couldn't tell if he was suffused with hatred or not. What he seemed to see was curiosity. And after a moment or two, he turned away.

'I need to drink,' he said. 'Please.'

Abdi hesitated, perhaps weighing up the options. Keep him thirsty? Make him suffer? Or give him a drink and extend his life? There seemed to be this tussle inside him that Joseph couldn't grasp.

He tried another tack. 'Clarice,' he said. 'Is she still here?'

Too late he watched the anger bubble up inside his captor, his hand clenching around the pistol. And then he felt the crack again with a force that twisted his neck round. He heard an involuntary groan and recognized his own voice altered by pain.

'What have I done? Why are you here?' It burst out of him like a poisonous boil exploding with pus. He knew it was his voice, but being tethered to the chair, unable to move, short on food and shorter on drink was having its effect. His voice now was weak, almost a squeak. He was frightened in a way he'd never experienced before because he couldn't understand the situation. The unknown was so much more frightening than a recognized threat. That he could have dealt with. But this dark void, letting his mind run riot, was terrifying. He'd never experienced such extreme vulnerability. The inability to defend himself, unable to duck when he sensed a blow was coming or reciprocate in any way. His fingers were useless, slowly puffing up with cold and inactivity. He had no gun to load, no reinforcements to call on, just this big black, hopeless nothing. A paralysed victim.

But he'd learned a lesson. Clarice was Abdi Daud's sensitive spot. Whether it was motivated by extreme love or hate he didn't understand. But he knew she was still here yet either unable or unwilling to help him. Maybe her fear of Daud prevented her from helping. He strained for some hint of her – that soft-slippered, steady step; the buzz of a vacuum cleaner; the scent of polish – but in fact the house felt dead already.

Was that his plan? Destruction?

4 p.m.

Jason had fetched sandwiches for them and they were all tucking in. Sitting around, with little to do, was making them all hungry. After the initial flood of information that had followed the first press release, things had quietened down, the phone lines staying stubbornly silent. Most of what had come in had turned out to be false or unhelpful. And the one thing that remained elusive was Joseph Holden's past. No one had come forward to provide any personal information on the elderly man. They'd released a statement nationwide that there was a hostage situation at Rudyard Lake in the hope that Joseph Holden's three friends might come forward, but if the news had reached them, they were staying out of view, possibly fearing they would be the next target.

They knew from official sources that Joseph had been a staff sergeant in the army, but he'd left the armed forces nearly forty years ago. And after that he'd largely disappeared from view. Fallen into a void. And that was what was troubling Joanna the most. Because she sensed somewhere in this background narrative were the answers she was desperate for.

Robbie's words rang in her head. *Find the narrative.*

Was this when he'd travelled the world, collecting treasures?

Here could lie the connection with Abdi Daud. He could have been in Somalia at some time before he'd moved to Cloud Mansion. According to Doreen Caputo, since he'd arrived, he'd mostly stayed at home, leading an almost reclusive existence. But only now had Daud surfaced.

The three buddies who visited a few times a year were almost certainly old army mates, but they had no idea of their names or current whereabouts. And yet they probably knew at least some of the answers to their questions, which would, in turn, lead them back to Daud.

Doreen had suggested that Joseph had been a cut above his three colleagues . . . captain of the troop?

Something bonded them together, but they were laying low.

She realized her focus was shifting away from the hostage taker, spiralling out now from the hostage, focussing on the question: who is this man? What is his connection? What is his life story? And her question was slowly turning around into: who is the villain here?

6 p.m.

Joseph Holden's chin had dropped to his chest. He was tired. So tired he wasn't sure he cared what happened to him. He wanted to sleep. But when he closed his eyes, his mind filled with images.

'I'm sorry,' he apologized to no one. 'I'm sorry.'

Hunched up in the corner, the gun cradled on his lap, Abdi Daud heard the apology and glanced across briefly, eyes flickering with some emotion. Scepticism? Disbelief?

THIRTY-FIVE

Joanna's focus shifted again, this time returning to Clarice Hani. The forensic team had visited the room she'd rented from Claudia Shannon and removed a hairbrush entangled with black hair. There had been no match on the Interpol site so she wasn't a known criminal, but it confirmed their suspicion that she'd entered the UK illegally.

There was no bank account; she'd been paid in cash and had only made cash transactions. She was one of the invisibles.

Joanna blew her cheeks out in frustration. Korpanski, working on the other side of the room, was watching her. She crossed to his side and dragged a chair to sit by him. It meant she could speak quietly, voice her insecurities, without being overheard. She focussed on his eyes. 'I'm still worried I'm going to make a hash of this and someone will die because of my incompetence.'

Had it been anyone else, they might have jollied her along, shored her up with false, insincere flattery. But it wasn't Detective Sergeant Mike Korpanski's way. He and Joanna knew each other too well. They'd never communicated through platitudes. Instead, he reached out and covered her hand with his own. 'Even with Robbie Callaghan's support?'

She shook her head. 'He's not here, Mike. *He's* not the one responding to Daud. I can hardly consult him during the calls, ask his advice on appropriate responses. Neither is he the one who Daud demanded handle the case.'

Korpanski was thoughtful. 'Maybe it's purely geographical,' he said. 'Daud had some reason for wanting to target Joseph Holden, who happens to live on your patch. Maybe that's the only reason he's marked you out.'

'Is that why he attended the course in the first place? To come to the UK and do some groundwork for his scheme – whatever that might be?'

'It's possible.'

She thought about this for a brief while. And it cheered her up. 'You think?'

Korpanski nodded, smiling now. 'It makes sense. It might not be personal.'

She sat back. 'Well, it does make me feel better. I was getting paranoid about being named in a hostage case.' She heaved out a heavy sigh. 'But the fact remains that we still have no idea what his demands might be and we need to bring an end to this situation. Joseph is in poor health. He could die simply from stress and natural causes. We have to bring this to a close, but I don't know how.'

Korpanski risked teasing her, his face serious as he said, 'But you have to bring an end to this before next Saturday so you can mind Jakob while Eloise is handed her degree.'

The leg pull eased some of her tension, and she laughed. 'Quite.' She stretched. 'I'm struggling, Mike. I'm tired. I want to go home, have a shower, put on fresh clothes, spend time with Matt and Jakob, go out on a bike ride as a family. Get my life back.'

Korpanski gave her one of his signature grins. 'Then bring an end to this, Jo,' he said softly. 'You can do it.' He changed that to, 'You *will* do it. And then take a bit of your own advice. Have some downtime, a holiday, the three of you. Take a break.'

She hesitated. 'You know what I really fear?'

He said nothing, but he knew.

'If Joseph Holden dies, I'll feel responsible. I'll always feel I've failed. His death will be on my conscience.'

He shook his head. 'How often have we been told we aren't responsible for the situations we find ourselves in? It's the perpetrators.'

She managed a smile and returned to her own computer, logged in and started composing an email to Robbie Callaghan, selecting her words with care.

Thanks for your help. I thought I should bring you up to date with where we are so far.

While your course was really great, Robbie, even with your guidance, I'm not up to this situation.

Mr Holden is in poor health, and I'm concerned for him. I feel I must bring this to a close before he suffers some sort of medical event. It's almost certain that Clarice Hani, his cleaner, is the hostage taker's sister, but we have no idea what her role is in all this – why she came to the UK when she did in the first place and how she ended up at Cloud Mansion, which seems to have been a stroke of luck. We believe she entered the UK illegally from Somalia but, as she apparently comes from a remote area near the Ethiopian border, we know nothing about her except that she does not have a criminal record.

Daud, a professor in political science at Mogadishu University, has made no attempt to conceal his identity. He has still made no demands. Which means I have no clear motive for the situation and no idea how to bring it to a close other than storming Cloud Mansion, which you constantly warned is a high-risk strategy and to be avoided if possible; in other words, if there is a clear threat to the hostage's life. I'm assuming the connection between the two men is historic and probably originates with some event in Somalia, Professor Daud's homeland. I am, therefore, trying to anticipate Daud's demands. Possibly a hostage exchange or something of that ilk? Mr Holden's background is sketchy, and we have no idea what he has done since leaving the British military around forty years ago. The connection between the three protagonists remains a mystery, but there's a possible link with a local antiques shop where it seems Clarice also worked. We intend to follow that lead up when the shop is open. Abdi Daud has claimed he has a gun. Considering his military background, my fear is he and Clarice Hani have even more weaponry. Possibly explosives?

So you can see why I'm floundering.

Specifically my problems are these:

DS Korpanski suggests that this isn't a personal vendetta targeting me particularly but Daud is exploiting the fact that his quarry i.e. Joseph Holden, lives in my area.

Daud's familiarity with your teachings puts him constantly a step ahead of me. And, of course, I'm constrained by police rules and regulations.

I know you advise me to be patient, to wait, but what am I waiting for? Some sort of bloodbath? Possibly displayed on social media? A political message?

Daud is an intelligent man. I don't believe he started this without a clear end point in mind. In which way he is well ahead of me. I wish you were here to deal with this instead of me, but as you're not, any helpful advice would be very welcome.

Joanna (DI Piercy)

As she was composing this email, Joseph Holden's mind was tracking in the same direction. If things went wrong, the inspector would be blamed. He recalled her voice – wary, unconfident, apprehensive, and yet with an unmistakable air of certainty as though she blasted, *I am the law – representative of the king.*

Then his mind crept along the questions he'd been asking himself for the past five days. What was going to happen to him? He risked glancing across the room at Daud, who was looking pensive now, in some sad world of his own, his lips moving. Joseph asked himself another question. Why had he taken Clarice on when he'd recognized that she came from a part of the world he'd been doing his best to forget for the past fifteen years? He'd recognized her bearing, her pronunciation of certain words, the way she stumbled and lisped over others. One day, he recalled now, he'd seen her studying an old photograph of himself and had been surprised when she'd asked him a direct question. 'This is you?'

Fitz had taken it, a year or so before he'd died, killed by shrapnel severing his femoral artery. He'd bled to death in minutes before their eyes. He'd been standing in front of the Hadful Mosque in deepest, darkest Mogadishu. He'd understood her surprise. He'd had a full head of hair then, one of the few features he'd been proud of. Thick blond hair that barely tucked inside a combat helmet. He didn't look like that now. The hair had thinned and faded to white.

He continued his surreptitious study of Daud and was certain they'd never met before.

His head dropped. He was deathly tired. But in his dreams there was no rest. Only memories he'd tried to bury . . .

His team was running in a crouch, throwing their index fingers forward. All five of them. He smelled blood and felt sand rasping between his fingers. The sand was a warning. Guns and sand didn't mix well, and Fitz's gun had jammed. His load was heavy on his back; the barrel of the gun hot in his hands. The heat was so intense that he felt as though the hand gripping his gun might melt. Sweat dripped into his eyes and evaporated almost instantly to a salty crust which he felt on his lips. Gunfire mingled with screams; there was the *tic-tic* sound of a tank creeping forward. The atmosphere exhilarated and terrified him in equal scoops.

But it was his natural environment, as much a part of him as a camel is suited to the desert or a vulture gravitates to a rotting corpse. His career. His life. And the souvenirs he'd collected along the way would provide him with a comfortable retirement – if he survived.

Thou fool.

THIRTY-SIX

Sunday 15 September, 3 p.m.

The day was passing painfully slowly with no word from Daud. A torpor was settling over the entire incident room. Waiting was more exhausting than action, inactivity more tiring than climbing a mountain. No adrenaline kicked in, the only real challenge the suppression of energy.

Keeping an eye on her work phone, Joanna rang home. Matthew made an attempt to be cheerful, but she knew the situation was taking a toll on him. He was trying not to ask her unanswerable questions: how the case was going, when she'd be home, whether she thought she'd be free by Eloise's graduation day. Was she safe? The conversation between them was stilted and awkward. Her mind wasn't on events at Briarswood, while Matthew was trying too hard not to ask the wrong questions.

Korpanski was having a well-earned day off and they were down to skeleton staff.

Taking the phone with her, she headed into the town. She wanted to visit the antiques shop, but it was still closed, as it had been yesterday when they'd checked, metal bars across the window. Poor old Pargeter, she mused. He'd tried to protect his antiques and still lost money.

Oh well, she thought, one more day surely wouldn't make much difference.

She returned to the boat house and sat for a while, studying the picture they had of Daud. He was handsome, with intelligent, dark eyes that stared out boldly, a full mouth and, from the little she could see, strong white teeth. But pictures didn't reveal secrets, and after a few minutes, she resumed her checking of the data they'd collected so far.

The day crawled by, inactivity and lack of stimulus making them all fidgety and bored, too aware of their lack of progress. The phone remained silent. A few times she thought she'd heard it ring, but it was an imagined sound.

Waiting was proving hard.

But the day passed.

Monday 16 September, 8 a.m.

Mike turned up early. And brought in his wake a sense of energy and optimism. He breezed in with a cardboard tray of welcome, decent coffee which, in turn, energized them all.

Today, Joanna convinced herself, would be the day they made some progress.

And as if to buoy up her optimism, she received a lengthy email from Robbie, which shored her up.

> *First of all, Joanna, this is not your fault. Your experience in this field is confined to the classroom and a brief introduction to the situation. But he's asked for you, and so you've acceded to his only request so far.*
>
> *Secondly, bear in mind that, apart from this, he's made no specific demands. Which means I can't take over or even show an obvious presence.*
>
> *I've thought about this, and I agree that Daud is likely to present a political demand, e.g. a prisoner swap or publicity for some cause rather than a general one as in money. Usually political demands are more complicated as they involve other agencies, lawyers and government officials. You just have to wait. Professor Daud isn't some guy who's wandered in from the street. He attended my course with a specific intent. Whether this is an engineered encounter between himself and Mr Holden, pursuit of his sister or, less likely, to have some contact with you, we can't know. Therefore, my advice is to keep searching for the narrative which lies buried. This was no chance event but something carefully planned with a specific outcome in mind. Keep digging into the years after Mr Holden's military career ended but before he arrived in Staffordshire. At a guess, he and his band of mates hired themselves out as mercenaries.*
>
> *As far as your fear of booby traps or more weaponry, I sincerely hope not. But Daud wasn't in the country long before he appeared*

at Cloud Mansion. He wouldn't have had much opportunity to arm himself.

This is the best advice I can give you. I'll keep in contact and try and help/advise as much as I can, but you are on the frontline. Have faith in your abilities, don't try and force the pace and, whatever the outcome, you're doing your best. You can do no more.

I trust you.

Yours, Robbie. X

She read it through twice and it partly mollified her. But on the heels of that was an overwhelming instinct to curse the fact she'd done this bloody course in the first place. Had she not maybe Daud would have picked another person to head this awful situation.

She closed her computer.

It was time to head out and follow that second possible lead. See where Clarice fitted in.

Were Joseph Holden and Pargeter friends? Business acquaintances?

She looked out of the window at the leaves shivering on the trees and the now silent lake, devoid of pleasure seekers, its surface tranquil and empty. Apart from the murmurs of her officers and the tap of fingers on keyboards, all around was silent.

Mike was on the phone, checking up with the officers surrounding the property. By the bland look on his face, she suspected there hadn't been anything to report. He caught her glance and shook his head.

She sauntered across. 'Mike . . .?'

He lit up. 'What's the plan?'

'Robbie's suggested Joseph Holden might have been a mercenary along with those mates of his. So let's get access to his phone records. Maybe we can track the guys down.'

She left Alan King to work on this one. Mobile phone operators were notoriously sticky to deal with. He'd spend half the morning trying to persuade them to give him access.

Joanna had remembered something else. She'd befriended another officer during the course, someone based in Birmingham with West Midlands Police. Over the four days, as they'd shared lunches, they'd exchanged gossip and compared experiences, sympathizing with each other over the problems of today's policing. And when the course had finished, they'd exchanged telephone numbers.

Now Joanna wondered whether Chief Inspector Aileen Spencer

might remember something about Daud because, hard as she might try, she couldn't visualize him or connect him to the course.

Luckily, Aileen picked up and recognized her voice at once, and the bonus was that she already knew some of the details of the hostage situation playing out near Leek. 'I wondered if you'd get in touch.' She laughed. 'All hush hush, I'm sure, but I bet it's strange putting all those wise words into practice. Has Robbie been holding your hand, giving you moral support? I hope he has.'

'Yeah.' Joanna heard the emotion in her voice.

'Poor you,' Aileen said. 'So how are you bearing up?' Without waiting for a reply, she added, 'We didn't think we'd ever be using those hostage negotiation skills, did we? We thought it was just a skive. A little feather in our caps. But here you are.'

'Here I am.'

Knowing she didn't have to swear her colleague to secrecy, Joanna told her that Robbie Callaghan had confirmed that their hostage taker had been on the course.

'What?' Predictably Aileen was shocked. 'Was he there to learn the skills?'

'Who knows? He's actually a Somali professor.'

Aileen was even more astonished. 'What?' she said again.

Joanna moved on. 'I wondered if you might remember him better than I? His name was Abdi Daud.' She gave her a brief description.

There was a short pause before Aileen responded. 'I do remember a black guy – or at least he was more Moroccan looking. Handsome sort of fellow but something dangerous about him.'

'He has a military background.'

'Doesn't surprise me. I tried to talk to him a couple of times. Asked him where he was from,' she finished limply. 'He was pretty rude. Patently did not want to talk.'

'Where did he *say* he was from?'

'He sort of side-stepped the question, asked me about Birmingham. He was definitely a bit cagey about his own origins. Why?'

'Aileen, he knew my name. He specifically asked for me to take charge of the case.'

'What?' Aileen said for the third time.

'Is there anything you can remember about him that could help? Did he seem an angry man, a political persona? Did he mention anything about politics or . . .?' And now Joanna was at a loss.

'No. Nothing? Oh . . . wait a minute. He had a picture of a girl. I was behind him in the dinner queue and it dropped out of his wallet when he paid for lunch. I picked it up.'

'Did you ask him who it was?'

Again, Aileen laughed. 'I did,' she said. 'You know me.'

'And?'

'He said it was his sister.'

'Did you ask her name?'

'I did. I said what a pretty name.' She paused. 'Clarice.'

So now they had confirmation. The connection between them was close. Had she been his scout?

'Actually'– Aileen's voice cut into her thoughts – 'I thought he had a bit of a thing about you. He kept staring at you. I assumed he fancied you. So that's your hostage taker?'

'Yeah. And I don't think he was staring at me because he fancied me, Aileen; I think he was already starting to plan this assault.'

'Shi-it.'

She thanked Aileen, cutting off her curiosity and best wishes and ended the call.

THIRTY-SEVEN

9.30 a.m.

And now she was wondering. What was the true story behind how Clarice arrived at Cloud Mansion? Why specifically there? She knew Doreen's version – a card in the window – a fishing expedition. Had it really been random chance? There was a connection, admittedly tenuous, between Clarice, Joseph and Noah's Ark. A neat full circle. Had the owner of Noah's Ark similarly responded to a card in the window?

It seemed unlikely that the cards in the window, the job at the antiques shop and her arrival at Cloud Mansion were all pure coincidence. But Mr Pargeter might be able to add something to their tiny pile of disconnected facts. So it was even more imperative that they visit the antiques shop again.

Korpanski was on the phone. She tapped him on the shoulder.

'Fancy a trip out?'

He nodded, finished the call and blew out a long, frustrated breath which told her it had been a waste of time. She knew he was similarly frustrated with their inability to resolve this case, which was taking up so many officers, so much time, such a huge amount of resources. What was even more difficult was the inactivity. They had little to go on, each sparse fact hard won, with little to do but wait.

Korpanski stood up smartly. Every day he seemed a little stronger. 'Anything to get a breath of fresh air.'

They were in the car in minutes, driving through the town, heading out on the Stone Road to Noah's Ark.

Pargeter obviously felt their visit was because they'd tracked down the thieves and recovered his lost money. He was smiling a broad welcome when the shop bell tinkled and they stepped inside, hope brightening his face.

'Hi there. Good to see you. Thanks for following this up.' Then he asked, 'Any news?'

Joanna tried to let him down gently 'I'm afraid not, though we have circulated descriptions of the three people involved in the theft of your money.' She tried to erase the look of disappointment. 'Actually, we've come about another matter.'

She had to hand it to Pargeter. He picked himself up quickly and led them again into his small, hot office which still smelled of damp and cigarettes. Korpanski's bulk seemed to fill the small area so it felt claustrophobic. They left the door open.

On the way over, she'd discussed with Korpanski how much they should tell him and they'd concluded that the more they explained, the greater the chance of his cooperation. She began in a roundabout way. 'You might have heard that there's a police presence around Rudyard Lake?'

'Yeah.' Now he looked worried. 'What's that got to do with me?' He spoke slowly, quietly, as though he didn't really want to hear the answer.

Joanna plunged right in. 'Two people are being held hostage by an armed intruder.'

'Yeah. I read that.' Now his gaze had dropped to the floor. He was clearly worried about his own involvement. He looked from Joanna to Korpanski and back to Joanna again.

'The two people being held are both known to you.'

There was no response from Pargeter. Wisely, he waited.

'Mr Joseph Holden, who lives at Cloud Mansion, and the lady who cleans for him. A Miss Clarice Hani.'

Joanna waited; Mike didn't shift his gaze away from the dealer. Who was still hesitating, shifty eyes aimed at the floor once more.

Finally he spoke. 'Mr Holden is – was – a customer. While Clarice, Miss Hani, cleaned and occasionally looked after the shop if I was away at a sale – or somewhere,' he finished lamely. 'I never really chatted to her much. She was from Africa – some-where. But her English was good, and she was honest.' He smiled to himself, but his eyes were still on the floor. 'She'd clean the place up a bit and was OK with the customers.' He was speaking quickly, as though he wanted to get this over and done with. 'If there was something she didn't know about the stuff, she'd just ring and I'd speak to the customer directly.' He paused before looking straight at Joanna. 'I don't – I don't see how this has anything to do with me. I didn't really know her. It was just a business thing.' He gave an unconvincing shrug as though shed-ding a cloak. 'Coincidence.'

'How did she come to work for you?'

Pargeter pursed his lips. 'Card in the window, I think. Yes. In the newsagent's, the one on the corner. I thought I'd give her a try. The girl before her was clumsy – broke stuff. And she wasn't terribly reliable either.'

'Did she ever talk about her home life, about when she'd arrived in the UK?'

Pargeter shook his head. 'I never asked.'

'Did you ever see any paperwork or documentation connected with her arrival in the UK?'

Again, he shook his head.

Even though she anticipated the answer, Joanna tried again. 'ID documents? A passport?'

'No.'

'When did she start working for you?'

'Just before Christmas.' He seemed to feel he should justify the timing. 'It's always a busy time,' he said lamely.

But Joanna was thinking Clarice had worked first for the shop and then started at Cloud Mansion. She tucked the fact away and moved on. 'And Mr Holden? You say he was a customer?'

Pargeter nodded and cleared his throat.

Korpanski butted in. 'Buying or selling?'

Pargeter switched his attention to the burly sergeant. 'Both,' he said shortly.

'What sort of stuff was he selling?'

'Foreign things. Stuff he'd picked up on his travels.'

He seemed keen to skate very quickly over this topic.

'His travels?' Joanna asked silkily.

'I think he was in the forces.'

Korpanski shifted his weight on to his other foot. Since his accident, standing still proved a trial. Joanna would have suggested he sit, but she knew Korpanski would rather stand – however painful or uncomfortable it might be.

'According to our sources, he left the forces many years ago.'

Pargeter shrugged. 'I think he continued to travel until he came here,' he said, frowning. 'That was the impression I got.'

'Did you ever visit Cloud Mansion?'

'Once or twice.' His face changed, and Joanna caught a look of avarice, a sort of oily greediness. 'Treasure trove of a place. Stuff from all over the world.'

Korpanski and Joanna exchanged looks. 'Specifically what countries?'

Now the dealer looked worried. 'All over,' he said uncomfortably, looking from one to the other, perhaps searching for the right answer, the one which would eject them quickest from his shop.

It was time to leak a little information in the hope that it would act like a worm wriggling on a hook, tempting a bigger fish.

'Was there anything there that had a link with Somalia?' Joanna felt she was putting her hand into a bran tub, with no idea what she would pull out.

Pargeter's face changed. 'Why?'

'Our hostage taker is a Somali national, as is his sister, Clarice, your shop assistant.'

Pargeter looked shocked – and a little frightened. 'His sister? What? I had no idea.' He actually looked around him, through the door, into the shop. 'You think *I'm* in danger?'

Joanna could have pointed out to him that Clarice Hani had had plenty of opportunity to survey Noah's Ark– and launch any assault on its owner in her own time. And Abdi Daud had headed straight for Cloud Mansion. And yet. And yet – they all knew there was a connection.

'No, Mr Pargeter,' she said gently but firmly, 'we don't think you're in danger, but we are searching for the connection between Joseph Holden, Clarice Hani and Abdi Daud. And somehow you appear to be a lynchpin. We're wondering what your role has been. And its connection with Somalia.'

She waited for him to process her oblique query.

Her quiet bore fruit. The dealer's face changed. 'Yes,' he said quietly, 'there is a connection.'

It was as though she'd hit a bell. The resonance had struck a memory.

It was one of the phrases Robbie had used to illustrate progress – agreement from the person you were interrogating.

That's right. There is.

She waited.

10.15 a.m.

If only he could move.

He tried to use one of the tactics they'd been taught back in his forces days. Abstraction.

Fly through the air.

And so in his mind he found that freedom. He cut the ties and sprinted out of the door then rounded the house, which observed him, silent, immovable as a fortress, unable to either help or hinder. He reached his little green van and yanked open the door. Spat gravel into the air as he accelerated up the drive and out, out through the gates, out on to the Horton Road where he put his foot to the floor. Freedom found.

And lost.

Daud's eyes flicked open, a moment's alarm, as he swept the distance between chair and door, and smirked.

As if.

Joseph sank back, beaten, as he mocked himself and his posses-sion, remembering how he'd once loved this piece of furniture, bragged about the solid weight of seasoned oak, the indestructibility indicated by its age – over two hundred years. He'd bought it at Stafford Antiques Fair – was it seven or eight years ago? It was a big, heavy piece, a piece whose arms were stout enough to imprison him, the carving torturing his back.

Once he'd loved it. Now he hated it. If he survived this, he would

personally enjoy sawing it into pieces and burning it. He would
have begged for a cushion; the seat was hard and unyielding under
his bony posterior, but he still had a remnant of military pride though
every single vertebra felt all of its seventy-six years. He believed
he could identify every projection and angle of the carving on the
back panel of which he'd once boasted, *Not later carved. Oh no.
This carving is contemporary to the chair's age.* His own words
mocked him. Who cared now? Not him.

   Thou fool.

'Somalia,' Joanna repeated.

   Pargeter flopped forward in the chair, hands supporting his head,
his eyes wide open. He was scared.

   'He had a lot of stuff,' he said cautiously. 'Masks and . . . things . . .'
He hesitated and then, gathering enthusiasm, he set off again. 'It
was genuine stuff. Not knock-offs from a few years ago made for
the tourist market. He had a good eye.' Pargeter leaned back in his
chair. 'Most of it was African, some Chinese, Japanese. He was
well travelled.'

   Joanna waited.

   Pargeter continued to enthuse. 'There were some lovely things.
Rare things. Early Korean celadon pottery, Ming, Jing. And the stuff
from Africa – well – another world. Real bone carvings, shells,
ivory, ebony.'

   Joanna voiced a horror she'd always had. 'Shrunken heads?'

   Pargeter smiled, perhaps recognizing the detective's fear. 'One,
I think.'

   'Somali?'

   Pargeter shook his head, smiling gently. 'Shrunken heads come
from the Amazon, Inspector.'

   He could have been scolding a schoolchild.

   Joanna took back control. 'So . . . the link to Somalia?' she asked
politely.

   He was cagey now. Evasive. 'There isn't a market for that sort
of foreign stuff round here.' He spoke quickly, evasion in every
syllable, anxious to skate past this subject.

   There was a moment of awkward quiet.

   'You haven't answered the question,' Korpanski prompted this
time – a little less politely than Joanna, the hint of a threat inherent
in his build.

'Last year I agreed to put a couple of bits in a London saleroom.'
Pargeter struggled to look at them directly.

'You took them down yourself?'

'No. A Sotheby's van picked them up . . .' Again, his eyes wavered.
'A courier calls by most weeks – if we have something we need
collecting. They took the masks – along with some other stuff.'

He'd hurried over those last three words. So there it was. Hidden
in plain sight. The clue. The link, the shame, the reason for his
hurrying past the subject. *Some – other – stuff.*

She repeated the phrase delicately. 'Some – other – stuff?'

'There was a Qolxad,' he said reluctantly.

'A what?' She would have liked to have told him: in English?
She recognized he was still trying to bury the detail in a foreign
word he'd known they would not understand.

'It's a sort of dagger.'

'Somali?'

'Yes.' He hurried past the admission, swamping her with details.
'Can be called a Jile or a Gile in Afar language. But in Somalia it's
called a Qolxad. It was a lovely thing with a carved handle.' He
looked apprehensive now, glancing from inspector to sergeant and
back to the inspector.

'Rhinoceros horn. It must have belonged to a . . .' His voice
trailed away. He'd been found out.

Joanna's voice remained as smooth as silk rather than interroga-
tory. 'Tell me more,' she invited. But she knew Korpanski would
have picked up on the alertness in her face, that almost quivering
of the muscles around her mouth. When they returned to their incident room, the first thing she'd be looking up would be the CITES
rules: Convention on International Trade in Endangered Species of
Wild Flora and Fauna, which were meant to protect endangered
species' body parts from ending up as dagger handles. Particularly
rhinoceros horn.

This might possibly provide an explanation for the hostage situation too. Animal rights campaigners were certainly capable of
taking an elderly gentleman prisoner to draw attention to the plight
of endangered species.

Joanna stepped forward. 'I believe there are rules about buying
and selling articles containing rhino horn.'

The dealer nodded miserably. 'CITES. It's OK if they were
worked pre-1947,' he added quickly.

'And did it sell, this Qolxad?'

'Oh yes. It made over nine hundred thousand pounds.' He hadn't been able to conceal the note of pride in his voice.

'What?' Joanna and Mike looked at each other, stunned. 'Nine hundred grand? More than a house? More than a luxury car? For a sort of dagger? How?'

Pargeter made a face – part ashamed, part gloating. 'The Chinese,' he said. 'Rhino horn fetches more than gold. As an aphrodisiac. And then there's the actual piece. Such a fine thing would have belonged to a village chief.'

'Then how did Mr Holden acquire it?' Joanna's voice was sharp.

Pargeter had his answer ready. 'I don't know. But . . .'

They waited.

'The chief wouldn't have given it up without a fight.'

Joanna dragged something from her memory. 'Don't you have to have provenance to sell something of this value?' She spoke carefully She was here to learn facts – not apportion blame. She didn't want his cooperation frightened off. But . . .

'Of course.' Pargeter seemed offended.

'And?' Mike prompted.

'He told me he'd' – here the hesitation exposed the lie –'bought it from one of the chiefs. Somewhere in the Ogaden region. It's somewhere in the horn of Africa between Ethiopia and Somalia,' he added helpfully. 'A lot of the people there are nomadic so verification was virtually impossible.'

A useful phrase that, *verification was virtually impossible.*

Joanna pursued the point. 'In your opinion, Mr Pargeter, *were* they legally obtained?'

Now the dealer looked shifty. 'That's what he told me,' he said. 'And once they'd gone to the London saleroom, it was up to them to verify.' He exhaled softly, perhaps thinking he was out of the woods. 'The auctioneers were happy,' he said with a smooth smile. 'And so was the buyer.'

Joanna was sure he would have taken his no doubt generous cut. 'As were you, I expect,' she said with a smile.

Pargeter acknowledged her comment with a dip of his head.

'Was that the piece that drew most attention?'

'Oh yes. It made good money. There were other pieces around the house: African masks, some gold jewellery, a couple of cuneiform carved tablets. Unusual because instead of the usual records

of sales carved into the clay, et cetera, they were about the
Babylonian king, Nebuchadnezzar. Not really my subject,' he added
hastily as though he expected to be quizzed on the subject. 'But the
market for those sorts of objects is pretty flat. They would have
fetched only a fraction of the Qolxad. That was the piece that had
all the international interest. They put it on the front cover of the
catalogue. Attracted bidding from all over the world,' he added
proudly. He'd obviously forgotten temporarily the reason behind the
visit, that the sale of the Qolxad had probably found its way to
Mogadishu and, in turn, was the likely trigger behind Clarice Hani's
arrival at the antiques shop, where she would have been able to
unearth the true owner of the dagger and was then followed by her
brother.

Seemingly unaware, Pargeter continued blithely. 'I had to have
it verified, carbon dated and valued. It all takes time – and money,'
he added pompously, looking from one to the other, his expression
changing as he picked up on their silent criticism.

Joanna knew they'd found that golden nugget.

If she used it wisely, it could possibly be the key to unlocking
the door of Cloud Mansion and freeing Joseph Holden. But she also
knew that the Qolxad had a story to tell.

THIRTY-EIGHT

11.40 a.m.

So now they had a timeline. The dagger had been sold by
Sotheby's almost a year ago, last October. They'd called in
the newsagent's on the way back to the station and learned
that Clarice had placed her card in the window in January. She'd
started working at Noah's Ark early February and Cloud Mansion
late March.

She must have had a way of contacting her brother and verifying
Joseph Holden's identity.

So the dagger formed an explanation but still didn't answer the
question.

Why had Daud come in such hot pursuit of the item?

Was it simply its value – that the people to whom it had belonged were poor and the money would have provided useful cash?

Was it because it had been looted or the people cheated out of its full value?

These were possible answers. But something Pargeter had said disturbed her. The dagger would have belonged to a chief who would not have relinquished it without a fight. As soon as they were back at the incident room, Joanna rang Robbie Callaghan and shared these newly gained facts – as well as her concern. What was Daud's ultimate motive in coming here? Revenge seemed the obvious answer. But if that was his aim, why involve the police in a prolonged siege? How dangerous and determined was Daud? And if his ultimate aim was Joseph Holden's murder, then they should consider storming the house. She put that to Robbie Callaghan too, and he was thoughtful.

'That's risky to your team, the hostage and to Clarice Hani as well.'

Next he picked up on another point.

'Daud is a professor at a prestigious university. He's an intelligent man, not a villain with a violent past. Bear that in mind.'

'So what does he want?'

Robbie paused for a moment before responding. 'At a guess some political response. Maybe a platform for some grievance. Possibly,' he added, 'vengeance for the death of the chief who owned this Qolxad.'

She noted that he was familiar with the word, not stumbling over it. 'You have experience of Somalia?'

'I do. And it didn't go well.' It was obvious he didn't want to elaborate.

Next, she mentioned their belief that Joseph Holden, on leaving the military, had earned money as a mercenary. 'Does that sort of explain his role, out there, in Somalia?'

'Very probably,' Robbie agreed. 'You say that this Qolxad comes from a remote region in the horn of Africa. The Ogaden?'

'That's what Joseph Holden told the dealer.'

'So if I were you, I'd start to learn about the area. See what conflicts there have been where mercenaries might have been involved. Anything you do learn will help you understand Daud – and his sister's particular beef with your Mr Holden. Remember old people haven't always been old. They simply have a longer past.'

She thanked him but returned to her mounting concern. 'Robbie, storming Cloud Mansion . . . How do I get the timing right?'

'Imminent murder. If it's publicity Daud wants, he'll let you know. Stay calm, Joanna. Remember your remit is the safety of the hostage – whatever happened in his past. It isn't for you to judge. If his life isn't deemed in danger – in other words if there's no obvious and immediate threat – you have to sit it out.'

She wanted reassurance. 'You're sure?'

'One is never sure of anything in this situation.' His tone was sober. 'In my experience, if you listened to the lecture' – she picked up on his tease – 'storming a building is more likely to end in tragedy than being patient.'

And on that note, they ended the call.

But the idea of storming Cloud Mansion was taking root in Joanna's mind and she was starting to discuss the possibility with Sergeant Zak Livingstone, the person in charge of the armed response team. He was young, muscular, in his early thirties at a guess, with a mop of dark hair and bright blue eyes. He also had a forceful personality that brokered no argument. He listened to Joanna's briefings but there was no doubt who was in charge of this side of the operations.

Abdi had come to a decision. Joseph could read it in the change in his posture – a straightening of his shoulders, a deepening of his frown. He kept glancing across the room at him, then, when their eyes met, he looked away quickly. He was flexing his fingers, no longer *loosely* holding the gun but fingering the trigger safety. Testing the weight to check the magazine was in place, flicking it in and out. Joseph recognized the preparation because he'd prepared for action in exactly the same way.

Clarice was standing in the doorway now, watching him curiously, almost as though he was an animal in a zoo. He stared back and read only curiosity in her face. No apology or empathy. It was obvious she wasn't going to intervene or try and intercept any decision Daud might make, whatever it was, but Joseph still hadn't fully convinced himself that his cleaner was part of his problem. Could he trust her? Instinct screamed *no*. Had she been the one to lead Abdi here? Again, instinct screamed, this time *yes*.

And yet the doubts remained, nibbling through his mind.

He flashed back to the day he'd first met her. He'd had no real need for a cleaner. Even when Doreen had suggested it, he hadn't been keen. But then she'd arrived and something inside him had shifted. It had been something in her bearing plus the mute appeal in her eyes plus something intangible. It was as though he'd recognized her. Not *her* personally. But there was something familiar about her. She'd seen him watching her and quickly dropped her eyes but not before Joseph had read something shameful cross her face. A sudden flush.

He turned his head and read that exact same expression in her face now.

So it was you.

5 p.m.

'I'll tell you what I'm interested in, Joanna.' He'd started to speak as soon as she'd responded to the call. 'How far along the route have you come?'

As if she'd tell him.

'There's a bit more to it than meets the eye, Professor Daud. I'm realizing that.' She had no intention of updating him on her progress. Neither was she going to make things easy for him. Let him worry, she thought. Let him wonder.

It was one of the few ways in which she could affect some control.

'Tell me what you know about Clarice.' Now his voice was velvety, interested, curious.

'She's your sister.'

'Wrong.' He laughed. 'Half-sister.'

It didn't seem a significant point.

'What else do you know? Or think you know?'

Engage with them, Robbie always advised. But this felt like a waste of time, nothing but an ego trip for Daud. She sensed it would lead nowhere.

She felt a sudden compulsion to bite back. 'It's pretty sure that your *half*-sister is here illegally, in which case she'll be deported.'

She scolded herself. *Unwise, Joanna.*

And yet it resulted in silence before he hung up, but she'd sensed, for the first time, his anger.

9 p.m.

Reasoning Daud wouldn't ring again she'd decided to risk a brief trip home, the phone, as always, by her side. She needed clean clothes, a proper shower and she wanted to have a glimpse, however brief, of normality, her husband and son.

She let herself in to a silent, darkened house. Had it not been for Matthew's car in the drive, she might have wondered if the house was empty. It certainly felt so.

She tiptoed into the lounge, and there he was – or rather, there they both were: Jakob fast asleep on his father's chest, the rise and fall of their chests in perfect sync. What a lovely sight, she thought. Far away from the stand-off at Cloud Mansion, the wily goading of Abdi Daud, the vulnerability of the hostage and the sense of something worse, far away, decades ago whose shadow still hung over them. But however much she might regret it, this was the world she was forced to live in now – the dirty water she must swim in, the people she had to mix with – and at times it was the beauty, peace and tranquillity of Briarswood, the love and security of her family that seemed the illusion.

She spent a few treasured moments absorbing the picture of peace, love and harmony before her, storing it in her memory.

And then her phone went.

She hurried out of the room as she answered it, furious, for a moment, with Daud for breaking into such a scene. She'd convinced herself that he wouldn't phone again – not this evening. She answered it as she closed the kitchen door behind her.

'Professor Daud.'

'Inspector.' His response was as controlled as hers.

She waited.

'I expect you're ready for a rest and a shower. A change of clothes maybe.'

Was the guy psychic?

There was a brief silence while he waited for a response she had no intention of making. Then he pressed forward in a voice soft and slippery as false friendship, his tone reflecting a fake smile. 'I'm right, aren't I?' He chuckled, which made her even more furious.

As before, she was tempted to demand: *What do you want?* But she said nothing. She would let him control the narrative – for now.

She took some deep breaths even as she watched the kitchen

door start to open. Slowly. Matthew, Jakob still asleep in his arms, was watching her, his head on one side, eyebrows raised, questioning. She shook her head and made a go-away gesture with her hands. He retreated.

Daud shattered the scene. 'I wonder what else you've unearthed about me.'

She realized this was a serious question, and she wasn't sure how to answer.

He continued, still probing. 'So easy to find one's past and present via a computer. On the condition,' he continued, 'that those details were posted in the first place.'

She could hardly argue against this.

He continued in the same vein. 'Everything there except the most important details.'

The temptation was to follow this strand, this most important detail. Instead, she gave in to another instinct. 'What is it you want? What are you here for, Daud?'

He ignored her, continuing. 'In time, the past is buried.'

She made no response.

He continued smoothly. 'You know when I say I will shoot Mr Holden it is not a joke.'

'I would never call this situation a joke,' Joanna said softly, hoping Matthew wasn't outside the door, listening; hoping he'd covered their son's ears with his hands so the words couldn't seep into his dreams.

'No. It is not a joke. And the reasons behind this scenario are not a joke either.' His tone had changed. For the first time in their interactions, she was sensing anger in his voice. 'With your efficient police force, you will know that I am here legally, in full view. Unlike my sister.'

'Half-sister.' It didn't even feel that she'd scored a point.

'I see you are listening to my narrative.'

She didn't respond to his statement but pushed on with one of her own.

'Mr Holden is in poor health.'

'I agree. It's possible he will not survive this episode even if I hold my fire.'

'In which case you will be held responsible. Let him go, Professor.'

Daud exploded with a loud burst of laughter. 'If he dies of natural causes, I cannot be charged with murder or manslaughter.'

But you will be held responsible. 'Why him, Professor Daud?'

'Soon, Inspector. Soon. But for the moment, forgive me, that is something I need to keep to myself.'

'I need to know he's still all right.'

'Rest assured, he is fed, watered, rested. That is all I can tell you for now. And now, my dear Inspector Piercy – Joanna – you have that much needed shower and a well-earned rest. We shall speak tomorrow. You may even have your wish to speak to Joseph Holden again granted.'

She tried once more, but even to her it sounded weak. 'Don't harm him. I don't know what he is or what he was to you, but now he's an elderly man in poor health. Whatever his past – and I think I'm beginning to realize it was a murky past – let him go.'

'To face justice?'

'I can't promise that when I don't know the facts.'

'So what can you promise?'

'That we'll look into it.'

'Really?' All she could hear was scepticism in his voice, and her mouth felt dry. Daud could see right through her empty promises. He knew he and his half-sister would be the ones facing charges. And she knew this too.

Silence followed. She heard Matthew climbing the stairs, his voice low as he talked to his son.

She was desperate to extend the conversation, to extract some sort of assurance from him. 'And Clarice? What do you intend doing with her?'

'Why' – he chuckled – 'take her home, of course. That's what you'll do with her anyway. I'm saving you a job. Goodnight, Joanna.'

And he ended the call.

Matthew was standing in the doorway again. He must have put Jakob to bed. 'Jo,' he said and held out his arms. 'What do you have to deal with?' The hug spelled out safety, security, protection.

He kept her folded in his arms for minutes.

A place where she felt protected from Daud's scorn, his cat-and-mouse taunts, the responsibility for lives, the decisions that meant life or death; Matthew's arms, encircling her, kept all of those away.

When he let her go, she looked into his face and read concern and something else, something she'd rarely seen before.

Fear.

THIRTY-NINE

10.15 p.m.

Having showered and changed as quickly as she could, Joanna was back at base though with little expectation that Daud would call again. Not this night.

Though he was a man of surprises.

She was too pent-up to sleep – she didn't even make any attempt to lie down and rest but paced the room downstairs. She wanted an end to this, a return to the normality she'd glimpsed briefly earlier that evening. She wanted her life back. Not under Abdi Daud's control.

But she also wanted Joseph Holden free, alive. And Daud and Clarice in custody. She wanted to wipe the smirk off his face. No, she hadn't actually seen it, but she'd heard it in his tone, in his silences, in his control of the situation. He was calling the tune, and she was forced to dance to it to save an elderly man whom she was increasingly suspecting of being less than innocent. But she could hardly share this doubt with Chief Superintendent Gabriel Rush. And to bring an end to it all, she had to learn what part the three characters had played. And so she revised the facts they'd gleaned and finally, around three a.m., she started looking into the Ogaden. (Thank you, Wikipedia.)

Then she sat back, closed her eyes and dreamed, picturing an arid area where the local population were largely nomadic and where oil – liquid gold – had been found as well as rare earth elements, necessary components found in mobile phones, computers, electric cars, flat screens, practically everything. And so the greedy world would fight over it and trample over the native population.

It was obvious why the Ogaden had become desirable and an area of conflict between Ethiopia and Somalia, who both claimed ownership, with different objectives, however. The Somalis were anxious for the region not to be developed while Ethiopia needed the money. So the Chinese had stepped in, financing exploration projects. There had been skirmishes, most notably in 1988 and 2007.

It didn't take a huge leap of imagination to picture mercenaries being hired to protect the area from the Ogaden National Liberation Front.

Had Joseph Holden been one of those mercenaries?

If so, what were Abdi Daud and his sister's connection?

Who was the criminal here? The easy answer was Abdi Daud. But why would he risk coming here, holding one of those mercenaries hostage and threatening him with a gun years later? Where was the connection? What was he hoping to achieve by coming here? The big question was always the same: how had this situation arisen? Not by chance. She'd worked out how they'd tracked Joseph down. The Qolxad had been advertised to attract attention worldwide. And it had. But one of the people who'd seen the auction catalogue had been either Daud or his half-sister. And that had brought them over four thousand miles to here. Clarice first, to check out the source of the dagger. And she'd done well, tracking down both the antiques dealer who'd entered the item in the saleroom and Pargeter's source, Joseph Holden, original owner of the dagger, an elderly man who had, for fifteen years, successfully hidden himself away in a remote house in the Staffordshire countryside. Her patch.

Daud had enrolled on Robbie's course partly to familiarize himself with the area, perhaps driving out here. And that had resulted in his brush with her.

More and more she wondered about Joseph and the sources of his collection of worldwide artefacts. Instead of seeing them as treasured acquisitions, she now saw them as loot. Plunder. The spoils of war acquired not always through bargaining but the result of violent crimes. War treasure.

So what was special about this particular piece? Yes, it was valuable, but she didn't feel this was a chase driven purely by riches. Revenge? She searched again and realized. A Qolxad, particularly one with a carved rhino horn handle, was a status symbol. She searched through the saleroom's archived catalogues and found the piece, staring at it. To her it looked quite ugly. Not only because a beautiful animal had died for it. But now it also represented conflict, violence, murder because it would have belonged to a Somali chief who would have died – and probably had – rather than sell it or hand it over to a band of soldiers. The auction house had catalogued it as possibly belonging to a clan chief. Would a clan chief have given up such a valuable and symbolic item? As Robbie had said, not voluntarily.

Were Daud and Clarice here to extract vengeance rather than Robbie's suggestion of seeking a public platform?

She'd hoped for a peaceful end to the siege – her first, and hopefully her last. The thought of having to go in sickened her for a moment, then she pulled herself together. If they were going to storm Cloud Mansion, she needed a detailed plan of the layout. And there was only one free person who might be able to supply it.

It was too early to call on Doreen Caputo now, but she had it marked as her first task of the day.

She should have slept, but her mind continued to whirr, preparing for what she now feared was inevitable.

If Joseph died either before or during a raid, she would feel she'd failed. The drama of an armed raid could increase the risk of a health crisis, plus there was the danger of being caught in the crossfire. Robbie had warned them repeatedly that barging in was messy, unpredictable and dangerous, occasionally leading to the death of the hostage through 'friendly fire'. A misnomer if ever there was one. To minimize the unknown, they needed that plan. Even then, however well they planned, there was an inevitable loss of control. And Daud already had a gun pointed at Joseph Holden's head. Daud was smart and prepared, no fool but an intelligent adversary who'd learned about hostage situations, enrolling himself on Robbie Callaghan's course so he knew the same facts and advice that she did. It felt as though he stood behind her, peering over her shoulder. He saw what she saw, the same pitfalls, the same advice, the same knowledge.

Negotiate, Robbie had emphasized right through the four days. *Negotiate, negotiate, negotiate. Listen rather than talk, use every vocal weapon you have and subtly manoeuvre yourself into a position of power. They want to live.*

Did he? And that was where she hit the unknown. Was Daud's desire for vengeance stronger than his instinct to survive? Something was driving him, and she knew there was a connection to his origins. But was there something more? Something even deeper? Even nastier? And what about Clarice? Did he value her life? Was she a victim, willing to sacrifice herself for this vengeance? Or was there a point beyond which she wouldn't go? Was she possibly a weak link?

She felt chilled. Of all the scenarios Robbie had discussed, one had stood out. His one – big – failure. *The most difficult to deal with,* he'd said, his face tense with the memory, *is the hostage taker who doesn't care whether he lives or dies, the risk taker with nothing to lose – not even his life.*

That had led to a discussion about suicide by the law.

Was that part of Daud's plan?

FORTY

Tuesday 17 September, 8 a.m.

She rang Robbie as early as she dared and poured out all her thoughts and misgivings.

He listened without comment until she paused for breath. 'I see,' he said. 'So what do you propose to do?'

She continued with her plan.

'OK,' he said finally. 'Well, you know how much I regret poor outcomes. If I were you, Joanna, I would confront him with the knowledge you've gained.'

'I thought you advised against that.'

'Normally, but Professor Daud has planned this down to the last detail. He's been planning this for almost a year – ever since the dagger came on the market and attracted such interest. Clarice has been here . . .'

'Since just before Christmas.'

'Exactly. Doing the groundwork, locating the seller of the dagger.'

She shared her instinct that there was some deeper dimension to this. And, as before, he listened.

'You may well be right, but it doesn't make any difference to your management.' He paused, thinking. 'Play it by ear. Trust your instincts. Had Professor Daud not insisted he deal only with you, I would have stepped in by now.'

'Why?' she asked curiously. 'Why me? Because I'm a rookie in this? Or is it simply because Mr Holden lives on my patch.'

'Pro-bab-ly' – Robbie dragged the word out – 'a bit of both. You were on the course so your level of expertise would match his, and you are local.' He paused. 'It's even possible it's because you're a woman.'

'Really?'

'I'm just putting that out there.'

'Robbie,' she said glumly, 'I have a bad feeling about this.'

'Then get on with your homework,' he said briskly. 'Those boys can't go storming into Cloud Mansion without at least a rudimentary floor plan. And, Joanna, stop trying to make moral judgements. That isn't your prerogative or your responsibility. There will be enough post-mortems in the future. You can depend on that –you won't be short of finger pointing. Focus on the advice I've given. Trust your instincts. Involve your colleagues. You have a good team.'

'How do you know?'

'I know,' he said smugly. 'Now get to work.'

8.45 a.m.

She gave Chief Superintendent Gabriel Rush an update on last night's telephone call and the data she'd gleaned about the background to the siege, as well as filling him in on the content of the conversation she'd just had with Robbie Callaghan.

He listened without comment then asked her for her plan.

She plunged in. 'I'm going to try and talk to Abdi Daud, but we'll be preparing for entry into Cloud Mansion.'

'Oh.' Even in that one syllable, she heard disapproval and hesitation. She'd always thought CS Rush might be humourless, but he was at least fair. She'd always assumed he'd watch her back. But this felt like a falling away of support.

She tried to convince him. 'Sir,' she said, 'I believe there's now too much risk to Mr Holden's life. He could die of a heart attack or something through sheer stress. I'm not even sure Daud would alert us.'

'Mmm.'

'Daud might even make an example of him.'

'You mean . . . put something online?'

'It's a possibility. He might be a professor, but his origins are in a tribal area, and the past conflict runs deep.' She remembered Robbie Callaghan's words as well as her own conclusion. 'He's stewed over this for some time, wondering where Mr Holden has hidden himself. And now he's found him. He's been planning this whole event for at least a year.'

CS Rush made no comment, so she carried on. 'There's something else.'

'Go on.' His tone was still terse, discouraging.

'Clarice is here illegally, but her brother has come announced. He's made no attempt to cover his tracks or hide his identity. He wants to go public. But I still don't know exactly with what.'

Silence on the other end.

'Sir,' she appealed.

'So what's your schedule?'

'Talk to him, get a plan of the house, brief the armed response officers. Prepare to go in.'

'When do you anticipate . . .?'

'Either tomorrow or very early Thursday.'

Rush was silent for a moment, absorbing her words, perhaps chewing them over in his mind. And then he said, very quietly, 'So be it.'

It was as good an endorsement as she was likely to get.

FORTY-ONE

10 a.m.

But however much Chief Superintendent Gabriel Rush assured her that the right outcome was the most important fact, she felt she was, somehow, mishandling the situation. That there was another way she could draw this siege to a close. The trouble was she couldn't find it. That silver bullet. She wished it was over. Being a puppet with Daud pulling the strings was horrible. This whole situation was dragging out when she'd hoped for an early resolution. Instead, she was being forced to wait.

At ten o'clock, her phone rang again.

'Professor Daud.'

'You sound tired.'

She let the comment slide over her. 'How's Mr Holden?'

'He's tired too.'

'And your sister? Sorry, half-sister. Is she tired?'

'No. She's fine.'

She waited before making an appeal she already knew would prove a waste of time. 'Professor Daud, please let Joseph and Clarice go. Whatever it is you hope to gain from keeping them both hostage, it won't work.'

His voice broke in, angry. 'Clarice is not a hostage. She simply prepared the way.'

He didn't expand, so she followed up with, 'Does she know what you intend to do?'

'She knows . . . enough.'

'How can you do that to her?'

'Do what?'

'Put her in danger.'

Silence. She knew she'd just given something away.

She took a deep breath and appealed to him. 'We want an end to this.'

'I'm sure you do. But . . .' He let the sentence trail away.

'I know there's—'

She didn't get to finish the sentence. He cut her short with fury – the first hot, real, uncontrolled anger she'd heard. 'You know nothing.'

She kept her voice low. 'I think I know more than you think.'

That stopped him in his tracks. 'I wonder.'

She pressed home her advantage. 'What is it you want out of this? For an elderly man to pay for an old sin?'

'Old sin?' He used the words delicately.

She'd gone as far as she dared – for now.

And so she dropped back into neutral. 'Is there anything you need?'

Daud laughed. A loud, mocking laugh as though he knew she was running out of ideas. 'No. I will let you know if we want something.'

The spectre of an assault posted online haunted her. She didn't want those ugly images of public beheadings, beatings, stonings to be connected with her. She appealed one last time. 'Please don't harm him. If there are old sins unpunished, let the law, our law, deal with him.'

'Your law?'

She heard the cynicism in his voice and didn't repeat the words.

'Old sins unpunished?' He'd picked up on the phrase and sounded interested. 'Why do you say that?'

She sighed. 'Because the origins of this siege lie somewhere long ago and far away.'

'Close,' he said. 'You're starting to impress me.'

She'd been about to follow on with a platitude, assure him that the law could and would deal with it, but she realized it would be futile. She couldn't guarantee it, and he would know that.

Which he proved with his next sentence. 'I don't believe the British legal system is in the slightest bit interested in a crime hard to prove, which happened in a place they think of as deepest, darkest Africa.'

'Crime?'

'War crime, to be exact.'

'That would be dealt with by an international court,' she said tentatively. This was outside her remit, as Daud would already know.

His voice was soft, almost kind as he responded. 'I hear you, Inspector Piercy, but you realize, as do I, that your powers and jurisdiction are very limited.'

The silence grew dense until Daud made a request of his own. 'You will be remaining on this case, Inspector Piercy?'

'I will,' she promised. 'I'll be available twenty-four/seven on this number. Until . . .' She left that one hanging in the air. She'd meant it as a threat, but it didn't sound like one.

As the call ended, she remembered Matthew's fear, recognizing it mirrored inside herself. Was part of Daud's intention to stream her own fate, her empty promises, together with footage from the armed officers' body cameras?

Mike was staring through the window in the direction of the track which sloped steeply towards the lake. He seemed lost in thought. Then he turned and grinned at her.

'You all right there, Jo?'

She sat beside him on a hard wooden bench, following his gaze down towards the lake's edge. Today it was quiet, the surface almost mirror-calm, the sun almost shining. She wondered what Luca Caputo thought as he stared out over the water. What moved through his mind as he looked at the same scene, day after day, the only difference wrought by the weather on the water's surface.

As they looked out, something in the trees shifted.

For a moment, she wasn't sure who or what it was until one of the armed response officers came striding towards them. She realized then how effective their camouflage wear was.

She heard the front door open and close, voices in the next-door room.

It was time to discuss their plan.

FORTY-TWO

10.20 a.m.

She outlined her thoughts to Sergeant Zak Livingstone who was leading the armed response, and he listened intently.

'OK,' he said slowly. 'You get us a plan and we'll be action ready.' He accompanied the assurance with a friendly grin as though he was heading for scout camp or some other schoolboy activity.

She felt she had to hold him back. 'I don't want to be doing this,' she said.

'Yeah, I know.' He didn't lose his air of excitement. 'But you know the drill. If it looks as though the hostage's life is in danger, we have no option. It's the only way – ma'am.'

Joanna hated being called ma'am, but it would seem churlish to remind the eager young officer of that. She was aware he would be risking his own life as well as the lives of his team.

'I'm going to try and learn the layout of Cloud Mansion through the neighbour who seems to have been inside.'

'You want me to come with you?'

She almost laughed. Kevlar bulletproof jackets were bulky. Add to that the camouflage uniform and big boots looked – military-looking and threatening – on top of his face make-up . . . If Doreen Caputo had been alarmed by two conventionally dressed officers turning up at her doorstep, she could imagine her response to Zak Livingstone in full combat gear.

He nodded and left.

'So,' Joanna said. 'Back to The Lake House.'

Mike stood up smartly, but she put a hand on his shoulder. 'I'll take Lilian,' she said.

Midday

On the way down, they passed two officers who'd prepared a stinger across the track just before it met the road. 'Just a precaution,' they said, even though Cloud Mansion could only be accessed from this approach by a four-wheel drive or a Land Rover.

As they walked, Joanna outlined the purpose of the visit. It didn't take much imagination to realize that, if they resorted to storming the hostage house, a detailed plan of the layout would prove vital.

Lilian, smart in her neat uniform, hair cut so short it showed the shape of her head, listened intently, her eyes focussed on Joanna.

'I hear our hostage taker is Somali.' She looked puzzled. 'How did he end up here?'

Joanna gave her a sanitized, edited version. 'We believe that this is rooted somewhere back in Professor Daud's country. We're also assuming that Joseph Holden, the hostage, had some connection with Somalia, in particular the Ogaden region, possibly as a merce-nary, possibly for a Chinese mineral exploration company.'

Lilian looked shocked. 'Wow,' she said, following that with, 'Somalia is such a troubled country. There's been so much violence and corruption there.' She gave a wicked grin. 'Gives Africa a ba-a-d name.'

No one could argue with that point of view.

Lilian's long-legged walk was quicker than Joanna's; she had to step out smartly to keep up.

'Tell me more about this Mr Abdi Daud.'

'He's a professor at Mogadishu University.'

Lilian turned to face her. 'And he comes here to keep an old man hostage. It must be some backstory?'

'Yeah. An educated man with status in his own country who doesn't have a criminal record, stirring up something over here that's—'

Lilian aimed a sharp glance at Joanna. 'It's good to hear you say that. You see him as a professor – not as someone who's come over here just to cause trouble.'

'I'm not sure I follow you.'

'OK.' Lilian held her hand up. 'Even in the so-called colour-blind police force, colleagues note my skin colour first, hear my accent second. Then I'm dangled as a lucky charm, a talisman. Look at how I got the job. Look at how I used the race card with Chief Superintendent Gabriel Rush. Then watch how people treat folk with different-coloured skin.'

Joanna was silent. But Lilian hadn't finished, and after a pause she continued, her voice soft now. 'I don't want special treatment. I don't want to be patronized, for the odds to be tilted in my favour. I want a level playing field. To be treated as any other British person. Not singled out because of my skin colour.' She laughed mischievously. 'Although it can be useful and, as I said before, I can occasionally use it to my advantage.'

They'd reached The Lake House, but Lilian put a hand up to stop Joanna knocking. 'Just watch how this lady treats me,' she said with a knowing look. Then she raised her hand.

Maybe Stevie Wonder was growing accustomed to visitors. He sniffed around Lilian, wagged his tail at Joanna and was quiet after just a few short barks. Doreen looked worried. She glanced from one to the other, biting her lip before she led them inside.

As before, Luca was sitting in a chair, staring out over the lake, his face expressionless. His wife had been shaving him using a soapy flannel and razor, which were laid out on a table to his side, together with a plastic bowl of water. She looked flustered at the visit but kept her manners, greeting them but with a modicum of curiosity.

'Is Joseph safe yet?'

'Not yet.' Joanna realized they owed Joseph's neighbour honesty at the least. After all, she had been the one who'd first raised the alarm.

'Everything is just as it was, Mrs Caputo. I'm afraid Joseph is still being held hostage. We know he's . . .' She paused, omitting the word 'safe'. It would have seemed like a mockery. Joseph Holden was anything but safe. They weren't sure what his crime had been. And as for Clarice, she might have been the one to locate the owner of the dagger, but they had no guarantee of her safety.

Doreen's shoulders sagged while her husband simply watched the surface of the water, perhaps reliving his fishing days, hauling in a catch of sardines. His eyes rested curiously for a moment on Constable Lilian Tadesse and then returned to the water.

'Oh dear.' Doreen shook her head. 'Poor Joseph.' Then she looked across at each of them in turn, her eyes sharply perceptive. 'So did you come here to tell me that?'

'No.' Joanna shook her head and leaned forward. 'We think you might be able to help us.'

'How?' Doreen was startled.

'How well do you know the layout of Cloud Mansion?'

'I've only been in a couple of times since he's been there.'

Joanna picked up on the one significant word. 'Since?'

'Well.' She finally came out with her confession. 'The thing is' – expecting judgement, her eyes flicked from Joanna to Lilian and back again – 'before – when it was up for sale – before it was sold – Luca and I did take a look around.' She held her hand up. 'It was all above board. The estate agent took us round.' Again, honesty forced the true version. 'Or at least he gave us the key. We weren't thinking of buying it,' she added hastily. Her face flushed rose-pink as she admitted with a smile, 'I suppose it was just neighbourly nosiness.'

'Neighbourly nosiness,' Lilian repeated and laughed one of her loud, open-mouthed chuckles.

Doreen looked affronted.

'So . . .?'

Doreen stood up, crossed the room, pulled out a drawer in a cabinet and took out a notepad and pencil. Then she sat down again and started to draw.

'Behind the front door . . .' Her brow wrinkled as she pictured the layout. 'On the right, there's a big square room. Joseph doesn't use it much. He hardly ever goes in there, he told me. He spends most of his time in the study, which is to the left of the front door. That's the room with those long windows that overlook the track that leads up from the lake.' She paused and sketched the rooms in as rudimentary pen lines, labelling each room like a Cluedo board.

'Those long windows,' Joanna said. 'Do they open?' She was covering escape routes.

'Oh yes. In the nice weather, Joseph has them wide open. He loves the fresh air.'

That brought her back to the moment. 'He must hate being . . . a prisoner.'

They allowed her a moment's reflection before Joanna asked her next question.

'We're assuming that Joseph is being held in the study as the curtains have remained closed since the start of the siege.'

'He lives in that room. Sits at his desk most of the day.'

'Is there a' – Joanna wasn't sure how to put this – 'fairly solid chair at the desk?'

Doreen laughed. 'Yeah,' she said. 'Big heavy ugly thing.' She chuckled again. 'He's so proud of it. Told me once it's more than four hundred years old. As if anyone cares.'

Joanna didn't join in the mirth. She was picturing the hostage tethered to the chair. Whatever his past, she thought, fury rising up inside her, this wasn't the way.

'Anything else?'

'There's a cloakroom at the back of the hall. You know – just a sink and a toilet.'

'Is there a window there?' Lilian had asked the question politely.

Doreen flashed a smile at her. 'Yes,' she said, 'there is.'

'How big is the window?'

Doreen was quick to pick up her meaning. 'Not big enough for a man to climb through.'

They were all silent at this.

'The kitchen?'

'That's at the back of the house.'

'Is there a back door?'

'Yes. The back door leads from the kitchen into the yard where he keeps his van and where I spotted the other car. There's a turning point before the track leads up to the gates and the Horton Road.'

'The gates,' Joanna said. 'Are they always left open?'

'Yes.' Doreen thought for a moment. 'They're all rusted up. I don't know if they would even close. I've never seen them closed.' She turned to the practical. 'I expect it would be too much trouble for Joseph to close them after him. It's quite steep there. And then he'd have to open them again when he turned in from the Horton Road. The road is narrow there, and there's a nasty bend. It's safer to leave them open.'

Joanna nodded. It made sense.

'Kitchen windows?'

'Yes, but I've never seen them open. If he wants air, he tends to prop the door open rather than open the windows.'

Again, she thought for a moment. 'They're quite high up. He'd have to climb on to the work surface to open and close them. Probably safer to just use the door.'

'Anything else on the ground floor?'

'There's a sort of lean-to on the side. I think Joseph has his washing machine and stuff out there. A sort of cloakroom. You know.' Doreen gave a rare smile. 'Coats, wellies, that sort of stuff, but it isn't connected to the house.'

'It has a glass ceiling?'

'Yes.'

They'd flown a drone over Cloud Mansion a couple of times, taken aerial photographs and seen it. And now they had a plan of the interior. Joanna studied Doreen's diagram.

'Is this helping? I'd like to think I had.'

'Yes.' Lilian and Joanna responded in unison, both officers obviously realizing Mrs Caputo needed that vital encouragement. 'Anything else on the ground floor?'

The encouragement worked. 'From the centre of the hall there's a big staircase up to the first floor,' she added eagerly, penning in some vertical lines as representation.

'Thank you. So . . .? On the first floor?'

'Three bedrooms, a bathroom and a sort of boxroom. Too tiny for a bed. The bedrooms are really big.'

'I don't suppose you know which room Joseph sleeps in?'

Doreen looked thoughtful. 'The curtains are always drawn in the bedroom at the back of the house,' she said slowly. 'I think he probably sleeps there.'

They were all silent now. Joanna was realizing how difficult was the task that lay ahead. Knowing the layout of the house was one thing. Knowing exactly where Joseph was being held, how close to Daud's pistol, covering potential access was another. And doing that while trying to anticipate Daud's plans was something else entirely.

'Is there anything else that might help us?'

Doreen shook her head. 'Not that I can think of. I'm so sorry. I wish I could do or say something more to help.'

'You've already helped us,' Lilian said. 'Thank you.'

Doreen nodded, but she didn't look convinced. They were preparing to go when her husband seemed to come to life. His hand began to shake, and he rocked in his chair, bubbling sounds coming from his mouth.

Doreen looked across at him, concerned, then kneeled by his side. 'Luca?'

Her husband's hand shook even more. He was trying to speak, obviously frustrated.

And then Doreen's eyes widened. 'Of course,' she said. 'Of course.' She patted her husband's hand. 'The cellar,' she said. 'There's a coal cellar. You see, when they used to deliver the coal, they'd put it in a cellar. There's a manhole in the yard just beyond where the cars are parked.'

That sounded promising. Joanna felt her pulse quicken. 'Where does the cellar come out?'

'In the kitchen. There's some steps down from a hatch into the cellar. The estate agent told us about it, but we didn't go down there.'

'Whereabouts does it come up in the kitchen?'

'In the middle. We saw the hatch, didn't we, Luca? Probably comes up underneath his kitchen table. I wonder if it's still used,' she mused, obviously not realizing the significance of the information she'd just handed them.

Her mind was heading along a different angle. 'Joseph probably doesn't use it anymore. It's possible he doesn't even know it's there. He had an oil-fired Aga put in not long after he moved there. He doesn't have open fires. He's got a couple of electric fires, but he said to me . . .' Recalling this was making her upset. She swallowed. 'He said to me that he was used to hot climates. Couldn't stand the cold so he needed a really efficient central heating system.'

Lilian and Joanna exchanged glances, acknowledging this new and unexpected knowledge could prove a game changer. A hidden access. Joanna wondered whether Clarice was aware of the cellar's existence.

They both stood up.

'Thank you so much,' Joanna said. 'We are really grateful for your help.' She would have added that, if Joseph was released unharmed, it would be partly, at least, due to her help. But that would have involved her in the converse too, which would also have her bearing some of the guilt.

So instead, she apologized. 'Sorry it's taking so long. But these things can't be hurried, you know.' She accompanied that with a wide smile to both Mr and Mrs Caputo, and she and Lilian prepared to leave.

Which was when Joanna's phone went off.

FORTY-THREE

12.45 p.m.

She answered it as soon as she was outside. She didn't want Doreen to hear any of this.

'Professor Daud.'

'Inspector.' He followed that up with, 'Happy with your recce?'

As before, she felt spooked, wondering how he seemed to have this almost supernatural knowledge of her whereabouts. But she managed to respond calmly. 'I would be happier if you would let both your hostages go.'

'You still make the assumption that Mr Holden and Clarice are *both* my hostages?' He hadn't been able to keep the surprise out of his voice.

'I'm giving her the benefit of the doubt.'

'Ah.' She sensed he was smiling. 'Of course. In your so civilized country' – his voice was rich with sarcasm – 'one is considered innocent until proved guilty. And so you continue to make a presumption of Clarice's innocence even though you know that as well as being my half-sister, she is here *illegally*.' He'd put heavy emphasis on the word.

'That's the law.' She made her tone stolid, uncompromising, unimaginative.

Which took Daud aback, as though he hadn't expected that from her. He'd thought she would engage in an argument. He paused, and she sensed he was considering what to say next.

Finally he spoke. 'I will give you a heads-up, Inspector.'

She resisted a sarcastic response of thanks.

'I will tell you what I intend. I shall let Mr Holden sleep tonight after a night or two in the chair. But he needs to be prepared and well rested, ready for tomorrow.'

Tomorrow?

'I need to have' – he hesitated – 'a conversation with Mr Holden.'

Joanna felt a moment of panic. Daud was bringing things to a head. Time was running out. At the same time, she was seized with curiosity – how she would love to eavesdrop on that conversation.

Daud continued smoothly. 'Depending on his responses, I can either shoot him or I can turn him in.' He sniggered, sounding unbalanced, quite unlike his previous self. 'At the same time, I could turn myself in – or not.'

He was tantalizing her, dangling in front of her the thing he knew she must want more than anything. She felt a chill and rubbed the back of her neck to try and fight it. At least rise above it. Detach. She'd hoped so very hard that it wouldn't come to this, and now that Daud had spelled it out, she was frozen. She couldn't find the right response.

'Why don't you let Mr Holden go?' It sounded lame, and she'd deliberately left out mention of Clarice.

His response was equally polite, his equilibrium restored. 'That is not possible, I'm afraid.' The polite apology made the situation worse. 'That would make my mission pointless.'

'So what *is* the point?'

Daud laughed. 'Not yet, Inspector. Not yet.' He paused. 'I want him to answer some questions. I also want to give him some answers. Some facts.'

By her side, Lilian Tadesse was watching, her expression curious.

Daud's voice came back, soft and slightly suggestive. 'So until then, goodbye, Inspector.'

Something at the back of her mind responded. She knew he was smiling. And then, quite suddenly, she could *see* him smiling. She'd arrived late to the lecture that day because the traffic into Birmingham had been extra heavy and so she'd tried to creep in, unseen, to the back of the lecture theatre.

Robbie had been showing slides of armed personnel storming a building, warning his students of the dangers. The students' focus had been on the front of the lecture theatre, absorbed in the drama; a few had been taking notes. One person had turned and locked eyes with her. He'd been sitting in the row directly in front, and as she'd slid into her seat, he'd turned and given her a wide grin, a knowing smile, as though he shared her secret.

She didn't know him and hadn't noticed him amongst the other students. So she'd stared back, embarrassed at her late arrival, resentful at the implied intimacy. He'd stared at her for a further minute as though committing her features to memory. He was young, younger than her, maybe mid-thirties. Impossibly handsome with neatly trimmed black hair, large, dark eyes, flashing white teeth, a Mediterranean complexion. Possibly Moroccan? The lecture theatre had been full, the lights dimmed for the presentation, and she couldn't remember anything else about him. When the lecture had finished, she'd joined the attendees queuing for coffee and hadn't seen him again.

The incident had been quickly forgotten. But now she pieced the two images together – stitching the passport photo back into her memory.

He'd known her.

FORTY-FOUR

1.15 p.m.

They returned to the boat house, Lilian wisely not commenting on the recent telephone conversation. Respecting Joanna's silence, she left her to her thoughts, though she glanced at her often and with curiosity. As they reached the door, Joanna looked straight at her. 'Thank you,' she said. 'I needed that time to think.'

Lilian shook the comment off with a casual, 'Yeah.'

Joanna's thoughts had been troubling. She was beginning to realize something she should have understood days ago. That the noose around Joseph, Abdi and Clarice was encircling her too.

The reason why might be unclear, but he'd expressed clear intent to murder Joseph Holden.

Which meant they had no option but to go in.

So her first action was to set up a meeting between herself and Sergeant Zak Livingstone, who took the news calmly, his forehead wrinkling as he began to lay his plans.

She put the drawing and notes of Cloud Mansion on the desk, watched Zak's face as he scrutinized it. He lit up when she told him about the coal cellar.

'Nice,' he said, grinning. 'So we have three potential points of entry. Front door, back door and coal cellar.'

'The hatches haven't been used for years,' she reminded him.

'They may have been nailed shut. But there is one other possibility.'

She told him then about the tall windows in the study. 'And they have been used recently.'

He nodded.

She couldn't help but ask, 'What about Clarice?'

'We'll treat her as a suspect.'

Seeing Joanna's troubled expression, he added, 'We have no option. She's certainly part of this though her exact role isn't quite defined. But if she gets caught in the crossfire, it's because she's there and she's stayed there.'

She nodded then described Daud's recent phone call about the 'conversation'. 'Honestly,' she said, 'he could have been describing any old Q&A session.'

Zak looked pensive, and she could tell his mind was already jumping ahead to the possible outcomes of their actions, trying to cover all priorities and eventualities. She could read only part of his mind. Locate hostage. Neutralize suspects. She studied his face, tense but calm. Caution, she suspected, would be his middle name. That was how he and his team would survive not only the drama but the scrutiny which would follow by folk sitting in judgement in a boardroom somewhere; coffee, mineral water and biscuits to hand, safe and far away from any danger.

But then Zak lowered his eyes, as though he didn't want her to read his thoughts. He moved over to the whiteboard and began sketching the ground floor of the house, an asterisk marking the position of the desk and chair in relation to the windows.

His team had filed in and were now engrossed in their leader's instructions. Some of them were frowning as they absorbed the challenges of the task ahead. Zak had left the details of the cellar until last, which was when finally she saw some of the officers' eyes light up.

'It might be a challenge,' he said before reiterating Joanna's comment. 'We don't know whether the hatch in the kitchen will have been screwed down at some point so it might not work as a point of entry.'

There were nods but few smiles until Zak himself smiled. The rest of the team had read the light of excitement in his eyes and the way he'd nibbled at his lower lip to suppress a smile and hold back premature optimism. Joanna watched from the back of the room, recognizing the professionalism of the armed response officers and the determination to do their best.

Next, Zak ran through some drone footage which showed the exterior and approach points of the house, marking out the position of Joseph Holden's van and the intruder's car, pointing out the probable position of the hatch which led through the coal cellar into the kitchen. He spent some time over the other points of entry: the back door, the stout front door and finally the tall sash windows into the study where they presumed their hostage was being held.

He didn't try to make the task any less hard than it would be. And his team listened. A few of them posed questions, largely about the structure of the two doors as well as checking on the weapons they knew Daud was carrying. Which was where Zak's expression became concerned.

'OK, guys,' he said, ignoring the fact that two of his team were women, 'he's told us he has a Glock. That may be true or not. He may have more weaponry, explosives. We can't be sure.' There were a few nods as well as a few worried eyes and deep frowns.

Zak turned next to the upstairs plans as described by Doreen Caputo.

'Do we know which bedroom Mr Holden is using?'

Zak turned towards Joanna, deflecting the question. All eyes moved towards her, but she shook her head. 'She thinks he slept at the back.'

Zak took over again. 'But we've noticed since the beginning of the siege the lights have gone on in the front bedroom, so we're assuming that's where he's been sleeping.' Again, his face became serious. 'On the nights when he does get to sleep in a bed rather than being tethered to the chair.'

Joanna wanted to add something about Daud's wiliness, a cautionary note that this could be a trick, a deflecting mechanism, but Zak did the job for her.

'Our hostage taker,' he said gently, 'is an intelligent man with a very deep and well-planned purpose here. He didn't just chance to wander into Staffordshire, to Rudyard Lake and Cloud Mansion. This is all part of a greater plan. Keep that in mind.'

She realized she was waiting, along with the roomful of officers, for Zak to tell them what this greater plan was. But he was looking at her for a cue, and she realized they were nearly there. The room was hushed now. Then she had a strangely inappropriate rogue thought. Today was Tuesday. If they entered Cloud Mansion tomorrow, just before dawn, which was the usual appointed hour, she would have enough time to make her reports and still be free to look after Jakob while Matthew attended Eloise Levin's graduation ceremony.

She smothered the image and looked at Zak, who was waiting for her.

'I'm in Daud's hands,' she pointed out. 'He either rings or he doesn't ring. I can't ever predict it.'

Zak nodded, his frown deepening. 'Any further thoughts, Joanna?'

She was frowning now. 'I'm just thinking about this . . . conversation he said he needs to have with Mr Holden. I get the feeling that the conversation is the whole reason behind him being here.'

She tried to put it into plain English. 'I think this *conversation* is his way of drawing the siege to an end.'

To an end. She knew those words would haunt her dreams in the future.

But Sergeant Zak Livingstone had made a vital decision. 'OK,' he said, his voice smooth and controlled. 'We hold back for twenty-four hours to give this a chance to end peacefully. As there's a clear potential threat to life, we go in on Thursday morning.' He issued a final word of warning. 'And don't even think of forgetting to turn on your body cameras. Understand?'

The team nodded, their eyes focussed, their manner determined as they filed out.

10 p.m.

The night was stormy – the branches on the trees waving frantically. The first hint of autumn brought in its wake a sense of unease as the wind whipped around the house, moaning like an Irish banshee.

Inside Cloud Mansion, Abdi Daud had drawn up a chair and was sitting facing Joseph, who, sensing that they'd reached a watershed moment, looked back uneasily. If he was to be shot, this was the moment. They could both hear the storm outside, rattling the windows, trying to get in. Behind Daud, Joseph saw the curtains billow and drop, billow and drop. The catch must be open, allowing a draught to sneak through.

It gave him hope.

Inside the boat house, Zak Livingstone was huddled in the corner with a few members of his team. They were conferring on the best strategy, which officers to send where, how many to focus on the entry points. They could have been directing a battle plan for a movie, each movement, each character carefully choreographed, timed to the second. Periodically, one of them stood in front of the whiteboard to study the plans before returning to the huddle. There was much finger pointing and discussion. Joanna could hear a few objections, but on the whole, considering the risk and drama of their proposed plans, the atmosphere was quiet and controlled.

Abdi fixed his eyes on Joseph, who, tired, hungry and uncomfortable as he was, stared back fearlessly. For moments, there was silence between them. If Clarice was still around, he had no idea where.

Abdi continued to study him, searching his face for . . . something.

Joseph was about to speak when Abdi said, 'You don't know me, do you?'

'No.' Joseph frowned. But something *was* tugging at his memory. 'How old are you?'

Abdi Daud smiled. 'Thirty-six,' he said in a quiet voice. 'I was born in 1989.'

'Where?' Joseph rubbed his fingers together, felt sand between the digits, fearing the answer.

'You know where.'

He asked the question.

'Who are you?'

FORTY-FIVE

Wednesday 18 September, 12.30 a.m.

The storm passed, leaving the night eerily quiet. The stillness inside the boat house was intense as the team took advantage of a few more hours' sleep. They had twenty-four hours' grace, but that only added to the tension. Joanna wandered outside, wanting to escape, wishing it wasn't coming to this. She'd hoped Daud would put down his gun, raise his arms and come out, but the more she thought about it, the more she realized that had been a vain hope from the start.

Korpanski was hanging around, watching her. She heard him follow her outside, but recognizing the still slightly uneven step, she didn't need to turn around.

'You should go home,' she said. 'Fran will be worried.'

He shook his head. 'I've texted her,' he said, sounding similarly tense. 'She didn't like it but . . .' He couldn't find the words. 'She's OK. She understands.'

'Really?'

He tried to laugh, but it sounded dry and unconvincing. 'Well, no, actually.' He switched focus. 'You spoken to Matthew?'

She shook her head. 'I don't know what to say,' she confessed. 'But knowing him, he'll sense that things are hotting up. If I try to put his mind at rest, it'll make him worse. And it won't help me.'

'Yeah.'

She sat on a staddle stone. 'I never was up to this, Mike,' she said.

'I get that.' His tone was terse.

She turned to face him then. 'I don't even know who or why we're protecting this guy. Daud is no fool. In fact, I suspect that if I had to make a moral judgement, I'd come down on his side.'

'What?'

She was staring into his face. 'He's come here for some purpose. I know the way he's done it isn't our way, but I think when we understand the entire story, our condemnation will be for Joseph Holden.'

Korpanski was silent, watching her without comment.

'He's here for justice, and that's what he'll demand from us.'

'Revenge? For a past crime?'

'Yeah. I think Daud will try to explain it all to us. Maybe even try to get us on his side.'

In the old days, Korpanski would have put his hand on her shoulder, tried to buck her up with one of his store of platitudes, a *Hey*, or a *Come on, Jo*, but since his accident, something in their relationship had shifted. He'd lost some of the confidence which came from being an Alpha male, equal to any physical challenge.

He wasn't sure he would be able to protect her any more.

Less than half a mile away, Joseph too was searingly aware of his altered physical state. Eight days of imprisonment, sleep deprivation, hardly eating anything, drinking less, as well as the stress of the situation were all taking their toll. Constantly bracing himself against a further assault and the dizziness caused by the two pistol whips had made him nauseated, exacerbating his vulnerability while his mind wandered through parts of his past. He was so weak now Daud hardly needed to strap him in the chair. Once he could at least have put up a bit of a fight, but that was before Anno Domini had robbed him of the little strength he'd had left, further weakening his heart and wasting his limbs. Much as he tried, his mind kept slipping back into the past.

1 a.m.

They were still outside even though the night was both damp and chilly.

'Try this on for size,' Joanna said. 'When he left the army, Joseph Holden became a mercenary. The pals who visit him from time to time were a team who worked for him. And I think at some point they worked in an area known as the Ogaden, which is disputed between Ethiopia and Somalia and is unfortunately rich in minerals.'

'Unfortunately?'

'Yeah. It's one thing to be a disputed area, but being rich in minerals escalates the conflict beyond animal herders' skirmishes. It attracts big money. There's been Chinese exploration there, and I think they might have felt their interests needed protection. Every now and again there's a skirmish and people killed. The last one happened around 2007, but there was also a significant one in 1988.'

She continued. 'The trouble is mercenaries don't exactly have an honourable code of ethics. At a guess, atrocities were committed. I think that's why Daud is here. For revenge.'

'Have you shared this with Zak and the team?'

'He'd worked some of it out anyway, but I haven't spelled it out quite like that.'

'What was his response?'

'He said the why didn't make a lot of difference. The situation was unchanged whatever the reasons behind it; whatever the hostage's past, he was being kept prisoner, and it's their job to free him.' She kept the next thought to herself. Free him from what . . . for what? To face trial?

'So how much does Daud know that you're aware of?'

She shook her head. 'I don't know, but he's smart, intuitive. He might have guessed I'd pick up on certain aspects of the siege. Perhaps he thinks I'd understand his mindset – the foresight, understanding and intelligence behind it. He has a solid reason behind his actions, but I don't know his final intent. Maybe the success of his mission will be to shoot Joseph Holden and then have his day in court, in front of the media, to explain why. Maybe he wants a platform to describe events from the past.' She paused. 'He could film Joseph's execution, which would make it a very public murder before it's taken down. He could film a confession, but I suspect there's something even deeper that I haven't worked out yet and . . .' She turned to face him. 'It's really frustrating me. He's still a step ahead. And I think he knows I have a moral conundrum. Who should I be protecting?'

Mike's response was like a rock to lean against. 'We're in the UK, Jo,' he said. 'The crime is being committed here. He's holding an elderly man hostage, possibly his half-sister too and that's against our laws.'

She laid her head against his shoulder. 'So dependable,' she said.

It was a compliment.

FORTY-SIX

8.30 a.m.

Despite the situation, Joseph woke refreshed in the front bedroom. For a moment, he stretched, savouring the freedom. But at the back of his mind was an instinct. Today would be the end.

In a way, it was a relief.

He heard Daud's footsteps outside the door and waited for a knock.

And when he met his captor's eyes, he read determination and a vague excitement confirmed by Daud's next words. 'Today,' he said.

'First you use the bathroom. And then I want you to dress properly. Smartly.'

Joseph took his time in the bathroom, listening to Daud fidgeting outside the door. When he returned to the bedroom, clothes were laid out. A shirt and tie; a pair of clean, pressed trousers. He glanced at Daud, questioning.

'Put them on.' His captor was unsmiling. 'Or I shoot. Maybe the knee first. And then elsewhere.' He put his face close. 'The time has come for us to talk.'

Joseph swallowed back the retort: *And I have a choice?*

But from the gleam in his eye, he knew Daud had divined it.

10 a.m.

Joanna's phone rang.

'Good morning, Inspector.'

'Professor Daud.' She'd continued to use his title in the hope that reminding him of his position would somehow civilize him.

'Joseph and I are having a necessary conversation today. He will be ready to make a statement at seven o'clock tomorrow morning. He will have something to tell you.'

'Tomorrow?' Was he playing with her? Had he realized they'd been making plans to come in?

Joanna looked across at Zak Livingstone, who was watching her. Slowly, reluctantly, he nodded and gave a thumbs up.

'OK, Professor.' She had a question of her own. 'How will Mr Holden be making this statement?'

'I have an iPhone. You will be able to watch.'

She stiffened. Something else they hadn't known. He must have kept it switched off since that first day.

11.15 a.m.

Joseph had been served bacon and eggs. It felt like a condemned man's last breakfast, and it tasted like sawdust – or sand.

When he'd eaten as much as he could, Daud strapped him in the chair, the zip ties tighter than usual. Then he drew up a chair for himself and sat, for a moment, studying his prisoner.

'It is time,' he said and rested the gun on his lap. He leaned back, his face relaxed. 'Let me tell you a story, Mr Holden.'

Joseph fixed his eyes on Daud and made a weak attempt at a challenge. 'Fact or fiction?'

'That is for you to decide.'

His eyes were fathomless, too dark to read. Joseph couldn't decide if they were hostile or not. Angry or not, filled with hatred or not. He waited.

'Once upon a time, in a place far, far away from this pretty area in Staffordshire, there lived' – Daud put his face next to Joseph's – 'shall we say, for the purposes of our story, a handsome chief of one of the local tribes. The tribes he belonged to roamed the area in a hot, dry place called the Ogaden.'

He'd known it.

Daud continued, his voice so soft and polite he could indeed have been telling a child an exotic goodnight tale of a prince and princess. A story with a happy ending – except Joseph already knew it was not.

'The chief was unaware that beneath his feet was treasure of immeasurable value. Heaps and heaps of minerals that were riches to the wider world. Normally riches bring happiness, don't they? But in this case, they attracted the worst of humanity. Rats, villains and criminals, as well as the rich people of the world, wanted those wonderful riches. But to do that they had to steal from underneath the feet of the people to whom those precious minerals truly belonged. The people who didn't care about the riches they trod on daily. They simply wanted their lives to continue in the way they had for hundreds if not thousands of years.'

Daud leaned back in his chair, smiling. 'Are you enjoying this story, Mr Holden?'

Joseph shook his head. His mouth was dry, and there was a strange buzzing in his ears as though the blood vessels supplying his auditory sense were trying to drown out this story and the ending he anticipated.

'The people who wished to steal and mine the area already had plenty of money. But they were greedy. And to quell the objections of the local people, they used their money to buy soldiers. The soldiers had guns and ammunition, and their job was to clear the area of the herdsmen ready for the accoutrements of exploration, the diggers and mines, the cranes and the towns to service the people who would work there.'

His eyes clouded over. 'The chief refused to move away from their cattle grounds.'

Now he stared into Joseph's face and, as before, something stirred inside him.

'Do you not recognize me?'

Joseph began, 'I left . . .'

The gun smashed into his temple.

'Try again.' The voice was coaxing, polite, soft and all the more threatening for it.

'The chief died trying to protect his people. The captain of the soldiers stole the Qolxad anyway. But worst of all . . .' Daud's voice was rising. 'Worst of all,' he repeated, 'the soldier . . . the captain raped the chief's wife.' He waited, but when Joseph made absolutely no response, he taunted him. 'The chief's wife became pregnant. Months after her violation, she gave birth to a son.'

He looked hard into Joseph's face. 'Do you not recognize me?'

Joseph tried to shake his head, but it wouldn't move.

After a pause, Daud spoke in a low voice. 'Nine hundred thousand. Not a bad return on something you stole. For what?' he continued, looking around him. 'This crumbling old mansion?'

And all Joseph could think was: *Thou fool.*

The shot shattered the silence, echoing through the trees, bouncing over the water. They all heard it – from the camouflaged officers dotted around the area, down to The Lake House where Luca Caputo sat in his usual chair facing the water, to the listeners in the boat house.

Who thought they'd been fooled by Daud. They'd left it too late.

FORTY-SEVEN

Joanna stared at Mike, appalled.

Responses around her were the same. Shocked paralysis.

Questions tumbled through Joanna's mind. Had their hesitation just cost a man his life? Would she carry this responsibility through the endless enquiries that would, inevitability, follow, as well as the one which would last for ever in her heart?

And then her phone rang.

'Daud?' No professor this time.

Silence.

He was daring her to ask the question.

But she didn't. Afterwards, she would try and convince herself that she'd kept silent as a refusal to engage. But, to herself, she could be honest. She was afraid.

It took her a few moments to speak again. 'Professor Daud?' Even to her, her voice sounded weak, frightened, apprehensive.

She tried to hang on to Korpanski's earlier words. *Jo, he's stuck up there with no hope of escape. All he has as a bargaining chip is the life of his hostage and his sister. He won't risk that.*

Zak Livingstone was watching her, his eyes hooded. No need to ask whether he'd heard it.

She tried to imagine what Robbie would do now.

Minutes ticked by. He was still there. She could hear him breathing, her own heart beating.

She asked the question. 'Is Joseph . . . alive?'

She got no response.

FORTY-EIGHT

Thursday 19 September, 5.45 a.m.

They weren't going to wait for Daud's deadline. Whether Joseph was alive or dead, the decision was made. They were going in.

Following that first call, the phone had remained silent all through Wednesday while their tension had mounted. The house stayed silent, and there had been no sign of movement.

So now preparations were being made. Zak's team had been fitted with helmets. The officers' faces were unrecognizable, darkened with camouflage paint, making their eyes look strange, unnaturally bright and owl-like, their teeth gleaming. Some were checking their weapons; others stood studying the whiteboard one last time. A few stood in contemplation, thoughtful but prepared. One officer was mouthing something, clutching a crucifix.

The darkest hour, it's said, is just before dawn, when the stillness and chill envelops the land. Birds don't sing; animals are somewhere safe for the night, and even the nocturnal creatures have headed home. It's no one's time. Yet through the woods there was movement – stealthy, slow and precise, each action measured and soundless.

Towards the house they crept and crawled on bellies, like snakes, or crouched, ape-like, making not even the mistake of a snapped twig – that traditional giveaway. Zak moved first, leading his team, while a similar task force were working their way round to the rear, two men peeling off to explore the manhole which might or might not lead into the cellar of the house and from there into the kitchen. If they were lucky. All were equipped with head torches, currently switched off, and body cameras, switched on. If events turned out badly, the record could protect them against litigation as well as either a warning or a teaching aid by lecturers such as Robbie Callaghan.

One learned as much from mistakes as successes.

Joanna had been told to keep well to the rear. *Out of the way* had been the phrase used, as though she was now viewed as a potential hindrance to the operation. Korpanski stood at her side, while a few uniformed officers, including DC Lilian Tadesse, waited at the bottom of the track, ready to guide in any emergency vehicles who might need access. An ambulance, if things turned out well.

Zak had decided to work on the assumption that Joseph was still alive. In which case where, in the house, was he? It was tempting to relegate him to a front bedroom, well out of the way. But Daud was a trickster who would anticipate any loose assumptions. And if Joseph was alive, Daud would keep him close to the firearm.

He also knew that Daud would know they were coming. So access had to be simultaneous and decisive. 'No pussy footing around,' Zak had said in his final briefing, smiling to rob the phrase of an insult. It wasn't the first time he'd spoken those words.

As they approached, Zak started to worry again whether, in one last act of defiance, Daud might have booby-trapped the house. He'd shared this worry with the men, telling them to be extra vigilant, on the lookout for stray wires.

The front door was stout and would take some battering to breach so, as they'd noticed the small crack at the bottom of the study window, they entered via three access points – the study window, the kitchen hatch and the back door – in sync.

The two who'd entered via the coal cellar found themselves in a pitch-black room that still suffocated like a coal mine, the atmosphere heavy, stale – an impenetrable black. But apart from a startled rat, it was empty. Slowly, they'd raised the hatch into the kitchen with surprising ease and found themselves underneath a rug thick with dust, which they pushed aside before climbing the steps into the kitchen, reuniting with the two who'd entered through the kitchen door. Torch in one hand, gun in the other, they flashed their lights around the room, which initially appeared empty, then they picked out a woman cowering in the corner, hands over her head in part surrender, part protection.

Steve Addison put a finger to his lips and inched forward, gun in hand, his sight trained on the girl. His colleague had her in handcuffs as fast as he could whip them out.

Steve spoke, his voice low and clear. 'Where's Joseph?'

She shook her head violently, though whether this meant she couldn't understand, wouldn't or couldn't tell, or she was telling them he was dead was unclear, and they didn't have time to inter-rogate her. The four nodded at one another, understanding mission accomplished so far by sign language.

Addison stayed with her while the other three stepped out into the hall, silent as cat burglars.

Ron Mason checked the downstairs lavatory while the others flashed their torches around the hall.

Empty.

Zak Livingstone and Art Butler had forced the study window open and climbed inside on to a soft, soundless carpet. They looked around the study, the probable scene of Joseph Holden's imprison-ment. Now empty. They flashed their torches around the room, picking out the chair Joseph had been tied to and a couple of zip ties on the floor. They scanned the walls, passing over strange objects, cabinets full of curios, weapons mounted: a sword, an old blunderbuss, a pale patch where something had been removed. The weapons gave the room the air of a torture chamber.

Zak opened the door a crack, peered through into the hall and met with the three officers. He pointed to the door opposite, and Ron nodded, forming a letter 'C' with his thumb and index finger before encircling his wrist and pointing to the kitchen. Zak acknow-ledged the gesture with a thumbs up and a nod towards the downstairs cloakroom. That drew a response from another one of the officers, who disappeared inside the second sitting room, then Zak pointed to the staircase. And so they faced the stairs, tall, wide, carpeted, weapons held in front of them.

One shallow, noiseless step at a time, they climbed.

The team reached the landing and faced five doors. All shut. No light or sound from any of them. Until . . . Zak picked up a glimmer of light from underneath one of the first doors they came to. A door into one of the bedrooms, according to the neighbour's plans.

Outside, Joanna and Mike were in a fret. Once the study curtains had been parted, they had picked out moving lights inside the house. But otherwise, there was no clue that six officers were moving stealthily through. It was silent. They stood still, feeling the chill of an autumn dawn creeping into their feet.

Inside, Zak kicked open the door and trained his gun around the room – and realized Daud was still playing tricks. The room was empty, a small light illuminating suitcases and little else. He closed the door, and they moved to the room at the back. Single bed, wardrobe, dressing table. The bed was hung with a valance. Zak shone his torch beneath it. Empty apart from a resentful spider who crawled away slowly.

Simultaneously, the others had kicked open the other doors. But it was in the last bedroom, the one at the front of the house, that they found their quarry tethered to a chair, Abdi Daud standing behind him, holding a gun against the back of his prisoner's head. It was a classic pose with a clear message.

Daud gave them a wide grin. 'I think we would call this check-mate,' he said.

FORTY-NINE

Zak motioned for his team to hang back. This was the tense moment, the fragile time when a snap decision, a wrong move or a moment's panic could result in death. He sensed Daud was calm – he didn't really care who lived and who died in the next few moments.

He glanced at the hostage. Joseph stared ahead, as though he was trying to abstract himself from the situation. It wasn't working. His whole frame was rigid, shoulders tense.

Zak moved his attention back to Daud.

And what he saw of him confirmed his earlier suspicions. Daud was here with a solid purpose. He had a design. And so he waited for him to call the shots.

He realized too that, as he'd sized Daud up, so Daud had been studying him with interest. At the same time, he'd kept the gun glued to the back of Joseph Holden's head. His grip hadn't relaxed; nor had his attention.

Daud spoke. 'Where is Inspector Piercy?'

'She's outside.'

Daud frowned. 'I thought I'd made it clear I would speak to no one but her.'

Zak nodded.

Daud risked a smile. 'I take it your bodycams are recording and not just for show?'

'They're recording.'

'You have radio contact with the inspector?'

Again, Zak nodded.

'Then invite her into the party. One of your men can open the front door.'

Zak spoke into his mouthpiece, and Ron Mason melted away.

Joanna wasn't sure whether to be pleased or terrified to be a part of this close action. Korpanski touched her shoulder. Through her jacket, she could feel his hand trembling. 'Hey, Mike,' she said. But his face told her all. Since his accident, DS Mike Korpanski had felt vulnerable, and nowhere was this more evident than here, at this moment, when she was about to enter the lion's jaws.

'I have to go,' she said. And managing a smile, she threw back, 'See you soon,' before she disappeared through the front door.

Ron Mason stood back and let her pass, indicating the stairs. 'Front bedroom,' he said and gave her a look which looked suspiciously like sympathy.

As the team had only minutes before, she climbed the staircase.

She saw the cluster of men standing by the door. They watched her skirt the landing and reach them.

Two of them looked away, reluctant to meet her eyes.

Zak Livingstone stepped back. So now she was facing Daud and his terrified hostage, who had his eyes tight shut.

She focussed on Daud. 'Hello.'

'Hello again, Joanna.'

She acknowledged the greeting with a nod and waited.

'You remember me?' he asked curiously.

'Not at first but' – she schooled her face into a smile – 'as you started reminding me more and more of Robbie's lectures, I did a bit of digging.'

Daud nodded in approval. But she noticed that his grip on the gun hadn't relaxed.

One small movement and . . .

She forced her mind away.

'Why all this?' she asked, keeping the tone of the conversation lightly curious. 'You have a life, a job, possibly even a family in Somalia. What on earth makes you focus on the past rather than the present, and why now?'

'You tell me.' His tone was equally polite and conversational.

She simply shook her head.

'Tell me something, Joanna. Do you think it wrong for a man to kill his own father?'

Whatever she might have predicted, this was unexpected. 'Sorry?'

'Let me put it this way. Is there ever any justification for a man to kill his own father?'

She looked at him aghast. 'Professor Daud,' she said, 'I have no idea what you're talking about. Are you trying to have a philosophical talk with a gun pressed against a man's head?'

Her temper was getting the better of her as she'd noticed Joseph Holden had shrunk in his seat.

Behind her, she felt Zak shift his weight from foot to foot, and she heard the sound of a gun being gripped. Behind her, she knew the five men were all armed, trained and accountable. They were on her side, but the situation felt edgy and dangerous.

'I had the feeling you'd have a bad temper,' Daud said. 'I guessed that when you arrived at the lecture late.'

But her mind had been diverted. She understood now what he'd meant.

Daud had been waiting for her to catch up while she studied him, and now she realized what had motivated him wasn't simple cruelty or greed. His vengeance held an unsuspected ingredient. A blood tie.

He tapped the top of Joseph's head with the gun. 'I told you Mr Holden has a story to tell. He knows the facts of that story. Now would be a good time.'

Joseph actually managed to swivel his head round to look into Daud's face. He seemed to be beseeching him, begging him. Had it been for his life, it would have seemed logical to Joanna and the watching officers, but it was something else. Joseph was panicking. He was frightened. But he was also ashamed.

Daud goaded his captive. 'Go on,' he said. 'Get on with it, Old Joe. Or would you like me to tell it? My way?'

Joseph looked at the floor. Joanna was tempted to prompt him, to tell him she already knew his story, but she held back. She'd read something in Daud's eyes, a need for justice. *This* then was what he wanted. A public confession recorded on the officers' video cameras. And, having held his hostage for nine days, he would get the publicity. She met Daud's eyes, and he gave her the tiniest of nods. He knew she'd understood, and she felt a rogue emotion. Understanding. Who *was* right and who was wrong? Both were wrong was the obvious answer, but one action had led to another.

Joseph started to speak, but his voice cracked. His throat was too dry.

Daud put a glass of water to his lips. It was an almost gentle gesture, but as he removed the glass, his words were anything but gentle. 'Now speak.'

FIFTY

Joseph's eyes darted around the room, resting briefly on Joanna before he quickly shifted his gaze to Zak.

'In the eighties . . .' His voice was weak, hesitant, but more ashamed than frightened, the words dragging out of him. 'Back in the eighties,' he repeated, 'I worked for a Chinese oil exploration company based in the Ogaden, a region between Ethiopia and Somalia.'

He gulped and stopped.

Daud prodded his neck with the butt of the Glock. It was a prompt containing a veiled threat. *Speak or die.*

'I was the captain of a squad of four ex-soldiers.'

Joanna took a moment to shift her focus to Daud's face. His expression intrigued her. Part fury, part hatred, but there was something else there too, something deeply buried but softer. She realized he was curious as to how Joseph would tell his story. But surely he already knew it?

Joseph lifted his head and looked at her, and she realized something else. There were officers behind her, but his eyes kept returning to her, apologizing only to her. As a woman.

Her focus switched back to Daud, whose finger, she imagined, seemed to be tightening on the trigger. She braced herself for an inevitable bloodbath. Daud's eyes were dark, too dark to read, but she sensed an icy chill behind them.

Joseph continued, his voice still wavering. 'We were paid by the Chinese to guard their facilities against some of the locals who were opposed to the development of the area. They wanted to preserve their way of life, which had been largely rural farming, its population nomadic with a few small villages.'

Daud nodded.

'One day we heard that some of the local villagers belonged to the ONLF.' He looked at the floor. 'The Ogaden National Liberation Front. They were regarded as terrorists.'

Again, Daud nodded.

'We – that is myself and my company of four – went to the village to . . . We . . .'

Joseph stopped, unable to carry on. Without warning, Daud smashed the gun down on Joseph's head, making them all wince. 'Tell the whole story, Old Joe,' he said.

'We – we attacked the village. Shot some of the men. One of my soldiers was shot in the leg. Another . . . didn't make it. We were angry. The chief tried to buy us off, but we took the stuff anyway after we'd . . .' And now it seemed he couldn't continue.

'I . . .' He replaced that with, 'The chief's wife . . .' He met Joanna's gaze then dropped his quickly, but not before she'd read the terrible shame in them. 'She was . . .'

Daud and the officers all waited, with a sense of what was to come.

'I raped her.' And now Joseph couldn't meet anyone's eyes for the judgement he was certain was to come. His shoulders were hunched, and he seemed to brace himself for either a blow or a shot.

Daud picked up the story, studying the group in the doorway, his eyes finally resting on Joanna. And now she knew why she'd been vital to this case. Not only because he'd met her briefly or even because she was a woman but also because she was a mother.

'I am the result,' Daud said, his voice a mixture of shame and puzzlement. 'Despite what had happened, my mother couldn't bear to have a termination. And out there that could have meant she'd die of an infection or haemorrhage. Somehow she grew to love me. When she told me how I had been conceived, I swore to her I would track him down and, if he was still alive, I would make him pay. She gave me all the details she had – that he had a head of straw, that he murdered her husband in front of her and stole his possessions, including the dagger, which she described to me. Because of the fact that she was carrying me, she became an outcast from her own people. She was seen as a traitor who carried the enemy's child.'

He stopped speaking for a moment, his eyes unfathomable before picking up the story. 'When the dagger appeared in a London saleroom, I recognized it and followed its trail. Clarice agreed to help me.'

Joanna was watching Joseph, who appeared dazed.

'In case you're wondering, Inspector, I sent Clarice over here to be certain. It was easy for her to collect a sample of hair. I have checked Mr Holden's DNA against mine. There is no doubt. He is the one.'

Joseph's head was bent, waiting for judgement.

Joanna broke the silence. 'So now what, Professor? You've tracked Mr Holden down, exposed his crime. Now what is it you want? Revenge for your very existence, for your mother's shame?'

'My dead mother's shame,' he corrected, his voice hard.

FIFTY-ONE

'I have a question for you.' Daud had addressed Joanna. Behind her, she felt Zak and his team's tension – quiet, controlled breaths in and out, feet and hands now ominously still. All their attention was directed towards the hostage, bound to a chair, head lowered, his slight frame braced for the inevitable, and Daud, who was controlling the events.

'Do you believe in justice?'

'I'm a police officer,' Joanna replied.

'You think the law will give me justice?'

'What's the alternative? If you shoot Mr Holden' – she was determined to give the shrunken man in the chair some dignity – 'you'll be charged with murder. Whatever the circumstances.'

Daud nodded.

Though she was horrified at the brutality of the story, she focussed on her mission: to save the life of the man in the chair. She kept her voice steady. 'Rape is a war crime, Daud, punishable by international law. Mr Holden can and will be charged with it.'

He'd sensed the weakness in her statement. 'You can promise that?'

Slowly, she shook her head.

And slowly, Daud smiled at her. 'You are, at least, honest.'

She felt a strange empathy towards him. Not what she'd expected or anticipated. International law was hardly her expertise, but she did know of the Taking of Hostages Act, which would land Daud in prison, possibly for a long time, whatever the extenuating circumstances. There was the fact that he'd been armed. She also knew that he was intelligent enough to have realized all this. For a moment, they stared at one another. It was a mental battle.

'I want him to face a public trial.' His voice was quiet but authoritative.

She started to say that she wasn't capable of ensuring this, but looking at his face, firm and intransigent, she simply shook her head.

'Put your gun down, Daud,' she said. 'I'll do what I can to ensure justice, but you know as well as I do that some things are beyond my powers.' She tried to alter the tone of the exchange with a light-hearted, 'Above my pay grade.' She smiled. Behind her, she sensed an intake of breath. Perhaps changing the tone had been yet another of her mistakes.

But she could see from a simple movement of Daud's mouth that he'd lost some of his certainty. At the same time, she realized honesty had been the only way they'd been able to talk at all. But now her honesty had unsettled him, made him undecided. However much he'd planned this entire operation, he hadn't quite worked out this last scene. Behind her were five officers, all armed, all fitted with Kevlar tabards, all of them trained and prepared for a shoot-out. And she was on the front line. Joseph still had his eyes tight shut, his shoulders braced.

For a moment, there was nothing in the room but silent tension as they all waited.

She wasn't a religious person, but she couldn't stop a 'Please, God' escaping from her lips.

She risked a glance at Daud and knew he was still uncertain. Behind her, she heard a soft, metallic click. Safety off.

Seconds passed, and then Daud laughed. 'You win, Inspector,' he said. 'But remember this: I have put my trust in you.'

He dropped his gun and held his hands up.

FIFTY-TWO

After that, he was quickly handcuffed and taken into custody. Joseph was led into an ambulance. But unlike Daud, he couldn't look Joanna in the eye; instead, he kept his gaze on the ground, shoulders hunched, wrapped in an NHS blanket. He shifted his eyes just once more to look back at Cloud Mansion.

As he passed, Joanna wondered. What would happen to him? What would really happen to him?

Clarice, sullen and quiet, joined her half-brother in custody, but though she'd played her part in this, Joanna hoped she would simply be deported. She thought that was likely to be Daud's reason for keeping her at the mansion, knowing she would likely be on a flight home soon after the siege came to an end.

As Daud was being cautioned, he gave her a bold glance, much like the one he'd aimed at her months ago in the lecture theatre. 'So, Inspector. Have you decided?'

She knew what he was asking; neither needed words.

Who is the real villain here? Who should be punished and how?

She simply shook her head.

Without waiting for her response, he climbed into the police van.

4 p.m.

The day was taken up with two phone calls and one text. Chief Superintendent Gabriel Rush didn't express any appreciation at the peaceful end to the siege and the fact that there had been no loss of life. He simply said, 'Right. Well. Glad that's over, as, I expect, are you.'

And she had to suffice with a, 'Yes, sir.'

If she waited for praise, she sensed she'd be waiting a long time.

Robbie Callaghan was slightly more appreciative. 'Well, Piercy,' he said, admiration clear in his voice, 'count yourself as one of the elite. Successful hostage negotiator. After a four-day course. Congratulations.'

Her response was heartfelt, 'I hope I never have another experience like that again.'

'I get it,' he said softly. 'It plays havoc with your sleep pattern, doesn't it?'

It was an understatement.

Unsure of his work schedule, she texted Matthew:

Siege over. Home later. Need a bath and a long sleep. XXXXX

It would soon be time to re-enter her real life, where her husband, her son and her stepdaughter – soon to be crowned a doctor – waited.

7 p.m.

Matthew met her at the door and folded her into his arms, where she could have stayed for ever. She looked into his green eyes, bright and warm with love; his smile was tender and protective. 'Don't make a habit of this, Jo,' he pleaded. 'I don't think Jakob and I could take it.'

Jakob trotted in behind him, arms held out, and she picked him up, nestling into his baby-soft skin.

'I won't,' she promised. 'Never again.'

Matthew looked sceptical. 'Really?' His smile broadened as he mocked her. 'Maybe, Joanna, you shouldn't make promises you might not be able to keep.'

She was still thinking about that as she luxuriated in a hot bath, scented with expensive Christmas-present bath oil.

You shouldn't make promises you might not be able to keep.

FIFTY-THREE

To Eloise's annoyance, Matthew had suggested she attend the graduation ceremony with Jakob, as though he couldn't let her out of his sight. 'Sit at the back,' he said to Joanna. 'There's always plenty of spare seats. If Jakob makes a noise, you can just slip out.' And in classic Matthew style, he'd tinged the suggestion with some humour. 'You never know. The solemnity and aura of the Great Hall might inspire him, Jo.' He'd ruffled his son's hair and dropped a kiss on the top of his head.

'Into medicine?' It was the first time he'd mentioned this aspiration.

But Matthew couldn't resist tucking in a sliver of criticism. 'Away from policing,' he said firmly, softening the comment with a kiss as well as smothering any response.

Initially, like her stepdaughter, Joanna had been appalled at the suggestion that she attend the ceremony. As well as Matthew's parents, with whom she'd reached a fragile detente, Jane – Matthew's ex-wife and Eloise's mother – would be there, together with her new husband and Kenneth, Eloise's boyfriend, whom Joanna had yet to make up her mind on. She would be relegated to the back.

And Jakob?

Unpredictable as ever, he seemed mesmerized by the occasion. He stared at the front, clapping as each graduate was handed their degree, occasionally turning those perceptive green eyes on to her, his head tilted to one side, questioning. She held him tightly though he was too much of a wriggler to sit still on her lap and let his mother stroke those fine baby curls.

'Eloise Levin.'

Jakob turned to her excitedly, laughing, clapping and pointing at the same time. 'Eloee,' he was shouting. 'Eloee.' He'd always been impervious to his half-sister's dislike of him. At the same time, four rows in front, Matthew had slipped his arm around his ex-wife's shoulders. Joanna felt a brief chill. For a moment, *she* was the interloper as they shared their daughter's success.

. Kenneth turned to look at her, his expression unreadable behind his thick glasses.

Maybe one day they would all be friends.

Some hope.

And Daud? He had his wish. Joseph Holden faced charges in an international criminal court whose long processes lay ahead. Daud was charged under the Taking of Hostages Act, the charge exacerbated by the use of a firearm. He was remanded in custody before finally being sentenced to five years imprisonment, though it was mooted that this might either be reduced or he could be deported to his native country. Behind the scenes, an international lawyer, Saloman Hitaba, and Daud were constructing a case against Joseph and his band of men: Craig, Stefan and Paulo. Months – years – of evidence would be considered by the International Criminal Court in The Hague. Clarice Hani, protective of her half-brother, was deported to her native Somalia, where she was instrumental in gathering the evidence needed to secure Joseph's conviction.

And somewhere in the Middle East, the hands of a wealthy collector cradled a twelve-inch dagger with a handle carved from a rhinoceros horn, while Cloud Mansion sat empty.

Acknowledgements

Joanna's 'skills' in hostage negotiation owe much to a book lent to me by my son Nick: *Never Split the Difference: Negotiating as if Your Life Depended on It* by Chris Voss.